PURGATORY'S BEST SHOT

TIME DIVING: BOOK 2

CRAIG ROBERTSON

PURGATORY'S BEST SHOT

TIME DIVING: BOOK 2

by Craig Robertson

Can Matthew ever make right what he did to the universe?

Imagine-It Publishing
El Dorado Hills, CA

ALSO BY CRAIG ROBERTSON:

* Podium Entertainment has produced audiobooks for all the below titles except the older standalone books.

For specifics as to the correct order for reading the Ryanverse, click here.

<u>BOOKS IN THE RYANVERSE</u>:

THE FOREVER SERIES (2016)

THE FOREVER LIFE, Book 1

THE FOREVER ENEMY, Book 2

THE FOREVER FIGHT, Book 3

THE FOREVER QUEST, Book 4

THE FOREVER ALLIANCE, Book 5

THE FOREVER PEACE, Book 6

THE FOREVER BOXSET, Part 1, Books 1 & 2

THE FOREVER BOXSET, Part 2, Book 3 & 4

THE FOREVER BOXSET, Part 3, Book 5 & 6

GALAXY ON FIRE SERIES (2017)

EMBERS, Book 1

FLAMES, Book 2

FIRESTORM, Book 3

FIRES OF HELL, Book 4

DRAGON FIRE, Book 5

For more information about Craig, his books, various series, or to see images and videos for some of his wild alien characters, please visit his website. You'll be glad you did: https://craigarobertson.com/

To sign up for Craig's newsletter to get announcements, updates, and his recommendations for other great Sci-Fi reads go to: https://preview.mailerlite.io/forms/2369493/188634426375144501/share

ISBN: 979-8-9860769-9-7 (E-Book)
979-8-9868105-0-8 (Paperback)
979-8-9868105-1-5 (Hardback)

Cover design by Alexandre
http://www.designbookcover.pt/en/

Editors:
Michael R. Blanche
Beth Lynne
Forest Olivier

Formatting services by Drew Avera
drewavera@gmail.com

First Edition 2023

I am dedicating this book to my friend, Michael Blanche. For years now Mike has helped me create the Ryanverse books. I can truly say they would not be as good as they are without his wisdom and his expertise. Thanks, man!

PROLOGUE

Un-hap-py birth-day to me,
  Un-hap-py birth-day to me,
  Un-hap-py birth-day, dear piece-of-crap I am,
  Un-hap-py birth-day days to me.

And a good time was had by none here in the State Hospital for the criminally insane, for yet another year. Why was I singing to myself on the anniversary of the dark day I was squeezed out of my mother's belly? Seriously? Who else would there be to possibly sing it for me? The guards? As if. The ones that work here because they're psychopaths and are *paid* to abuse defenseless patients? No, they hate everyone. How about the so-called medical staff, who work here because they have no other career options? Not likely. They have one job and one job alone. Do not get your ass fired. Would singing happy birthday to a patient get you fired? Who knew, but why the hell take a chance?

I'm Matthew Dunsratty, thirty-four years old today. I'm a man in his prime, right? Yeah, fifty pounds overweight, pasty complexion, and a mind like a steel trap. Well, a steel trap that's been beaten with a sledge hammer then cast into the ocean several decades ago. The

1

tepid oatmeal I'm forced to eat every single morning has more on the ball, more alertness and intellectual prowess than I do on my best day, which, for the record, is never.

Hey, when I was thirty-four *before*, I was a man with a plan, in great shape. Yeah. I had a wife that loved me, kids who idolized me, and a job that kind of sucked, but mostly it did because of my lousy attitude. Sometimes when I've been thirty-four, I even had more kids. But sometimes I didn't have a wife that loved me. Nope. Mostly my soulmate left me a few years earlier because I was a complete mess. I was that run-over squirrel you see on a busy road on a hot day. Hell, if I could have, *I* would have left me. Can't blame Shannon. I can only miss her.

It's funny, I've been locked up nineteen or twenty years, and can no longer see Shannon's face. I sort of remember her voice, even though we never met in this life, only past ones. But her sweet, angelic face. It's gone. Ah, well, twenty years of heavy psych meds, zero intellectual stimulation, and no friends or family must do that to you.

I do have one claim to fame. I was the youngest person in this state to be tried as an adult, convicted as an adult, and sentenced as an adult to the loony bin for the rest of my natural life. Yay, try and top that! Seriously, society? I was a fourteen-year-old boy with raging hormones who thought his sex-maniac girlfriend was leaving him for another guy. But the jury of my peers (like there were twelve homicidal teenage jurors available to select) felt I had "displayed serious intent and forethought in the planning and execution of his crime." Are you kidding me? A teenager with serious intent and planning in anything? I would have been the first in history. But no one asked my opinion, so here I languish.

Did I deserve to be punished for what I did? Absolutely. In the heat of passion, I accidentally killed a kid. Francis Taylor. Granted, he was the biggest phony, the loudest braggart, and the most revolting waste of space ever to darken with his shadow the face of planet Earth. But his only crime was to flirt too much with my Stacy.

I ... er, overreacted a bit. I stabbed the jerk in the chest with my toy sword. Turns out it was better made than it should have been. Sorry, Francis. Then I was railroaded through the justice system without a single advocate. My parents disowned me. Stacy disowned me. Hell, my public defender disowned me.

Twenty years a prisoner. Maybe I should write a book? That's a snappy title. But, hey, no one would ever read it, mostly because I couldn't ever publish it. The staff, dedicated to my rehabilitation, would never allow that. Someone somewhere might object, and they could get fired. And that's not going to happen.

So what does a person do for twenty years in a state hospital for the criminally insane? What educational and entertainment options are there? Well, let me see. My main goal each day is to not be brutally murdered by my fellow inmates. No, we're not inmates. I keep forgetting. We're *patients*. Anyway, it dawned on me my first day in this hell hole that the state had gone to a lot of trouble to assemble the most dastardly mindless killing machines into one cramped location. You name it, someone here has killed it. Pick a diabolical method of torture and murder, and probably *several* people here have done that one. So I made it Job One from Day One to not be singled out and butchered.

In my favor is the fact that every patient here is constantly on staggeringly high doses of powerful psych meds. It's Zombieville, really. Drooling, shambling, and grunting are about all anyone can muster. The guy two doors down from me is Freddie Dobson. You have to know him. The Buzz Saw Killer? Fred would tank up on methamphetamine, kidnap four of five random people at a time, and take them back to his parent's basement for "Buzzsaw Hour." That's what he called it. And darn if he couldn't cut them all to tiny pieces with a Skilsaw in less than sixty minutes. Well, you should see Fred now. He's so medicated that he passes out whenever he sits up. If he tries to walk, he falls and often breaks something. He's not a threat to kill anyone now because he has so many casts on at any one time that he can't wipe himself, let alone operate a power tool.

The weird part about my imprisonment is that I'm not always sure it was *me* that killed Francis. I know *a* Matthew Dunsratty did. I just don't remember if it was *this* one that did. Years ago, and lifetimes ago, I learned how to time dive. Using meditation, I discovered how to contact a younger version of myself and force that Matthew to change some event in my past. I tried to correct all my greatest regrets. What I did was fry my reality and alienate everyone who had ever cared for me. The woman who was my wife most of my lives, Shannon, Stacy, all my kids, even my parents, all of them dumped me. Quickly after my crime, everyone connected to me realized I was a pariah.

I've lived *thousands* of lives. I've met and married Shannon, and I've never met her. I've killed Francis a few times, but mostly I don't. In some life, I did kill him and was convicted and landed here. But I don't know if it was this me that actually murdered a Francis or not. I'm too brain addled and confused. All I know for sure is that, whoever the hell killed Francis, I'm taking the fall for it. As I see it, there's two ways for me to get out of this nightmare. One is if some doctor decides I no longer require medication. Will that ever happen? No. Because if a doctor made that call and anything bad happened, they'd get fired. And, seriously, do you think anyone is going to unmedicate The Buzz Saw Killer so he can take up his messy ways again? No. And neither will anyone take a chance on me. The second way I'm getting out is feet first in a body bag.

Want to hear something ironic? This mental hospital is so old, guess what they have out back? A graveyard. Yeah, so, in reality, I'm never ever leaving here. Shit, I can't even leave these walls when I die. Now that's priceless. If I had the mental wherewithal, I'd laugh.

ONE

I heard the footsteps coming down the hall. With one eye, I spied up at the clock. Four fifty-five. Right on time. My gut twisted with nausea. I guess I should say *more* nausea, since the damn meds they had my mind vaporized with had me nauseous twenty-four-seven. I hugged my slip of a pillow harder and tried to burrow into my prison bed.

The footsteps stopped just outside my doorless door frame.

One - two - three ...

"Hey, Rat Man, git outta bed," came the same order in the same Alabama drawl from the same revolting man. He took the five steps needed to reach the foot of my bed and prodded my sole with his riot baton. "It's suppa time. Git your lazy rat ass up."

"I'm not hungry," I grunted in futile protest.

Tucker backed into the hallway and shouted, "Did som'on go and give da Rat Man permission to refuse a meal?"

Three - two - one ...

"Nope, ratty tat tat, no one seems 'a done dat, so rise and shine. I'm 'a count to three, den I'm 'a make you git up," he announced with rising enthusiasm in his voice.

5

"Not worried. You can't count that high," I mumbled just loud enough.

As a good sadistic medical staffer in a psych hospital, Tucker had learned all the tricks. He could torture a patient overtly, covertly, with marks, without marks. Whatever struck his current fancy. He reached over, took firm hold of my thin mattress, and pulled me crashing to the floor.

"Tank you for yur compliance wit' da house roos, valued patient a dis state," he taunted.

The piece of shit.

I slowly stood. "Can't you cut me a break just once. It's my birthday," I foolishly appealed.

"I know it yur burday, ya nitwick dick. Dat's why I got you dis present." With that he slapped me hard on the back of my thighs with his baton.

I crumbled to the deck, hissing in pain.

"Aw now ya just tryin ta piss me off. You done lied yurself down again."

In spite of the pain, which I was very used to after all my years of confinement, I stood quickly. It was possible I could avoid the next blow if I moved fast enough.

"Datz betta, burday rat. An I'm on KP today, so I'll be 'spectin' yur plate wit' *eagly* eyes."

I shuffled down the hall and around the corner to the torture chamber with a sign over the doorway reading Dining Hall. It was the place food went to lose all chance of being appealing or nutritious. I snagged a tray—which was filthy—schlepped down the line and selected the least dirty cutlery, and did what you had to do to survive the Dining Hall. I dropped my eyes to my feet. To look at the disheveled staff or the anti-food they were assaulting us with only served to make a horrific experience worse.

"Evening," Martha mouthed with less emotion than a rock on the southern pole. She then slapped something wet and weighty onto my plate. "Next," she then dismissed with even less interest than her greeting had expressed.

I slid my tray down to Clarice. She was the assistant head appetite killer and generally in charge of side dishes and desserts. Every day, the menu posted outside the hall suggested that varied and nutritious fare was to be served. Every day, Clarice doled out the same thing. Her laziness and contempt apparently knew no bounds. She *combined* side dish with dessert. Thus, every weekday, we were suffered to gag down Chocolate String Beans Surprise. The surprise was, by the way, not that it was offered up, but that it tasted worse each and every time it was prepared. Only because Clarice took weekends off were we spared that revolting concoction every day of our sorry lives.

I took a seat. One advantage of dining with a cadre of incarcerated psych patients, as opposed to, say, your high school cafeteria, was that no one minded if you sat at their table. They didn't know *they* were at their table, so they sure as hell didn't notice company. That was, except for Rolando Johnson's table. Wherever he sat, no one joined him. If he sat at a crowded table, it became an instant ghost town. In our den of psychopathic monsters, Rolando was universally feared and fled from. The man had been a laborer, for which he was perfectly suited. The African-American man stood nearly seven feet tall and weighed in around three hundred fifty pounds. Think John Coffey in *The Green Mile*. One day, with no explanation or previous violent tendencies manifested, he ritualistically murdered his family. And by family, I mean *family*. Wife, children, parents, siblings, aunts, second cousins, even a great-great-grandmother. And after his arrest, at his trial, and to this very day, he has never spoken. Not one word. Yeah, even the most sociopathic guards treated him with cautious kid gloves.

As I stared aghast yet again in disbelief at my meal, I looked up and noticed Tucker entering the hall from the kitchen. He was mauling a huge piece of fried chicken, a food product I had not seen, let alone tasted, in twenty years. As he intermittently wiped the back of his sleeve across his greasy face, he casually strolled around the room. He rested his free left hand on the handle of his sheathed baton such that it stuck up significantly. As he passed behind the diners, the stick would bounce off shoulders and backs. It didn't do so painfully. No, it was just him pissing on everybody because he could.

When he came to me, he stopped. Yeah, he always stopped where I sat. He, a man of no intelligence or creativity, had a small set of abusive routines he would subject me to. I never knew which cruel stunt he'd pull, but I knew them all well enough for my skin to crawl.

"Well, burday rat, how's your special burday suppa? I had Chef Edgar make dis up specials fo ya."

I poked at my slop and said nothing. I knew the drill. If I talked, he escalated, and I was punished. If I didn't talk, he escalated, and I got punished. Why bother participating, right?

"I din's hear dat, ratzo. Do ya maybe tink yu betta dan me? You my betta today, rat shit?"

I froze. Whatever was coming was coming.

"I ... I'm a proud man, ratter tatter. Makin' fun—"

He fell silent. That wasn't part of the usual script, so I idiotically glanced up.

"Could ya does me a favor and hole dis for me for a sec?" He handed me the partially consumed chicken thigh.

I dared not accept it. That would be to actively disrespect him. But the son of a bitch wanted me to touch it, feel it, smell it. The fried chicken I'd never get to eat again in my life. I pinched the now slimy meat between two fingers.

"Na, don't ya be droppin' it, rat pus." He bent down to untie and tie his boot. As he nonchalantly rose, his annoyance baton whacked the piece of chicken, knocking it from my loose hold. It thudded to the floor.

The entire room froze in place. All breathing, heart beating, and thought processes self-arrested in the span of one second.

The fried chicken had come to a stop against Rolando Johnson's bare foot. Any unknown in the context of this mountain of a mass murderer was due cause for concern for every mother's child in the room.

Normally, Tucker would have berated me for dropping his chicken after specifically ordering me not to. Then I'd be brutalized. But since his cruel prank had now drawn in Rolando, he was rightfully concerned.

Tucker licked at his lips nervously, his attention jetting between Rolando and me. Then insane rage settled into his eyes. Shit, the monster had come to a decision.

"Rat man, you in a heep a trouba now. Go and fetch me my fried chicken and do it right quickly."

My sentence was to enter Rolando's personal space—something never done—and to remove a piece of delicious food from where it physically touched his body. That meant there were any number of justifications for Rolando's violent response to my intrusion. Even the ocean of mind-deadening medication couldn't suppress my fight or flight response.

"*Today*, ratsy," Tucker shouted. He drew his baton. Several other monitors drew theirs and trotted in our direction. Who didn't enjoy a good beatdown?

I slid back off the bench and stood. I slowly took the three steps necessary to bring myself up right behind Rolando. The big man then turned his head to stare up at me blankly.

"Sir," I began, ready to pee myself, "I have been ordered to retrieve that piece of chicken." I pointed toward his foot. "Would it be alright with you if I did that?"

Rolando continued with his white-shark stare. Then he slowly rotated his eyes to Tucker.

"Don't give us no trouble, boy. Ya understands me?" Oh, Tucker, you Southern racist moron. What you just said.

Rolando rose like a volcano being birthed from the sea. He towered over me and I knew that my life sentence was, for better or worse, about to be concluded. He glared at Tucker with all the contempt and hatred due him and volumes more. Then he stooped over, picked up the chicken, and tossed it in his gaping maw. Slowly, he chewed the skin, meat, and bones. After a full two minutes, he swallowed. He licked his greasy fingers and sat back down, focusing again on the nothingness of his mystery meat and chocolate bean dinner.

Tucker, stunned beyond rational thought, shook his head once and then walked away. Once he was ten or twelve prisoners away, he stuck out his baton and began harassing defenseless humans again. I collapsed back onto my bench and started to hyperventilate. I hadn't felt so terrified, or so alive, in the last twenty years. So distracted was I that I wolfed down my slop and departed silently. Tucker didn't even have a chance to chastise me for not finishing what I was served. Happy birthday to me.

Instead of returning to my bed, I prowled the common room like a wraith on a lifeless moor. The TV was on. It was an ancient cathode-ray tube behemoth mounted six feet up into the room's far corner. It received four broadcast channels poorly. No cable. No video tapes. No remote control. The staff had set the volume to as loud as possible in a manner that it still could not be clearly heard. A few patients sat in the decrepit lounge chairs facing the TV. Others slouched in wheelchairs pointed randomly in any direction but toward the screen. No one in the lounge moved, no one chatted, and no one knew what program was playing. Gosh, I lived in an upbeat place.

The totality of the indoor space accessible to us inmates was the dining hall, this large common room, and four long hallways that led to the guest suites. If I were able to move at a brisk clip, it might have taken me three minutes to make the rounds. Even in my drug-induced walking coma, it only took me five minutes. So, like a caged tree sloth, I shambled my universe again and again. Luckily, obsessive behavior was the accepted norm in the insane asylum, so at least no one made an effort to stop me.

After God-only-knows how long of my aimless wanderings, a giant hand locked onto my upper arm from behind. I was so stunned, I kept walking, and subsequently, my feet went out ahead of my center-of-mass. I'd have fallen on my butt if the hand hadn't been attached to impossible strength. Like in a horror film, I slowly looked down at the appendage restraining me. It was a black-skinned hand the size of a catcher's mitt. I reflexively began to mumble a Hail Mary and lifted my eyes upward. Rolando's expansive eyes met mine. In them, I saw all his empathy, all his ability to love and nurture, and all of his pain.

"Sorry," he said as a gentle whisper.

I began to wonder if his apology was intended as a preface for my brutal dismemberment. But his eyes told me that was silliness on my part.

"No problem, man," I was finally able to respond. Mind you, I had no idea what he was apologizing for, but I was overjoyed to dispense a blanket and unqualified acceptance of it.

"That was your chicken."

"No ... er, it was—"

He placed a tree-stump finger over my lips. "No, he made you do it. But if I didn't eat it, he'd a tanned your hide."

"Oh, right. Thank you," I replied gingerly.

"Figured the screw wasn't 'bout to hassle me."

I snorted. "No, he was not going to hassle you, Rolando."

He pointed to my nose. "Watch yourself, Mr. Dunsratty. This place ain't too forgiving."

"Thank you. Thank you very much, Mr. Johnson."

He released my arm and I strode away slowly.

Nice guy, that Rolando. But he was still scary as shit.

TWO

Back when I was alive, I was like everybody else. I had good days, bad days, pointless days, and bone-crushingly boring days. And I never once realized how that variety was a blessing. No, we take it all for granted. We wish away today, because it's not rising up to some arbitrary previous expectations. But tomorrow'll be better, we tell ourselves. Tomorrow will be sunny and warm. Tomorrow, I might get laid.

I don't think like that anymore. No, not when every day I live is a precise carbon copy of every other day I've ever lived. Well, sure, I already said we didn't get green bean surprise on weekends. No, we got mixed vegetables, seasonal. And the separate dessert was always Jell-O mold, with or without canned fruit. Yeah, every time, it was as exciting and scrumptious as it sounds.

But basically, all my days are interchangeable. Morning meds are at 08:00, promptly. Our facility's one registered nurse, a weathered and defeated man named Nurse Ed, hands out a paper cup of pills to whoever's next in line. All the while, he whispers something, presumably to himself, about *Zanzibar and all the sweet little people.* No one asked, so no details are known. If the patient requires an injected medication, they're generally out of luck. Early in his tenure, Nurse Ed told a pharmacy tech that needles scare the demons awake. When she shared this insight, we all assumed Nurse Ed was speaking of *our* demons. But no one asked, so no details are known.

Weekdays then phase into *Group Good Morning*, led by a sweet man named Robert, no last name, of indeterminable national origins, who is as energetic and ebullient as he is unintelligible. Seriously, if I catch three words for every ten minutes of his sparkling rhetoric and hand gestures, I consider myself lucky. He sure means well. And I always wonder what words of wisdom he has for us irredeemable psychopaths. Shit, maybe he's a genius and his words would transform mental healthcare delivery. Wouldn't that have been useful? Anyway, that group is scheduled for 09:00, generally gets rolling around 10:30, and the hour session is over by 11:00.

Since there's only an hour until lunch, nothing else is planned for the mornings, which is fine by absolutely everyone. Staff, patients, cockroaches, hell, even the walls appreciate the hour of non-intervention. Most patients return to bed. I assume the employees do so also, but I'm never vertical to verify that suspicion, so don't quote me. After lunch, what little attention we can muster through the burning haze of our indigestion is occupied in *Life Skills. Can't Live Without 'Em. Can Live With 'Em.* I am continually intellectually insulted by the Melba toast, banal tone of that title. It oozed the post-frontal lobotomy spirit. But, if you ever met Sarah May Hampers (I kid you not; the name's even a truthful sentence) LCSW, you'd partly forgive her. She was the group's leader and sole content contributor. Blessed she was not with looks, interpersonal skills, common sense, or brains. I mean, what's left for a girl to work with? And to think she was still single well into her sixties. Sarah May, who insisted we all address her as LCSW Hampers, has post-acne scarring on her ashen face, she never looks up when speaking, and she actually thinks we all appreciate her lessons. Appreciate? With a gun to my head, I couldn't tell you one thing that was said during any of her ninety-minute infomercials for the damned. Maybe she meant well. Then again, maybe she was a current patient who'd been accidentally mislabeled and given an office.

So, now it's 2:30 or 3:00, we're all on mind-crushing medications, we're reeling from LCSW Hampers's séance with practical skills, and you have to know that whatever's next is guaranteed to be a blur. So that's when we meet with the doctor. Not the doctors, plural. The doctor. Not the psychiatrist. The doctor. He's a spry man for being in his late eighties, aside from his limp and weepy eyes. And his tendency to drool. And the fact that he hasn't bathed this decade. But, he has two factors pulling for him. One, he is presumably licensed. Two, he is definitely the only practitioner who will come to our land of the mentally disgraced. Or maybe it's that his physical limitations prevent him from *leaving*, so he's counted as staying for employment purposes? That might explain his loose relationship with current medical practices and lucid thought. But Doc, he probably means well, or, you know, did back in the Roaring Twenties. Oh, and he apparently had a name. Faron P. Wigglesworth, M.D.. At least that's what it says on his name tag.

And that's my every day, my life, my curse. Sometimes I wish I were dead. But I learned long ago to never say those words, dare not speak those however valid thoughts. Because, if anyone does, zap, they're on Suicide Precaution. The staff loves it when you're on those. If everyone could be on them all the time, they might even not hate their jobs. Yeah, when you're on The Watch, as we call it, they throw you in a padded cell with a hole-in-the-floor for a toilet and no furniture. You're stripped naked and meals can be slotted anonymously under the door. If you return the used tray via the slot, they remove it. If you don't, they pile up inside your cell. How could the care for a criminally insane ward of the state be easier? The best part for the employees is the cleanup. If they don't clean the room between users, just exactly who is the patient on The Watch going to complain to?

What I outlined above I stated was for weekday existence at the state hospital. Weekend care was simpler. There was none. Nurse Ed had weekends and holidays off. Robert had those days off. LCSW Hampers might have had them off, but then again, maybe she just stayed in her room. And good old Doc Wigglesworth, well, who knew if he was there when he was in fact present, or present when he was in fact deceased? We were most likely offered two or three meals on weekends. None of us could say for certain. But we were never triple blessed and given no meals. A day that splendid we would have remembered in spite of being head-fucked by pharmaceuticals. But to live a day starving from not having to choke down Jell-O mold, with or without canned fruit. Ah, it is the stuff of dreams.

So, it must have been a weekday when I first noticed it, or rather, him. I think it was because I remember distinctly I was trying to pick green bean string coated in chocolate from between my teeth with the fingernail. I couldn't, of course, because none of us were allowed to have any nails, since they were a scratching risk if left to grow. Robert, of *Group Good Morning* was somehow tasked with clipping all the patients' nails. Given his bombastic energy and nonexistent language skills, we all stayed straight as statues for fear of losing fingertips. His success at the unwantable job ensured that it was his forever, the poor bastard.

Anyway, one of the secretaries, the people who worked on the other side of the Psycho-Divide, aka, the real world, was orienting a male, or not far from one, to the facility. You could tell the secretary was from the real world because of two reasons. First, she had on high heels. That was a strict no-no in Crazyville. You could put an eye out with one of those if you knocked her down and ripped one off, assuming you then had enough time to run to the nearest patient and actually hit his eye socket before the guards beat you senseless. That could happen.

Second, you could tell she was a visitor from the real world because she was walking quickly. She did so because—duh—she was scared out of her gourd. What sane person wouldn't be, what with our population of killers, rapers, killer-rapers, and raper-killers? It was a proven fact that no employee on this side of the Psych-Divide ever walked quickly. If a coworker were on fire, they would first have to check their watch and only then *wander* over to an extinguisher. And would a patient ever walk quickly? No way. Between the meds and the life sentence, rapid anything was not gonna happen.

So, anyway, Susie Cream Cheese is walking fast, pointing indistinctly, and leading around this short, rotund maybe-male. He's in what he must perceive to be street clothes, since he's certainly not wearing a standard issue hospital uniform. But even a convicted schizophrenic such as myself had to notice that his pink jeans, skin-tight mesh shirt, and Mexican tire-tread sandals, and an ascot made up an eclectic-to-say-the-least ensemble. But, living for years in a state hospital teaches you an essential lesson. To each his own. If you think that guy's weird, look in the next mirror you pass.

But, like everything else in this land-locked ship-of-fools, I promptly forgot about the gender-ambiguous new-hire with severe fashion retardation. Hell, he was probably a hallucination in the first place. Man, were my hallucinations badly disappointing. I wanted Sophia Loren at eighteen, but I got Elmer Fudd's socially repressed second-cousin. Life, can't live without it, can live with it. Hey, some portion of LCSW Hamper's class *did* rub off on me. Now to find some turpentine to try and remove it.

The next few weeks passed as a blur, which was standard operating procedure. All time blurs in the state hospital. I only knew vaguely that some span of time had passed, but not to any specific extent. The guy who turned out not to be a hallucination was now working as the sole night med tech. He had a uniform, black tennis shoes, and even a name. William "Billy" Shovellbottom. Seriously, that was his name and that is how it appeared on his name badge. I wonder if he ever got teased as a kid?

The job of a night med tech was poorly characterized. Presumably, he was there to monitor our status and report any emergencies that might arise. But, realistically, every inmate slept the sleep of the dead every night. We were all dosed with a powerful sleeping pill, Doriden, to hold hands with the paralyzing psych meds we were all tanked up with in the first place. If there was a fire at night, I guarantee none of the patients would even stir in their comas.

To his credit, Billy, who was issued the standard medical riot baton like the rest of the staff, took it off as soon as the rest of the employees had split for the night. It meant he hadn't taken this horrible job in order to beat other people senseless with impunity. Med Tech Shovellbottom was a man with perchance a modicum of integrity. I gave him two weeks, tops, before he quit or was killed by the other guards.

Maybe in his third week on the job, or maybe a decade later—time was real fuzzy for me—I noticed that Billy was being nice to me. Even through my chemical confusion, kindness I recognized. In my twenty years of institutionalization, no one, including myself, had ever been nice to me. At first, it was little things, like Billy saying good night as he passed my door frame. In no time, he was stopping to have brief discussions with me. How was I doing? Did I need anything? Could he get me a warm blanket?

That last offer sounded so preposterous, I had to take him to task on it. I asked where he would get a warm blanket for me if I said that I did want one. He said the blanket warmer was full of virginal blankets all heated to one hundred and thirty degrees. I was stunned. I asked when the unit had been delivered. Billy said he didn't know, but the date on the machine's label read 1938, so it was presumably a long time ago.

Now I knew Billy was either a serial liar or just another cruel hack. I dared him to quickly fetch me a blanket warmed to the pleasing temperature of one hundred and thirty degrees. Within a minute, he was tucking me in with not one but two such mythical blankets. As I lay there feeling toasty and loved, I asked why, in my twenty years of incarceration, I'd never been offered one before. He replied he couldn't say, but that the staff used them regularly when sitting at their workstations. Those sons of bitches, I say for the second time.

And it became a nightly ritual of ours, Billy tucking me in with a warm blanket. It took me longer than it should have, but I finally realized that a lot of Billy's "tucking-in" involved his hands running over my central body, which, anatomically, is far from the established tuck-in zones. I began to suspect he had ulterior motives that involved more than my creature comforts. But, hell, I'd have let him eat my left leg if it got me nightly warm blankets.

My relationship with Billy grew slowly but steadily. He started asking about my LBI, my life before incarceration. That violated a big taboo. One, it showed he cared, which was not only impossible, but it was frowned upon. Two, if you ask an inmate what he did to receive his or her sentence, the answer will automatically be first-degree murder, several counts if you can believe it. That's because all us inmates run scared all the time. If you are in for criminal insanity that involved, say, embezzlement, you'd be viewed as weak, and hence, victimized. If, Heaven forbid, you were doing time for child abuse, there'd be a line of inmates to take turns putting a shiv into your back. So all of us claimed to be coldblooded murderers. In fact, many were. But for a staffer to ask about my past, wow, that was undiscovered country.

So what did I tell Billy? I immediately began editing my life's tale into one that would reveal that I was tender but weak, caring but misunderstood. Why did I hit-the-road-lying? Because in almost a quarter century of incarceration, I had learned well how to survive as an inmate. Game the system, lie in case you can leverage that lie into even a small advantage, and, most importantly, lie. Come on. Criminally insane here, right?

So, I was a high school teacher, but instead of science, like I had, I taught music and art to disabled kids. And I led a class in the Equal Rights Amendment, because we all deserve our rights. Oh, and dance. I taught interpretive dance because we all had an inner self crying to get out, and dance was one of nature's best medicines for showing the world our true essence. I never mentioned my sexuality, but I did have a brief relationship with "a fighter pilot." But it didn't last because not all souls were made to fit together forever. I, um, I kind of impressed myself on how prodigiously and how well I lied. After a while, I wanted to be in a relationship with me.

And poor Billy, he lapped the drivel up like it was the last water in the desert. He would spend more and more of the night in my room, pining and gushing, dreaming and confessing. It wasn't like he was going to get in trouble with management, since no one was ever around to monitor his work. But it was insanely cruel on my part. I know I'd been sentenced here because society thought I was a homicidal maniac. But I knew I wasn't. I was no more insane than any other schlep trying to make it through another tough day. In one act of teenage passion, I accidentally killed a kid. That doesn't excuse my action. It was wrong. Even that dildo Francis didn't deserve to die because he was a pompous narcissist. But everyone back then misinterpreted my screaming and ranting after I did the deed, thinking I had to be loco. But I was just overwhelmed with the depth and implications of all the time diving I'd done in all my uncountable lives.

But I played Billy like a dime store tin whistle because it might just lead to something that would benefit me. There could be some unforeseeable way I could parlay his sniveling devotion to me into even a small gain, then I was all-in. Sorry, Billy. It's not personal. It's just life in the slow lane here at the state hospital for the criminally insane.

It was kismet more than planning or brains that led to my flash of brilliant insight. As the nights passed, Billy became more and more overt in expressing his desires to take our beautiful rosebud of a relationship to the next level. I knew the level he was referring to was horizontal. As much as I wanted to use the dweeb, I have to say my basic nature kicked in unbidden. He began to gross me out. That blossomed into him creeping me out. After all, he did have a prodigious erection most of the time we were chatting and tucking.

One night, Billy came right out and asked. Did I want to do it like wild stallions in an open prairie? I took his meaning unequivocally. My snap response was that *of course* I wanted to, but that I was incapable of any sexual desire, let alone performance, because of the stultifying burden of medications I was subject to. He frowned and grew very contemplative. For a second there, I was thinking he was going to retrieve his baton and use me as a practice dummy. But to his eternal credit, he remorsefully admitted that he understood fully. If there was anything he could do to lighten my load, so to speak, he instructed me to simply ask.

Over the next few days, I began to piece together a plan. What had gotten me into my cursed state was my continual time diving. In any number of lives and life stages, I would place my older thoughts into a younger version of mine's head. That Matthew would do my bidding and my world would slowly devolve into a cesspool. Once I was institutionalized, the potent medication I was forced to take crippled my ability to time dive. It required an inordinate amount of concentration and meditation to pull it off. And I'd always known I was trapped here until I died of natural causes, since my medication levels would never be allowed to drop below toxic.

But ... what if Billy could rig the medication system? I was ninety-nine percent certain Nurse Ed was either dispensing the same meds to each of us, regardless of our prescriptions, or mixing the pill cups up randomly due to his mental inadequacies. But, what did I have to lose in asking Billy if he could intercede? I was pretty sure that if I was off the poisons for even a few days, I would be able to time dive back and prevent young Matt from ending up in this hell.

Yeah, this might just work. Hot damn!

Once I had a firm plan in mind as to how to avoid being remanded to this dump, I began my assault on Billy's integrity. I almost wished I felt bad about my actions, but I didn't. I guess too much time in the loony bin rubs off on a fellow.

One night, Billy comes into my room, warm blanket in hand, and sits on the corner of the bed like he always does. He starts rubbing my nearest leg. When he touches me, I stiffen. *What's the matter,* he asks with all due concern? *I'm not worthy of you,* I bemoan. *Of course you are,* he defends gallantly. *But we can never be together,* I respond, tears beginning to flow. *Don't cry,* he pleads, *it breaks my heart to see you cry. If only there was a way we could be together,* I wail, *but we can't because I'm overmedicated. Time,* Billy reassures, *give us time. All will be as it should be.* He rubs more passionately and higher up my leg.

If only there was a way we could be together, I wail for the second time, *but we can't because I'm overmedicated. I love you just the way you are,* assures Billy, proud, protective, clueless Billy.

If only there was a way we could be together, I wail for the third time, *but we can't because I'm overmedicated.* I wanted to *spell* the word overmedicated so he'd maybe notice.

Wait, Billy finally catches on. He says thoughtfully that maybe there is some way he can work it that I'm not given the medications I'm supposed to take.

What is this? I marvel at his wisdom. What brilliance has my man hatched from his ginormous mind? Is there some way to have me take a placebo? Or to be handed an empty cup for several mornings in a row? Or to have me not be required to line up for Nurse Ed's pillapalooza? Maybe I could be reported off as too ill to attend or excused because of a physical limitation like a badly sprained ankle or broken limb that in reality were just fine?

Billy rubs his stubbled chin. *Maybe,* he thinks out loud, *I could tell Nurse Ed you are too ill to come to the med line. I could volunteer to bring you the meds, so Nurse Ed doesn't have to leave the line and waste time? Billy, you're so smart,* I marvel. I expressed a conviction that it was quite unlikely that the broken Nurse Ed, already deeply immersed in a sea of medical malpractice, would object to such an arrangement. *Why, if you could ferry me the meds for just three or four days, why, I was certain my little admiral would be able to salute again.*

Billy's face pruned up. *Was I in the Navy prior to my incarceration? And, even if, what did that have to do with the topic at hand?* I admitted that I was just joking around. But if I was medication-free for a few days, I was sure I could not only achieve a satisfactory erection, but that I'd be quite passionate about wanting to put it to good use.

Billy was all-in. He was hooked. Heck, the hook was set in his lower intestinal tract, so firmly hooked was he. He teared up, told me he'd do anything, risk anything, to help us. I told him there was no I or him in us, just us. By God, that melted him.

Man, was I a bad player. But, if Billy had read the fine print in our contract, he'd notice the part written in red. *The occupants of this state mental hospital for the criminally insane are ... criminally insane.* Caveat emptor. He had, if he realized it or not, fair warning.

That very dawn Billy came to my room and issued me the only orthopedic device authorized for patient use. An ACE bandage, minus the sharp metal clips, naturally. It had to be affixed by tucking in the loose end. He advised me to moan a lot and writhe in bed maybe. He would hang around the extra hour and then ask Nurse Ed about him being trusted to administer my morning meds. I told him he was my hero, landing on the beach of life fighting for our future. I reminded him that there was no I or him in us. Come on, the line was too absurd not to pound him with. I might not technically be insane, but I was admittedly pretty much a dick.

At ten minutes to eight, Billy came into my room. The dude held before him an institutional white paper cup. Nurse Ed not only jumped, figuratively speaking only, at the chance to not have to move, he handed Billy the nearest cup a few minutes early. *The little friends know when you're pimping and when you're keeping it real,* he told Billy in a circumspect manner. Whether that was an explanation or sage counsel, we will never know.

Billy rattled the pills, all the while grinning from ear-to-ear. It hit me then with a thud. I truly hoped dental insurance was part of the benefit package offered to the employees here.

22

"Patient Dunsratty," he said, trying to sound authoritative, "I am going to count and verify these doctor-prescribed medicines and then pass them to you so you may swallow them."

I nodded.

He dumped the pills into his hand, counted them with a finger, then pretended to place them back into the cup. As he was a simple man, as he handed me the empty cup, he flashed a glimpse of the pills squirreled away in his palm. Then he winked.

I faked throwing back the pills. Billy stood to leave, but I cleared my throat. He puzzled at me.

"You're supposed to look in my mouth to see if I actually took them."

"Ah," he grunted, and judiciously inspected my open mouth.

Of course that evening, Billy's first task was to come to my room and ask if "it worked." I had to let him down—probably literally. Honestly, one day's break from brain poison was not enough to think straight, let alone get anything else straight. How long? he asked. We'll just have to see, I bemoaned. He lingered a bit, but had to withdraw. He confessed he did not want to break down in front of me. It might loosen my resolve. Whatever he meant to express, I agreed and went back to sleep.

By the fourth day of my drug holiday, I could tell a massive difference. For one thing, my mouth wasn't as dry as a desert and I was actually hungry. What's more, the revolting offerings in the dining hall actually made my mouth water profusely. Who'd a thunk it? As I went through the day, with me alert and able to think, I set about planning my impending time dive. I hadn't done one in twenty years. I knew that was going to be an issue. Sure, in all my lives, I'd done thousands of them, but they were never trivial. So not only did I need a plan as to how to abort my being remanded to this hellhole, I needed a backup plan in the event that I faltered. I could put Billy off for only so many days. If I wasn't able to vanish quickly enough, I was facing a legitimate call to pay the piper. I mean, I could suppose, but the prospect was ... well, it was unappealing. I'm a firm believer in to-each-his-own, but he wasn't part of my personal world-view, if you take my meaning.

What specifically got me sent here was my accidental killing of Francis with my plastic toy sword. Stacy had wrapped it in a bunch of aluminum to make it look more realistic. I was supposed to be her knight-in-shining-armor for her costume-themed birthday party. Obviously, she'd added enough bulk to make the blade lethally rigid. I had felt the need to assault Francis at the party for a few reasons. One, he was a dick to me. Two, he was massively flirting with my girlfriend. Three, and most critically, a much older version of me had time dived back and placed a thought in that much younger Matt's head. My idiotic intent was to have me break up with Stacy. Why? Don't ask. I had some cockamamie notion that I could win back Shannon, my first wife and soulmate, if Stacy and I were never too involved.

I knew when I'd planted the thought in young Matt's head. It was right at the end of Stacy carving up her birthday cake and passing out pieces following some nauseating dedication to the recipient. Right at the moment when I most feared I was losing Stacy, I placed this thought in that poor boy's addled mind:

You don't have to take this, Matt. Get mad. Get very mad and make Stacy feel bad she lost you. Stacy hates you, Matt, can't you see that. Stacy hates me. Get mad and make them all so very sorry. It is all Stacy's fault, Stacy and that Francis fellow.

What a horrible man I had been. Through all the years and the Great Wall of Medication, I recall that suggestion verbatim. What an asshole.

Anyway, I had to either push young Matt along an entirely different path before the cake-moment, or really pull off a miracle and redirect him after that incendiary thought was implanted. I was likely only going to get one shot at this. Billy would quickly grow suspicious. Hell, even the pudding-for-brained Nurse Ed had to, at some juncture, raise an eyebrow. So I faced not only a tough time dive to begin with, but had to do so after a very long hiatus. If I had no time pressure, I could start practicing my transcendental meditation skills here in the lockup. But it would kind of stand out and be noticed. No one did anything healthful and proactive in this bleak house. Worse, word of my odd behavior would quickly find its way to Billy, and even that doe-eyed dolt would have to get suspicious.

For better or worse, I decided late tomorrow afternoon was Zero Hour. Everyone, staff and inmates, would be mentally sailing in the doldrums. Mostly, we were supposed to hang around and await the summons to meet with the doctor. If I slipped away, no one would notice until at least the dinner bell. Even my worst detractor, Tucker, was in the habit of stealing an hour nap between three and four. There was a custodian's closet near the end of one hallway where I could hide well enough. We had one janitor, Woody. On the days he bothered to show for work, he was perennially drunk. I'd know well in advance if the closet would be unused. If Woody did show and wasn't too inebriated to function, I could always hide in the least-frequented restroom, which was near the end of the opposite hallway. Okay, I had that part of my plan.

On what was hopefully my last day in hell, I awoke refreshed and clear-headed. How ironic. In the very center of Kill-The-Brain City, I was hitting on all cylinders. I ate a light breakfast and skipped lunch. I wanted to be sharp for my attempt. Hunger would help sharpen my focus. Staying awake, let alone on my A-game, was really hard as I waited the eternity to get through LCSW Hampers' mind-numbing drivel. But make it I did. Woody had called off ill, so the closet was mine for as long as I needed it. Once Tucker was up from his snooze and dinnertime neared, it would also be one of the last places he'd search for me. That wasn't just because he was a moron. He'd also made no secret of his disdain for cleaning products, and cleanliness in general, so he was loath to visit the janitor's closet.

Not wanting to draw undue attention to myself, I snatched a blanket off someone else's bed to sit on. With it tucked under my arm, I slipped into the closet completely unnoticed. I pushed Woody's mess to one side of the space, set down my blanket, and sat on the floor. I was still in my early thirties, so I was still able to pull off a full lotus position. I wasn't sold on the fact that it helped, as opposed to just sitting, but I needed all the help I could get.

There I was. Clear-headed, alone, and able to fix the tragedy that put me in this hopeless place. I had literally dreamed of this for decades. Show time. I knew better than to try and rush any part of this. For ten full minutes, I just sat there, relaxing. Then I started the breathing exercise, which was to basically start not noticing my breathing. With luck and an advancing state of consciousness, my respirations would slow further, but without any active input on my part. I thought of happy times in my past. And, in spite of the mess I made of the past, there were many to browse through.

Then I nudged myself to ...

Bang - bang - bang ...

The closet door flew open. Someone tumbled in, panting and whimpering.

Shitshitshit. I was outed. After all my ...

I looked up to see a stunned Gabby Patterson. He was more surprised to see me than I was to see him. Gabby was a harmless soul. He'd been locked up here for nearly fifty years. Apparently, he'd abused drugs, though no one knew which ones and how much. He is said to have been a big drinker too. Aside from that, it was unclear why he was a co-resident of mine. Knowing him superficially, I kind of figured he was put here for no particular reason and he had no particular interest in ever leaving. Gabby once tried to organize a bingo night. That was where the man's head was at. It failed because most potential players fell asleep by the third ball out of the blower. But he meant well.

"M ... M ... Maatt, wha ... what're you doing in h ... here?" he asked. Oh, yeah, he had a bad stutter too.

"Gabby, I'm beating off. Can I have some privacy, please." First thing that shot into my head. Sorry.

"Oh, g ... g ... gotcha. S ... ssorry. B ... but Ji ... Jimmmy just threw up. T ... Tucker said I b ... bb ... better get a mop s ... so Ji ... Jimmy could clear it u ... uup."

I pushed the rolling bucket toward him with one foot. The mop was still in it. "Here. Go. Hide it in your room when he's done, 'cause I need some time, dude."

"Sh ... sure thing. I unders ... understand completely." He pulled out the tools and softly shut the door.

Man, how I didn't need that. Deep breaths, Matt. Deep breaths.

I started back with where I was. I was about to begin focusing on happiness as an abstract and separate entity. I sought serenity. I needed ...

Damn it. I forgot to toss the floor cleaning solution into the bucket. When Tucker noticed it was missing, he'd cuff Gabby's ear and send him back to retrieve it. I grabbed it and almost set it out in the hall. But then I thought, what if Tucker doesn't send him back? Then some asshole'll notice the gallon of cleaner in the hall and put it away, disturbing me yet again. I'd never be able to meditate with that over my head. So I slid it as far away as I could and tried to calm myself down. It wasn't easy.

I'd been in this farcical place way too long and for no good reason. I wanted to get out and make things right. Hell, I wanted Francis to grow up and be able to father many really annoying children. It wasn't fair. The world was unfair to me.

Fairness was ... was a goal. Everybody should be fair, to themselves and to others. But what was fair.

Yeah, before you know it, I was spacing out, contemplating *fairness*. And damned if it didn't work. There's a point in meditation, at least my TM, when I know I'm in the zone—where I need to be to time dive. I was there. I had to be careful. Even thinking too specifically about achieving the goal would burst the bubble and I'd just be sitting on the floor in the janitor's closet.

I knew where young Matt was at the party. He was in the corner. The one near the open picture window, where the couch ended. The green felt sofa with wear so bad, it was bald on the armrest. Matt was sulking, and he was mad. I knew he was thinking of Francis' treachery and Stacy's infidelity. I eased toward Matt as he stood there, seething. We were fit to be tied. We wanted to be anywhere but here. Stacy, she shouldn't be doing this to us. I didn't deserve to be humiliated in public. I had been a loyal boyfriend. I had never so much as ...

Matt, walk out the front door. Walk out the front door. If Stacy loves you, she will follow. Prove her love. Walk out the front door.

There, I sent the message. The rest was up to fate and ...

My head!

My head, it's going to explode. It did. My head exploded like a thermonuclear bomb.

I can't breathe.

I can't see.

I can't ... be ...

THREE

Ooooh.

Oooo ... oooh. What the fu ...

Where am I? It's dark.

No, I'm blind! My head. Oooh my aching head.

I ... I thought it had exploded. That's right. Apparently, it did not. Or Shannon was correct all those years when she said I seemed to operate without a brain.

Achy-ouchy-mama.

Where ... oh, I'm in the janitor's closet. That's where I am. How long have I been here? When Tucker finds me, he's going to beat me to within an inch of my life and then insist my meds get upped. If I'm on more mind crap, I won't function at all. Just as soon be ...

"Matthew," a young girl's voice called out in a panic. "Matthew, are you okay, sweetplus?"

Nobody calls me Matthew anymore. Haven't heard that for ... years. And sweetplus? No one ever ... well, Stacy did, back in the Dark Ages. I don't even recall where she ...

Stacy? Was that Stace's voice? Wow, I guess my head did explode.

29

"Matthew, can you move?" the angel's voice cried out. Slight, tender hands slipped behind my head and lifted it to the angel's chest. "Oh, Matthew, don't be sick. I couldn't stand it if you were injured or ill." She roughly turned my head so our faces were inches apart. "Can you hear me, love?"

My eyes fluttered open. Shit on sushi rice it *was* Stacy. It was … it was impossible. But there she was.

"Oh, Matthew, say something," she pleaded.

"You know it's probably not wise to twist the neck of a person found unconscious on the ground."

Yup, I was in the loony bin for decades, hadn't seen Stacy in who knows how many lives, and the first words out of my mouth are an absolutely lame attempt at first-aid humor. Strong work, Dunsratty.

She released me like I was radioactive and I hit the ground hard. I heard a distinct thud when my head met concrete.

"Oh, Matthew, I'm so sorry. Did I hurt you?" She bent over and draped her partially exposed breasts over my face. Oh, yeah, she was wearing the silly English wench dress, wasn't she?

"I'm good," came my muffled response. I mean, my head hurt like hell, I think it was bleeding, and my vision was still wonky. But, yeah, I was perfect.

"Matty, Matty," she cried softly, "why did you leave my birthday party? I was just about to—"

I sat bolt upright. I could not be at her birthday party. I was thirty-four-year-old Matt confined to the state hospital.

No, wait, I was able to time dive. I tried to stop myself from killing Francis. But, if I succeeded, I shouldn't be here. Time dives always left me in the adult form I would have been at the time of the dive if it were successful. I never … *stuck* back there in time. And I didn't remember time dives. If I did try to dive out of the hospital, I shouldn't remember that at all. Sure, toward the end, I started recalling snippets of time dives. But never real-time ones.

Shit, crap, damn. This cannot be real.

I grabbed Stacy's shoulders. "How's Francis?" I shouted harshly at her.

"Francis?" she said, clearly blindsided by that query of all the possible things I might have said.

"Yes, Francis. Francis Taylor. Big guy, bushy, bushy blond hairdo."

"I know who he is," she snapped back.

"Is he dead?"

"Good Lord, Matthew," she sat back up, "what's gotten into you? He's not dead. I just handed him some cake when you ran from the r—"

My head started spinning.

Then it started tornadoing.

Oh, yeah, hurricane class five now. I vomited into Stacy's lap. She yelled something, I think it was "gross," but I wasn't all there. I began to float, to levitate. Then my entire body turned inside out. Oh my, that hurt. I was nowhere. It was dark and it was frigid. I started shivering. I threw up again.

Then the seizures hit me. I remained conscious, but waves of convulsions racked my core and I was certain I would be killed.

Then, as abruptly as it began, it was over. I was lying quietly on a carpet. No, a couch. Had Stacy moved me to a couch?

"Stacy, are you there? Stacy," I moaned.

"Matt? Were you calling me, honey?" It was a woman's voice now. I knew that voice.

"Stacy, where am I?"

"Stacy!" she exclaimed. "If you think you're with Stacy, you'd better not be doing it on our living room couch, Matt. I'd haul you into divorce court faster than you could say *I need an attorney.*" She chuckled playfully.

In spite of my headache to end all headaches, I risked peeking out of one eye. Was that ... "Shannon?"

"You were expecting maybe your fairy godmother? Or that Stacy Kaufman you dated once or twice during high school? Because if it was, boom, we're going to court." Now Shannon laughed joyously. "Honestly, Matt, honey, I'm so glad I married you. You really keep me on my toes."

I was so confused. I opened both eyes and took in the room. It sure looked like the second house we lived in after we got married. I was on a revoltingly Victorian sofa with all the leather tacked back so there was no way to not be in pain. And the living room. Same coffered ceiling with the gaudy tin tiles. I'd forgotten how very much I hated this room, this house.

"So, Matt, is nap time over or are you planning to sleep through until bedtime?" she teased lovingly. "I mean, if that's how you want to spend your Saturday, far be it from me to object. But it does seem an awful waste of time if you were to ask my opinion."

"No, no. I'm up." I slid my feet to the floor and took a few quick deep breaths.

"You really did have a doozy of a nightmare, didn't you?" Shannon remarked with a trace of concern.

I looked at her squarely. "You would not believe it in a million years if I wrote it in my own blood."

Poor Shannon. Her eyes nearly bugged out of her head.

"Sorry. Yeah, it was a doozy." I shook my head in disbelief.

Unless I was dreaming, I had pulled off the escape of the century! I was thirty-four years old still, but I was Matthew Dunsratty, high school science teacher. Dull, boring, and not incarcerated.

Oh. Hang on. I was living in state-forced celibacy for over twenty years. Here I sat staring at the woman I loved in the prime of her life. And look, she was bending over to pick up a toy. Nice behind, still. Or again. Or newly nice. Hell, I had no clue, I just wanted to ...

"Daddy ... Daddy?" A toddler by the sounds of him. Oh, crap, that must be Edgar, our first child.

"Yes, honey," I shouted. "Daddy and Mommy are in here." Not having sex, I added to the sentence in my head.

He burst into the room and wrapped his little arms around me. Nice.

"Yes, Edgar, what is it?" I asked lovingly.

He got the oddest look, sort of a crooked confusion, all over his cherubic face.

"Daddy, who's Egar?"

"Edgar, honey. You're Edgar. Named after my great-grandfather Edgar Dunsratty. Remember?"

"I'm Clarence, not Edmer."

"Honey," Shannon chided, "don't tease him like that. He's only three and hasn't learned to ignore your sense of humor yet." She led him away by his cute little hand. "What can Mommy get for you, sweetie?"

"Daddy said he'd fix my swing," whoever the hell that kid was said as they faded into the kitchen.

Clarence? I named my son Clarence? Anyone with a functioning brain named their kid *Clarence?* What the fuck? I know I'd learned to be self-serving and cruel in the state hospital, but even then, I'd never name a *shoe* Clarence, let alone a human being. Clarence, Clarence, there were no Clarences in ... Oh. No way. No, no, that'd still be cruel and unusual punishment. Once, years ago, I asked Shannon who she admired most in the world. Naturally, I expected her to say her dad. But no, she said it was the family mailman when she was growing up. He was tall and handsome in his blue suit and always tipped his hat to Shannon when he saw her. Yeah, the mailman Clarence was her childhood vision of a hero.

My son was named after some 1950's mailman? God, I was a horrible father already. I ... and there was no way I could ever make it up to the kid. He was doomed and I would be damned. Clarence Dunsratty. Oh the shame.

"Matt," came my wife's sweet voice, "after lunch, can you and Clarence go fix his swing?"

"Sure thing," I called back. Maybe I could rig a noose next to it while I was at it and hang myself. But, as the saying goes, hanging is too good for the likes of me. I named my son Clarence.

But I'm back! I'm not confined to a state mental hospital. I never killed Francis. and, come hell or high water, I'm getting lucky tonight.

But I'm ... I'm not supposed to remember all this. It's what, 1987. I'm not supposed to know I got here by time diving. And I'm sure as heck not supposed to know that the Berlin Wall falls November ninth two years from now or that my beloved Giants win the World Series in 2010, 12, and 14. Go, Giants!

Then again, I've never time dived after being on a quarter century of drug-induced sedation, not to mention a few sessions of electroconvulsive and insulin coma therapies. Yeah, my brain has been pickled, fried, and starved. That has to cause some real damage. Maybe this is a new time diving? If so, man, that's a scary prospect. Before, I'd come up with some scheme, mail myself a letter describing my intervention, and include a detailed biography of my life at the time of the dive attempt. But for decades, I never knew—as in recalled—that I did such a time dive.

Now, I was the Matt there at the end of my life who planned the bungled time dive that caused me to murder Francis.

You don't have to take this, Matt. Get mad. Get very mad and make Stacy feel bad she lost you. Stacy hates you, Matt, can't you see that. Stacy hates me. Get mad and make them all so very sorry. It is all Stacy's fault, Stacy and that Francis fellow.

That was what I said that got me into so much trouble. But now I was thirty-four-year-old Matthew Dunsratty, maybe even living my original timeline. No, wait. Crap, this wasn't the original Matt. No, my firstborn now has the same given name as the guardian angel in *It's a Wonderful Life* and the father of frozen packaged foods.

Oh, man, am I confused. In fact, what else is critically different? Am I even still a high school teacher? Do I have other kids? Am I a drummer? What other hells am I in? Maybe I could ask Shannon over lunch. Pass me the chips, and oh, what's my line of work? Yeah, that would go well.

What if I work Sundays now, like, I sell shoes at Sears or some horrible numb death like that? And if I do show for work tomorrow, I don't know where the stupid shoes are in the back and I can't ring up any sales because I have no clue how to. I ... I don't even have an employee number or code. Damn, what do Sears shoe salesmen use to ring up a sale? Crap, are the cash registers digital or the old National registers with the big thing on the right you hit and the numbers that spin around. Oh, God, how am I supposed to work tomorrow? I don't even know the store hours. Noon. I think Sears opens at noon on Sunday. No, they stopped the Blue Laws shit in the 1980s, right? Oh, who can I check with to know when I need to show for work? Google? Holy hell no. It won't be around until ... it does not matter when Google's invented. Matt. You need to know Sear's Sunday store hours today.

The yellow pages? No, they don't list hours. Do they? No. I ... I could call Sears. Yes, as soon as I get a free second, I'm ... I'm using the yellow pages to find Sear's number and I'm calling them on our rotary phone. Or touch-tone phone. I can't remember. No, rotary phones were out by the 1980s. Yes. If we have a phone, it's a touch-tone. We have a phone, right? Of course we do. I bet we have a couple. I'll check later. I can check now. Where would I put a ...

Shannon was staring at me like I had three heads. Her mouth was even agape.

"Uh, hi, hi there, wife of mine."

Still she was with the stare and the agape.

"Say, where's that boy of mine, Cl ... Cla—" I pointed to the kitchen, "the one you were just here with?"

"What has gotten into you, Matthew Dunsratty? First you think I'm that floozy Stacy, then you can't remember your son's name, and now you're having a conniption fit or something."

"I ... I can explain. I ... I want to explain." I pointed to the couch. "I had a bad dream."

"And?" she sort of demanded. "Explain."

"No, that's it. I had a bad dream. It started the ball of my day rolling downhill. Now, I'm ... I'm out of sorts, sort of." I buzzed my hand toward the floor like it was a dive bomber. "Downhill out of sorts."

"The ball of your day rolling downhill?" she asked incredulously. She glared some more and took a few deep breaths. "I'm going to put Edg ... Clarence down for his nap." Shannon balled up her fist and turned around twice like she was playing pin-the-tail-on-the-donkey. "I am so mad at you. Now you've got me calling my own son by the wrong name." She forced herself to calm down over a minute. Then she knifed a hand toward the stairs. "I'm putting Clarence down. Then I'm coming back here. You and I are going to have a come-to-Jesus meeting, Matthew. You started this weird behavior a few years back. I threatened to leave you then and I'm reminding you of that fact now. You seemed to improve, but maybe you were just fooling me because I'm so trusting and because I love you. But I'm a mother now. I do not love you enough to risk my child's safety and secure future if you're going to take a dive off the deep end." She panted a few seconds. "I will be back in five minutes." Shannon stormed out.

I - guess - there - was - some - history - at - play - here. Ho, boy. Whatever I said five minutes from now probably shouldn't include asking if I sold shoes at Sears. No. I'd rifle my study, look for pay stubs or something. Maybe there was a phone book in there, one with yellow pages. And a phone.

Hmm. Did I have a study?

FOUR

Well, I survived the Shannon Inquisition, but not by much. The overarching takeaway I was left with was that I was not, contrary to my ardent hope, going to get lucky tonight. Those who sleep on the couch—the tack-studded uncomfortable couch—do not *get* lucky. No, they arise unrefreshed with a sore neck and skin mottled with odd depressions. And they arise as horny as they were when they laid themselves down to rest. I guess it was better than another night in state prison. Maybe. The food here was better. But that Shannon, she was beginning to remind me a little bit of Tucker. Note to self. Check and see if there's a riot baton in the house. If so, get rid it.

After fixing Claren's swing. No, that contraction didn't work. Clar's? No way. That's a girl's name. The kid'd have enough baggage to carry without being a boy-named-Sue too. Claren ... Claren ... setti? Wow, that was so stupid. Clarenosis? Stop it, Matt. Claren-bomb-barren. Claren .. aw, shit, it was going to be Clarence. Maybe I could call him Bubba? Or Champ? Lots of dads call their sons Champ. Sure, strong and masculine. Champ! Bubba Champ. No, crap, that sounds like Bubba Gump, which, of course won't be a known phrase until the mid-nineties.

After fixing my young son's broken swing, I discovered that I did indeed have a man cave/study. It was sparse by my future standards. Worse yet, it had all the old furniture Shannon replaced elsewhere in the house. I had old-lady chairs with vinyl coverings over the paisley-silk fabric, and a hutch. Oh, boy, I had me a hutch. I could display all my guns and fishing tackle in that-there Ethan Allen cherry wood hutch. Oh, well, it beat the heck out of the hospital day room, so stop complaining, Matt.

The computer was an already decrepit, out-of-date Commodore 64. And the internet hook-up was so slow, I could walk to somewhere to learn about it faster than I could download the info on it from the net. How did we live like this? Anyway, since Shannon would not be distracting me with conversation or affection, I was free to spend a few hours trying to figure out what the hell was up with me.

My first considerable relief came when I found a letter from my school principal. Good old Hank Bayer. Dull, bad breath, intolerant to a fault, but he was my boss—still and again. I worked at the high school, taught science and the occasional math class, and was vice-chairman of the Building and Facility Committee. Wow, I was a power broker in this timeline. That one was a new notch in my gun belt, let me tell you. Oh, and it was Saturday, March 20, 1987. I was due back in class bright and early Monday morning the twenty-second. That was a tremendous relief. If I behaved at home, my life might just return to a semblance of normal. Well, normal for a guy with about a thousand copies on himself in his head and the ability to fly through time.

In my original time line, Shannon and I had a boy named Edgar first. Then we had some girls and boys, ended up with five offspring, the last being Matt Jr. Sorry, kid. Maybe that was why he was the one child who had, ahem, *issues*. He eventually went to prison for embezzlement. Anyway, I decided then and there that I was not going to try to tailor my family to my liking or to match some arbitrary configuration just because it was the initial one. Nope, if this life was poker, I was staying with my hand. In fact, it would be really wise of me to never time dive again. If I wanted to keep my Shannon, I was going to have a hard enough time of it since I knew the future. Yeah, I needed to sell her on the fact that it was no biggy that we were phenomenally rich. I was just lucky when it came to investments. And gambling. And politics. And guiding technology. Maybe the entertainment industry too. What, we were looking at the 90s coming up. I could, you know, sell Kurt Cobain the lyrics to the songs that made him famous before he ever came up with them. Just sayin'. And what if I just happened to buttonhole Bill Murray at a cocktail party and challenge him to write a movie about a man reliving the same day over and over until he got it right. Hmm, for a slight fee, I could suggest a location that would guarantee it would become a classic.

Oh, yes, fame and fortune would be mine ... I mean ours. But mostly, I had to settle in, learn the nuances of my current state, and wait for the river of fate to bring the opportunities to me. Yeah, I had it pretty good. Wait, what am I saying? I had it superbly great. I was no longer a victim of our fine state's hospital for the criminally insane. I wish those memories had been wiped away when I changed the past, but they were as vivid to me as the miserable days I lived them.

Maybe someday I'd go visit the dump. I'd love to introduce myself to Tucker, him having no clue about our history. And Nurse Ed. It would be so cool to walk up to him and whisper in his ear, *I'm one of the sweet little people and I'm here for your brain.* Brilliant! I mean, I doubt they'd let me in. They didn't have guided tours the entire time I was there. But a guy could fantasize, right? Plus, in the end, there was nothing and no one I actually cared to look in on.

Well, wait, there was Rolando Johnson. He had been kind to me, which was a rare commodity in that hellhole. What's more, there was always something about his case that troubled me. Here he was, for all intents and purposes, an upstanding if unremarkable member of society. Never jaywalked or even got a parking ticket. Then, one day, he brutally murders those he loved the most in the world. He was a superstar in reality TV circles, with endless documentaries about Rolando and his possible motivations. The one show Keith Morrison did, *Dateline*, featured Rolando so many times, he should have paid him a salary.

In fact, I probably knew Rolando better than any person alive. Hell, I was the only one he'd spoken to in decades. That's a trip. I was best friends with the most notorious and mysterious mass murderer in US history. He ... I don't know, he seemed like a pretty decent fellow. If he really were the meet-you-chop-you-up kind of guy, why would he cover for me with the fried chicken incident? From what I was led to believe about Rolando, after he snapped up Tucker's chicken, he'd have eaten me. But he wanted to deflect the sadistic guard's attention from me to himself. That says nice guy to me, not butcher.

He committed his heinous crime, what, in the mid-seventies. Maybe 1974 or 75. I was in prison and drugged up, so I didn't catch a lot of the details. But I had time and a sucky internet now. I decided to look into Rolando's case a bit.

It didn't take long to discover he murdered most of his family on Friday, June 13, 1975. So much for debunking superstitions, right? As I remembered, he lived in Reseda, California, in the San Fernando Valley just north of LA proper. Born and raised in Detroit, drafted into the Army and sent to Vietnam in 1968-69. Returned to the States and settled in Reseda. Maybe it was Vietnam that screwed with his head? He got a job at Ace Moving and Storage, where he was a strong back. In the five years since he returned from overseas, he'd married, had three kids, and joined the choir at the Antioch Baptist Church. One biography on him mentioned he was about to be made the head of the Trustee Ministry, but then he went off the rails just a little bit. On the surface, the Rolando Johnson I discovered in my research seemed an awful lot like the guy who gave me assistance when he didn't have to. A nice guy. What nice guy murders his entire family? In fact, in all the exposés, inside looks, and conspiracy psychobabble pieces I read, no one could document one single instance of Rolando ever being anything other than what he appeared to be—a straight shooter and a model citizen.

So what happened on that dark day back in 1975? And trust me, you don't want to know the details. They are scary ... terrifying, in fact. He moved to Reseda because his mother's family was from there. As a consequence, when Rolando went nuts, he killed a total of thirteen people. Spooky, right, thirteen people on Friday the Thirteenth? Wife, kids, grandmother, an uncle, two aunts, two cousins, a second cousin, a niece, and a nephew. And Rolando did not own a gun. He said many times after returning from the war he would never hold one in his hands again. So he offed his family the good old-fashioned way, with a blade.

But guess who he did *not* kill with the same knife he'd carried through the jungles of Vietnam? His wife's best friend, who was over for coffee that morning. His grandmother's live-in caretaker, who witnessed the entire gruesome scene and testified as to what she saw in court. And there were fourteen other non-relatives he did not kill who were eye witnesses present from his knock on the door until the last flash of his knife. If you're going to fly off in a homicidal rage, why spare anyone, let alone more people than you actually did murder? It made no sense. I guess that's why the press so loved to tell and retell the story. It had an unanswerable element to it, a disconnect. Those made any form of wild speculation not only possible but marketable.

Rolando was a secret member of an occult religion. He was in reality a space alien. Drugs. Rolando Johnson was a druggie, just some bad shit, and that caused him to go crazy. PCP mixed with strychnine was the most common speculation. Of course his toxicology reports were all negative, but, come on, since when do facts interfere with a good conspiracy theory? In fact, his negative tox screen *confirmed* that whoever dosed him with whatever had a sinister motivation to cover the facts up. Muahahaha. It was sickening to read all that crap about a guy I knew to be a good man. It also pissed me off.

Rolando had done me a solid. Maybe I could return the favor? Let me see, what was I doing in mid-1975? I had finished my teaching credential a year earlier and had my first paying job as a teacher. I worked as a long-term substitute for a woman who went on maternity leave right in the middle of the school year. Aragon High School in San Mateo, that's where I was in mid-1975. And the school year ended the very same Friday the Thirteenth that Rolando went on his rampage. I remember it vividly because I met with the principal that last day and he handed me my final paycheck personally. He praised my efforts and repeated his claim that he would have loved to keep me on permanently. But the economy was going through a down spell in the mid-seventies. He couldn't make the numbers work.

Why did my buddy kill his family? I did not know, but I intended to find out why. And, if I was very good and very lucky, I might just stop him from ruining so many lives. Win/win in my book. I know I was on thin ice with Shannon, but since my time dives wouldn't involve this family, there was no way she'd catch wind of them. Not if I was careful.

FIVE

All of my past time dives in each of my past lives involved the same basic principle. Focus back on a Matthew Dunsratty that I knew to be in a specific location at a specific time. I then meditated to help place a fairly simple thought in that Matt's head. *Go to Stacy's for sex* was the very first one I ever told a much younger me. Sometimes the idea placed was more complex, like when I left instructions for me to save John Lennon. But most of the details and planning had to be carried out by that Matt. I was just the initial spark. He was responsible for the bonfire.

What I wanted to do for Rolando was to have a past me investigate the man. And then what? Write his findings down and put them in a time capsule so I could find them a decade later? I had no clue how to set up that type of time dive. And if it ever came down to me needing to attempt an intervention, that would be crazy difficult. What, would I be asking a past Matt to step into the middle of a mass killing and stop it? Talk about that Matt assuming some personal risk. In fact, the more I stewed over it, the more I came to realize this wasn't a very good idea. I was at the point of wishing

Rolando the very best in his killing spree and forgetting about my meddling.

But then I realized—come on, Matty—that I really had nothing to lose. No. If I made some rudimentary attempts and they failed miserably, what was I out? Nothing. If I wasted a little of 1975 Matt's time, so what? I wasn't all that busy back then. Remember, the school year ended the same day Rolando did his deed. As a teacher, I knew the last couple weeks of class were mailing-it-in time, with everyone just waiting for the curtain to fall. And that summer, I went camping with Shannon. Talk about non-urgent use of time. Yeah, that Matt had some spare time to help out a friend, even if he didn't know him from Adam.

So, what day could I return to? I clearly wanted to avoid that awful Friday. At least my preliminary interactions needed to be a week or two earlier. Maybe I might visit Reseda much earlier and try to befriend Rolando. That way, any intervention I made later would be greased by the familiarity we shared. No alternate plan seemed better or worse than any other, so I decided on the simplest and most direct course. I would determine the timing of my action based on what events I recalled the best back in that general period, say a month or two before that dark Friday the thirteenth. Of course, just as my son Edgar was named Cl ... Clar ... you know, what he was named now, there was no guarantee what had been a sentinel event of that period would remain the same. So, the bigger the event I aimed for, the better.

Hmm. What stands out in my mind? Late May to June 1975. Huh, I do remember watching several replays of what happened June 1. President Ford arrived in Austria to meet with Egypt's Anwar Sadat. He slipped and fell on the stairway while descending from Air Force One. Yeah, that was quite the image. But I wasn't there, and can't associate anything specifically with it in my life. Oh, I do remember one. I should warn you, it may seem dumb, but I was crushed. May 4, 1975 was the day Moe Howard died. Born Moses

Horwitz, he was the leader and last survivor of *The Three Stooges*. I found out that evening after work. Later, I went into the bedroom and cried my eyes out. Moe especially had been such a huge part of my childhood. His loss, and the definitive end of *The Three Stooges*, it meant a lot to me. And then Shannon, who had wondered where I was, found me and comforted me. By comforting ... *ahem*, how to say this, it progressed into a pleasing ... oh, hell, I'll just say it. We had massively great sex. There. So, now you see why I sort of recall that specific time and place. Of course, trying to plant a thought into any male's head in the middle of sex would be an act of futility. Nah, man-brain no worky during.

But, if I placed it before Shannon found me, it might stick. The unsettling concepts bouncing around in that Matt's head might make the good part that followed not ... be proceeded to. But I guess I could spare one roll in the hay to help out poor Rolando. Man, when this was all said and done, I was letting him know he owed me. Well, no not that he owed me *that*. No, just that I did him a big favor and I'd apprise him of that fact.

What to tell myself to do? This was a tough one, as I'd alluded to earlier. I could either tell Matt to tail Rolando, find stuff out about him, or I could have him go to Rolando and introduce himself. That third one would be awkward as hell. It would be easiest to have younger Matt snoop Rolando out. That would be a good starting point. Then, after he did whatever he did, I'd see what I remembered. Of course, I'd write myself the typical pre-dive letter, so I'd know if I acquired any new knowledge. Okay, a plan.

Whoa, Matty Boy. Rolando lived in Reseda. You lived in the San Francisco Bay Area at the time. How was I going to follow the man around from four hundred miles away? Again, I needed to not set off Shannon's hair-trigger antennae perpetually scanning for signs on me acting crazy. What could I do? How could I be in LA? Oh, wait, this was easy. My job in San Mateo was ending. I could actually arrange an interview in LA, maybe even Reseda. A sad fact here.

There are many schools in impoverished neighborhoods that are always critically short of qualified teachers. All I had to do was have that Matt solicit an invitation from one of those places, and my trip to LA would be one-hundred-percent above board. Okay, *now* I had a plan.

That evening, Shannon was out with her friends. She had a cadre of old friends that got together every week for wine and whining. Hey, that's what they called it. Don't blame sexist me. Four of the five gals went to one of their houses and sipped Mateus rose (gag me with a wine opener) while baring their souls. You know that old expression, oh to be a fly on that wall? Yeah, if I was a fly on one of those walls, I'd go looking for a spider web.

Anyway, I had a few hours to myself. I got out the standard school envelope I used to send myself time dive updates. Those were sure to be confidential because Shannon never opened my dull school announcements. I wrote a fairly detailed biography, at least what I knew about the time-period version of me, along with the following message that I would place in that Matt's head:

Write this down. Get an interview at a school in Reseda in May. Seek out a man called Rolando Johnson. He will commit a crime. See what he's like. Remember it.

That seemed vague enough, but would get me started. Then I could base another time dive on the results if I felt it was still worthwhile. I mailed the letter at the box down the street and returned home. I plopped down on the living room rug and set about getting in the mental state to time dive. First, I relaxed, then I focused on a simple act. In this case, I picked *loving*. I know, I know, corny. But I'd found meditating on positive concepts was more useful than most other matters. Meditation about taxes or a leaky faucet were bad segues to a calm focus. Once I was in the zone—whatever that means—I probed the cosmos. I was picturing the Matt of 1975, lying on the bed, sad about Moe Howard. I moved toward that Matt. As I'd done this so many times, it was becoming second nature, so the process moved along quickly.

Then I began to *see* 1975 Matt. I don't mean I *imagined* him. No. I saw him in some strange voodoo way, and moved toward him. As early as my very first time dive, I'd learned that once my meditative, disembodied head overlapped with a past physical one, I could transfer the thought. Then the Matt doing the time dive would pass out. Me, in this case, would find himself blacked out or asleep in some odd place and I'd have no memory of what led to my present state. Generally, I'd assume I'd time dived, but that was only based on experience, not specific knowledge.

I inched closer to 1975 Matt. I focused on his head. I passed through his skull and floated toward his eyes. As I assumed the position where his eyes were, I saw I was clutching my personally autographed photo of Moe. I'd forgotten to mention that part. Silly fan boy.

Then, my virtual eyes fused with his and ...

Whhhham. I was staring down at the framed photo of Moe. It was one of those standard studio publicity shots. But Moe signed it for me at some convention, so I treasured it. I was so sad. I wished I could have ...

WHAT - THE - FUCK!

I wasn't back in 1987 on the floor vomiting. I was in 1975 being an immature dolt, pining over the loss of my ...

"Matt, honey?" Shannon's voice queried.

I flopped onto my back, still clutching the picture.

"Ah, there you are. I've been looking all over for you," she said softly. "What are you doing?" She sat on the end of the bed.

Ho, boy. I knew how this scene ended. Guilt exploded in my brain like a flash-bang grenade. I ... it wasn't right for me to take advantage of this Shannon. It was too creepy.

But, wait. She was my wife. We were about to have passionate sex. I was the one who'd *had* passionate sex with her. So how could it be wrong for me of the future to ... er, enjoy the moment?

As I was constructing idiotic pseudo-morality controversies, Shannon reached out and began stroking my thigh. "Matt, what's the matter?"

Oops, my physiology was stirring.

"I'm ... I'm just sad," I said. I honestly can't remember what I'd said twelve years earlier. But that didn't matter because I was saying something now.

"About what?"

More thigh rubbing. More physiology going woo-woo-woo.

"Moe Howard died today."'

She got a puzzled look. Yeah, she, like most women, couldn't fathom my passion for the biting, slapping, and blinding antics of The Stooges.

I showed her the photo.

"Oh, that Moe Howard, the clown one."

I was totally confused. I had actually lingered in 1975, as opposed to planting a thought and vanishing. There was no way that should happ ...

Whoa, I'd briefly lingered back in the 60s, with Stacy. Oh my goodness. This constituted a new phase of time diving. How very unwelcome. Nausea swelled along with, you know, the physiology thing.

"I'm so sorry to hear that, sweetie," she purred. "I know you loved his shows." Then her eyes fixed on ... well just above where she was stroking my thigh. She had a sort of well-I'll-be-damned look on her cute little face. At least back in the day, Shannon was really pretty into sex and stuff. Time passed, we got old, and things changed. But, back in 1975, before kids, she was a fan.

"He was a giant of the entertainment industry," I stated for unclear reasons.

She maintained her focus.

"I'm so sorry," she purred. "Maybe I can help?" Her hand slipped up higher.

Yup, that was a bit of alright. I squirmed a little, well, because I was such a moron.

"I met Moe once, you know," I said very loudly.

Shannon crawled up the bed and came to rest on top of me, her hand remaining however at its post. "Yes, I recall you mentioning that once or twice."

"He sure—"

I mumbled a bit before I stopped blabbering. Shannon had planted an open-mouthed kiss on me.

I ... yeah ... I stopped avoiding the issue at hand ...

The next morning, as I stood in the shower, I determined that I was *still* in 1975. This was so bizarre. How could I linger? And what the hell was happening with the Matt of 1987? If the 1975 version was in that head, wow, was Shannon of the future going to be not amused.

It was Monday, May 5, 1975. I was inside an ancient version of myself's head. And, oh joy, I had to go to work. This just absolutely sucked. We had lived in Redwood City, just south of San Mateo where my school was. I knew there was a beat-to-crap 1966 Volkswagen Bug parked in the street that belonged to me. It used to be tan. Now it was mostly rust-colored on account of the rust. I knew I had to be at Aragon by 09:45 for my first class at 10:00. What we were studying, where the hell were the classes, and similar would-have-been-handy details were missing. Come on, for this me, I was a whole *bunch* of Matts, many of whom were FODs. Excuse me, fat old dudes. I couldn't remember specific details of my day-to-day life in my personal antiquity.

"Matt?" There was a loud knock on the door. It was Shannon. "Matt, if you don't get out of the shower, you'll be late for school. Come on. I need to get in there too."

Yes, I confess, the thought of extending her an invite did flash through my testosterone-poisoned brain. But I let it pass. I needed to get to school to figure out what end was up.

"Coming, honey." Crap, that didn't come out sounding too good, did it?

I opened the door as I toweled my ear. "Morning," I greeted her.

Um, she hadn't bothered to ... ah, to like dress since our Moe Howard Memorial Sexcapade. Man, was she hot. Young and hot. I started up the rationalization generator in my head. What was the school going to do, fire me? With a week left and I was a substitute?

I stood up straight and made a serious face. "Excuse me, ma'am," I said in a low voice.

She raised her eyebrows.

"Were you aware that you were naked in the presence of a man dressed with only a towel?"

She grinned energetically. "Why, officer, I was not aware that was against the law."

"Oh, yes it is, ma'am," I puffed. "And are you aware of the penalty for such a transgression?"

She nodded playfully. "I have a pretty good idea, yes."

I dropped my towel. "Then you understand that I'm just doing my job, ma'am?"

She set her hands on my butt and pulled me in. "Oh, yes, officer. I fully confess my crime and accept the—" Yeah, the kissing thing truncated the dumbass role-playing, thank goodness.

Half an hour later, with my hair dripping on the steering wheel, I was trying to remember how to shift my ancient car as I jerked away from the curb. It stalled twice before I made it to the intersection where I needed to make a left. I checked my watch. Yeah, I was going to be late. But ... that was fine, all things considered.

I lurched and screeched into the parking lot just as the 10:00 bell rang. Okay, I had ten minutes to figure this out. My first class. Which was it? I had physics, introduction to science, and biology, including bio lab today. I think physics was ... no, intro was first. Crap. I jogged to the office.

"Morning, Mr. Dunsratty," the aging secretary greeted me cheerfully.

I pointed at her. "Good ... morning—"

Her name plate. It was right in front of her. "Ruth. How's your day so far?"

"Monday. End of the year. Surging teenage hormones. You tell me." She grimaced.

"Gotcha. Say, I was wondering ... if ... if I could get a copy of ... like my schedule."

An eyebrow shot up. "You've forgotten your schedule after this many months?" she asked incredulously.

"No, no, silly. I just want a ... a document. You know, for when I go on job interviews and such."

"They might want to see your last schedule?" she asked *more* incredulously.

"I don't want to think. I want to be prepared."

The ten-ten bell rang. We both looked up.

"Mr. Dunsratty, in thirty-five years of employment in this office, never once has a principal asked to see an interviewee's actual schedule." There, she was calling my bluff.

I leaned onto the counter, smiled for all I was worth, and said, "Yes, Ruth, but the times they are a' changing."

She blinked twice.

"I'll put one in your mailbox when I get a chance," she stated by way of dismissal.

"Gosh, see," I pointed a hand at her, "there you have it."

She blinked once.

"Er, say, you wouldn't happen to have a chance to do it ... like now, would you?"

She blinked no times.

"Do you have an interview with another school in the next few hours?" she asked, channeling the Rock of Gibraltar.

"No, Ruth, I actually do not. But I tend to obsess. I obsess a *lot*, in fact. It's kind of a character flaw, just between you and me. If I go to class now," I gestured over a shoulder, "and just keep obsessing about that darn copy of my weekly schedule, why, I think I might be short-changing my students. Now, I don't know about you, but me, I worry over such a dereliction of duty."

"Mr. Dunsratty, if I go get you that copy, will you promise to leave so I might try and avert the next disaster that is surely coming in the form of a soon-to-graduate-senior prank, a soon-to-be-a-senior-*junior* prank, or a mass cutting of the next period?"

I crossed my heart. "I do."

She rose quickly, pulled a sheet from a filing cabinet, and stepped over to the Xerox machine. In no time, I was on my way to ... I checked the schedule ... Physics in Room 1001. Hey, I remembered. It was in Building 3. Sweet.

As I opened the door to Room 1001, my first thought was to close the door and back away quietly. No one would even notice. There were paper airplanes, wadded up sheets of paper, spit balls, and a smallish student flying through the air. The screams and shouts made it sound like someone farted on a crowded New York subway car. And the smell of marijuana was overpowering. Welcome to the 70s, Matt.

I walked to my desk and took in the energy that was America's youth, our hope for a secure and prosperous future. A really nerdy-looking kid in the front row was looking at me, pencil raised, binder open, and his mouth as well.

I cleared my throat. "Okay, so that is not in your texts and it will be on the final. Let's move on."

Three-quarters of the class froze in place like my words were an ice storm. Nice.

"Next order of business," I said business-like. "I want a show of hands. How many of you in this class are seniors?"

Almost all the hands went up. Now even that rambunctious last quarter of the class quieted and mostly raised their hands.

"And as of this moment, who exactly has accepted a spot in the freshman class of a college or university?"

Almost all the raised hands stayed raised. People started finding their places and sitting down. I slid the top drawer of my desk open and pulled out whatever was on top. I raised it, blank side facing the class. "This is a standard acceptance letter from an American school. Did any of you read all the pages of your acceptance letters?"

Hands neither rose nor fell, but they wavered.

"I thought so. On page two," I pulled another sheet from the drawer, "it states clearly that your acceptance is contingent on you completing this semester successfully. It also reminds you that a copy of this acceptance letter was sent to your present high school, for their records. If this class would prefer to behave like monkeys on Monkey Island, fine. But if you do, I shall go directly to the office, pull everyone's file, and contact your would-have-been dream schools and inform them of your short-sighted folly. Any questions?"

The kid up front, the only one who'd been listening intently, raised his pencil. "Will that be on the final too?"

A wad of paper bounced off the back of his head.

"Who threw that?" I asked firmly.

Slowly, painfully, several students turned to look at one particular pupil.

He lowered his head. "I did, sir."

"Name?"

"Jim Stelling, sir."

"Jim," I said paternally, "normally, I do not condone violence in my classroom. However, you made the right call just now. You get five points extra on the final."

To the rest of the class's moans and complaints, Jim grinned and thanked me.

I pointed to the nerd. "Name?"

"Gus Van Bockland. You know that, sir, because you yell at me every class, *Van Bockland, you're so darn annoying,* your words not mine."

"Is Gus short for Gustav?"

"Yes.

"Fine, I knew that too. For five extra points on the final, where did we end up last class?"

"The coefficient of static friction. That's on pages three hundred and three through three hundred and fourteen of our text book, *Physics: Concepts and Structure*, published by Jossey-Bass. Would you like to see my detailed notes?"

"No, Gustav, that won't be necessary, but thanks anyway." I paced back and forth slowly. "Who can tell me the other coefficient of friction?"

Gus's pencil shot up.

"Anyone besides young Gustav here?"

One of the two girls in the class raised a tentative hand. I pointed to her. "The coefficient of *dynamic* friction."

"Yes, a fine mind you have there ... er—"

"Melissa."

"Melissa. I see a bright future in STEM for you."

"Thank you," she said almost apologetically. Then she had to ask, "Sir, what's stem?"

Oops, ahead of my time here. "That, Melissa, is what you are likely to be a pioneer in."

She nodded uncertainly.

"Now, can anyone tell me *why* the two coefficients are different? I mean, why should friction be based on whether a body is in motion or not?"

All eyes shot to Gus, who slouched in his desk.

"Well that's the rub, now, isn't it?" I asked rhetorically. I'm going to step out for ten minutes. When I return, I will ask each discussion group to give me their best explanation. If your last name is from A to F, go over there. You are Group One. G through M," I pointed to another corner, "N through S," I pointed, "and whoever's left over," I pointed to the final corner. Back in ten. Fair warning, I expect to be amazed."

The groups were chattering away before I left for the library. Back in those days, school libraries had big fat phone books for many

US cities. Why, I could not tell you. None of the kids were going to be making calls from the library, but there you have it. I found one that included Reseda, in the Greater San Fernando Valley book. In a flash, I had three schools' numbers. I approached the librarian, who was seated behind a stack of books on her counter that rose like a defensive parapet. I peered over. "Ah, does this phone dial out?" I asked.

She sheepishly looked at the phone, then my chest, and then lifted the phone over the barrier that protected her from the rest of the world. As she didn't speak, I didn't bother to thank her. Perhaps she was, in addition to a high school librarian, a nun who had taken a vow of silence. Carmelite, I think. Anyway, if so, I shouldn't want to tempt her.

Each high school I called expressed first stunned amazement, then obsequiously fawned over me. I thought two of the schools were going to send a helicopter to pick me up immediately, they so wished to secure my talents. In any case, I scheduled three interviews on the same day on this Friday. I returned to class fifteen minutes later than I had predicted. My model students were all seated, hands folded on their desks, and eagerly awaiting me to not threaten their futures any further. Hey, this teaching gig, it was pretty easy.

"Thank you all for delving into the mysteries of modern physics," I said as I sat. "The answer is, because a body at rest has formed covalent bonds with the surface it rests upon. To move, not only must the body overcome the dynamic friction inherent in the system, but it must break those electrostatic bonds. Clearly, once in motion, the net creation and cancellation of those bonds are in balance, so add no more friction. Are there any questions?"

"But you didn't ask if any of us got the answer right," someone anonymously chided me.

"Did anyone, in fact, come up with the correct response?"

No one budged. "Alrighty then, onward and upward. I will now discuss a really important aspect of physics. Can anybody tell me the best way an average American can apply physics to their daily lives?"

I gazed upon a sea of confused looks. I searched the faces. I knew he was out there somewhere, the ambitious one who was taking physics because he knew it suggested to prospective colleges that he was clever, not because he cared for the sciences. Ah, yes, there he was.

I pointed to him. "Name?"

"Curtis, sir," he said with poise and confidence.

"Curtis, I wish you to answer honestly, not how you think I would want you to respond. Can you do that for me?"

He was uncertain a moment. Then he squared his shoulders. "Yes, sir."

"How would you like to apply the knowledge of physics you learn in this class to your daily life? By that, I mean, what would you *ask* of physics, were it yours to command?"

"You mean like a genie?" He chuckled.

"Sure, like that."

"I'd ask it to make daddy some money."

The class laughed. They knew Curtis well.

"Thank you for your forthcoming response."

"You're welcome."

"Have you, Curtis, ever heard of a semiconductor?"

"You mean like a transistor?" he asked.

"Yes, exactly." I stood. "We all know about computers. The big ones use reel-to-reel tape to function. Soon, all computing will be done by way of microchips, which are just really, really small transistors. So, let me ask you this, Curtis. Applying physics to your daily life, if you knew the name of the company that will come to dominate the world chip market before the turn of the next century, what would you do with that information?"

He looked to the students nearest him. Then he smiled. "Are you shitting me?"

The class erupted in laughter.

"I shit you not."

"I'd sell naked pictures of my older sister to get more money to invest in that stock."

I held up a finger. "That is the correct answer, my friend. You'd go all in."

"But I can't know that," Curtis protested.

"What?" I countered. "You can't know about *Intel?*"

He looked to his friends again and grinned even bigger. "I'm stopping at the camera store on my way home."

That evening, I told Shannon over dinner that a few school districts in LA had contacted me for job positions. She was not overjoyed, but only because she knew LA and had zero interest in settling there to raise a family. I was with her one hundred percent on that, but, hey, this was all a scam, so I had to sell it.

"I realize Southern California is not our preferred location to put down roots, but I think it's worth my going there and at least hearing them out."

She set her fork down with gravitas. "I hear what you're saying. I also realize that, as of now, you don't have a permanent job offer on the table. That said, honey, life's a slippery slope. We move there for a defined period, rent and do not own, but time passes. I just don't want to wake up one day two decades from now to realize we'd spent our lives in LA." She voluntarily shivered. "Such a soulless place. You're never more than a block away from a liquor store or a want-to-be movie star." She looked to me passionately. "It's just no place to bring up kids."

I threw up my hands in surrender. "I know, I know, and I couldn't agree more. *However*, if I got a great offer at an okay school, it'd look great on my resume. That's all I'm saying."

"I see your point," she conceded unhappily.

"And they're paying for the airfare and car rental, the whole nine yards. So we've got nothing to lose." I was about to tease that they'd offered to cover the cost of hookers too, but wisely deleted that mirth. Shannon would not appreciate the humor, or lack of therein.

"Now, am I invited too?"

Danger Will Robinson! I did not see that coming. "Er, ah, no, dear. This is a professional, feeling-each-other-out interview." I sliced a cross over my chest. "But I swear on my grandmother's grave that before I accept anything, you and I will tour the area exhaustively."

"Matt, your grandmother's not dead."

"She's in a nursing home and doesn't know she is. The old gal thinks she's on the *Queen Mary II* sailing for England. In my book, that's close enough."

The look on Shannon's face indicated she'd switched gears. "Well, I suppose there's no harm in you *talking* to these schools."

"None whatsoever," I lied confidently.

"So when are you going?"

"This Friday. I have an interview then and two on Monday. It's possible I might need to stay an extra day, but that'd only be if one of the prospects was looking especially enticing."

"But you will not *commit* without discussing everything with me, correct?"

"Absolutely. This is about our future, after all." And not Rolando Johnson's massacred family. No. Man, I was becoming such an accomplished liar.

I let my school know the next day I'd be unavailable. On Friday, I was dressed in the best off-the-rack suit Sears had to offer and I was whisked by Pacific Southwest Airlines to LA. Because I was being cautious, I actually met with the principal and vice principal at Mt. Vernon High in Reseda. I did so early to keep most of my day available for snooping on Rolando. I had his home address from the library phone book, so I drove there. Parking half a block away, I started watching his house. I knew he was almost certainly at work, but as he was mostly a driver, I couldn't very well watch him do that. But maybe he came home for lunch.

By early afternoon, I'd finished all the magazines I'd bought at the airport and I was getting hungry. Apparently, Rolando did not come home for lunch. I headed to a local mall and ate. Then I nostalgia-window shopped for a couple hours. Man, the clothes we wore back then. What *were* we thinking? I returned to Rolando's, hoping to catch him coming home. At half past four, he parked in front of his small 1950s bungalow. As he stood, I was even more impressed with his physicality. When I knew him, he'd been a mute in a psych hospital for years. Though he was still huge back then, now, at his prime in 1975, the man was a mountain.

Unsurprisingly, he walked up the short path to his door, entered, and was gone.

I considered sneaking around his yard, trying to listen to his interactions with his family. But the picture in my head of him catching me and what he would subsequently do to me persuaded me that was a *terrible* plan. So I returned to my motel and settled in for a dull night. The next morning, I parked a half a block in the other direction in front of his house, and began my vigil. He was up and out much earlier than I'd have thought. I followed him to Captain's Pizza Parlour, spelled presumably with a "U" to lend a continental flair to the establishment. It was nearing nine in the morning. I walked past the front door a few times. The place didn't open until eleven. What was he doing in there?

I went around back and was surprised to find him taking out large plastic bags of trash. Rolando was employed at Captain's. Huh, what a hard-working guy. Full time weekdays, then part time on Saturdays and what looked to be a full day at church the next day. Not my typical preconception of a serial killer. I hung around until the place opened. When there was enough of a crowd so I didn't stand out too much, I ordered a pie and a pitcher of beer, and sat myself in a dark corner of the restaurant. I caught the occasional glimpse of Rolando. He was definitely on clean-up duty. He was mopping, scraping, and making trash runs all afternoon. I got tired just watching him. Fortunately, his duties rarely brought him to the front of the house, so he didn't have a chance to notice me lingering.

Around four, as I was nursing my second pitcher, he finally spoke to who I knew by then was the boss, and then Rolando split. I followed him out from a distance. He drove to a three-story office building a couple miles away. He went down to the parking area below the building and opened a locked closet. Shortly after, he pushed a large mop bucket out, loaded with cleaning supplies. He called the elevator and waited. I slipped around to the other side of the building and watched him take the elevator up to the third floor. Damn, he went from one custodial gig to another on his day off. *By the livin' Gawd that made you, You're a better man than I am, Gunga Din!*

I returned to my car and watched him. Occasionally, he'd pass a window, generally while mopping or sweeping. It took him three hours to clean the building. I was growing so bored, I began to question my sanity for following the man around. I almost didn't notice when a black 1974 Mercedes-Benz 600 Kompressor pulled up near the underground parking's entrance. When I was originally in the 1970s, I never saw a car that luxurious. It exuded excess wealth and an indifference to cost on the part of the owner. I was immediately struck with a thought. I, in my cheap-ass rental, didn't match this neighborhood's demographic. What was priceymobile doing slumming in these parts? I was rather pleased to have a "mystery" to ponder, since I was about ready to start pulling hair out due to acute boredom.

Rolando reappeared with his mop bucket and the rest of the stuff he'd taken with him when he set out on his duties. He deposited several plastic bags in the dumpster, and walked back across the abandoned parking lot to put away his gear. Then, without obvious reason, he stopped dead in his tracks. He wasn't resting or noticing some trash that needed picking up. He was frozen to the spot he stood on. Most peculiar. I chanced to glance back at the Mercedes. The rear window facing the building was open. I was pretty sure it had been closed before. Then I checked out Rolando. The man was trembling. Now that was odd in the extreme. I mean, he wasn't shivering or seizing. He trembled as if he were very mad, or tormented in some manner. Then, as quickly as his worrisome state had befallen him, Rolando shook his head once, then proceeded to store his cleaning equipment. I wondered for a few seconds what had just happened. My eyes wandered back to the Mercedes. It was gone.

SIX

I lay in bed at the motel, trying to decide what to do next. After I followed Rolando home, which was completely uneventful, I watched his house for a while. When it was clear that nothing worth noting was going to happen, I left. Plus, hunger was calling. I stopped at a diner named Zig's. The sign said it was the home of The Bullet, so you know I had to try one. A big cheeseburger with grilled peppers. It was filling, I'll give Zig due credit there.

So, in summary, I'd tailed Rolando in a half-ass manner for a couple days. All I knew was that he was a hard worker. My return on invested time was pretty marginal. I either had to get more directly involved with him or give up this enterprise. In the back of my mind the entire time was the worry as to when I'd return to my "new normal" time of 1987. I had precious little experience with these *sticking* time dives, as I was beginning to call them. I didn't know if I had any conscious control over their length. I feared I would be whisked away at any moment, so I needed to make my time here count.

Well, tomorrow was Sunday. I knew enough about Rolando's history to know he was a church-going man. And church is an open, welcoming experience. Maybe I could back myself into actually meeting him tomorrow? It was the perfect setting, where social barriers were set aside by most participants. Sure. Why not? It would be interesting to maybe chat up the silent hulk I'd known for a few years. Maybe the pre-murder spree guy was funny, even gregarious?

In my future, I would have checked the internet for the times of the services at Reseda Antioch Baptist Church. But as I was years away from that convenience, I could either call the church (I did have a phone book in my motel room), or I could make a guess and show up then. If I called, I might get a recording of the schedule. Then again, this was the low-tech 70s. Instead, I elected to arrive a little before eleven. That was a fairly traditional service time for Sunday services. And if this particular church met at ten, I'd at least catch them dispersing.

I drove past the church at a quarter to and found a lot of cars out front maneuvering for parking spaces. I had been correct about the eleven o'clock start. I found a spot a block away and walked slowly toward the building. Based on my estimates, considering the structure's size, a good crowd was amassing. Around five 'til, the group gathered out in front began filing in. As seamlessly as I could, I mingled into the flow. As we slowly ascended the steps, I noticed Rolando was a greeter on the left. On an impulse, I directed myself in that direction. As I came alongside him, he reached out a massive hand and I shook it.

"Welcome, my friend," he said with a warmth and conviction that nearly caused me to hug him.

"Thank you," I mumbled back, still shaking. "Ah, this is my first time here,"

I added hesitantly, "Is there any order to the seating?"

Rolando's smile was as large as the crescent moon. "There is no plan to the seating. But I would be honored if you would choose to sit with me and my family."

"Ah, wow. Are you sure?"

"There is no doubt in my heart, my friend. Please," he released my hand and took me by the elbow, "follow me."

He guided me through the crowd of people chatting and hugging as they found their spots. He stopped by the second pew from the front and gestured to the group sitting there quietly.

"I'm sorry, I did not ask your name," he said with a guilty grin.

"Matt. Matt Dunsratty."

"Matthew Dunsratty, let me introduce you to my fine family. This is my treasured wife, Dorothy."

She rose halfway and shook my hand daintily. "Pleasure to meet you, Mr. Dunsratty."

"And these are my gifts from God." He signaled for two young children to stand. "The tall one is my Jesse, and the shorter one is Marcus. Between them sits my little angel, Angela." She was in a car seat carrier.

I waved to the boys, who slightly bowed their heads.

"Please, have a seat, Matthew. I shall return directly."

I slid in next to Dorothy, but left plenty of space between us for Rolando. The organist began playing softly, as a signal to the gathered that the service was about to begin. Rolando returned and scrunched past me to sit by his wife. Once he was settled, he gave me a joyous smile. "Thank you for joining us, Matthew."

The music volume shot up, and we were underway. I'd never been to a Baptist service. I actually had been to few churches of any ilk in my younger days. My parents weren't particularly religious, so neither was I. Right off the bat, I was impressed with two things. The gathered faithful here were energetic and gleeful. The choir was superb and the musicians quite competent. I was also impressed by the fact that while I wasn't the only Caucasian present, I was definitely one of the very few. But not a single person so much as glanced over to me. It was all good.

The pastor made his presence felt after the music. His sermon was passionate and it was ... er, how to say ... *lengthy*. My limited experience was with a short, structured homily. This was free-wheeling and extended. But it was nice. Was I an instant fan? Maybe. Soon enough, the service was over and everyone filed out. Rolando and our group lingered until most of the crowd was gone, then he extended an arm toward the exit. "If you will, please, Matthew," he invited.

As we headed out, Dorothy and Rolando greeted several others. The place was definitely one big, happy family. Near the door, Rolando extended a hand to me. As we shook, he said, "Thank you again for joining us, Matthew. There is a coffee and cookie reception in the hall if you'd like to meet some of the others."

"Oh, I don't know—" I began uncertainly.

"Please, I mean, who doesn't like cookies?" He grinned mischievously.

"Well, you got that right," I affirmed. "As long as there's enough for unexpected guests."

"Here, my friend, there are no unexpected guests." He wagged a tree-trunk finger. "God moves in mysterious ways. That is especially true where cookies are involved."

We shared a chuckle. Then his family and I headed over to the meeting hall. There was a modest group chatting and laughing by the time we arrived. Rolando excused himself from his wife and asked me to accompany him. I could tell that for Dorothy this was a routine occurrence. He led me to where the pastor was laughing with a few others. He had a cup of coffee in one hand and a large homemade cookie in the other.

"Pastor William," Rolando interrupted. "I'd like to introduce you to our new guest, Matthew Dunsratty."

William quickly set the cookie down so as to free up his right hand. He extended it to me. "Brother Matthew, so wonderful to meet you."

"The pleasure's all mine," I responded with a nod.

"And what did you think of our celebration?"

"Very impressive," I replied honestly.

"Well then, perhaps you will grace us with your attendance again some time?"

"I'm not a local, but who knows what the future holds?"

"Truer words, my friend," he concurred. "Just know our doors are *always* open, especially to any friend of Rolando."

"Thank you, pastor," I concluded.

William was pulled away by other social obligations. Rolando pointed to the refreshment table. "Let's get a cookie before they're all gone. My missus baked all day yesterday, but she can never quite seem to make enough to satisfy this crowd."

Massive cookies and cups of weak coffee in hand, we rejoined his wife and daughter. The boys were off in a corner horsing around with some of their buds. There was a lot of yelling and running involved. Ah, to be young again.

I took a bite of the cookie and was stunned. It was what a cookie aspired to be, but so few made the grade. It was moist, yet crisp, sweet, but savory. The chocolate chips melted just as you bit down on them, and the nuts then greeted your palate with an oily good-ness. My immediate reaction? I needed to get back to that table and grab a few more. Did they have bags available?

"Dorothy," I exclaimed, "this is the best cookie I've ever tasted. How ... who ... I ... these are blissful."

"Thank you, Mr. Dunsratty. You're too kind."

"No, seriously, these are the best ever. Would it be too much to ask for your recipe? My wife's a decent baker. I know she'd love it."

"Why, of course, Mr. Dunsratty," she replied with a modest turn of her head. "As chance would have it, I have many copies of that recipe available. People have been known to request them before."

"I bet they do." I turned to Rolando. "You are a lucky man, my friend."

"Don't I know it," he thundered in response.

After that, Rolando and I chatted a bit, mostly about the weather and our family's health. Then I thanked him again and made my way back to my car. In my afterglow, as I drove to the motel, I was tormented by a singular impression. There was no way on God's green earth Rolando Johnson could ever kill that lovely family of his. None. Not even remotely possible.

But it happens in less than a month.

Why?

SEVEN

I was whooped when I got back to my room, so I decided to take a nap. When I awoke, I'd worry about a late lunch. I was that tired. To the clunking rattle of the window-mounted AC, I drifted off, still wondering about how Rolando could have possibly done what I knew he was about to do. I remember sleeping fitfully, tossing and turning more than was typical for an afternoon siesta. I don't recall dreaming. That was probably just as well. I'm sure they were dark, unsettling, and ended poorly.

As my slumber broke, I felt better. I had a notion that I was going to feel refreshed. Even my pillow was softer, the room with a crisp homey scent in the air. I think I smiled before I even opened my eyes.

"Matt?" a woman's voice called to me softly. "Are you awake yet, honey?"

My eyelids shot open like cheap window shades. There was no woman with me when I laid my head down to nap. My first thought? Call the police? No. Bolt for the door? Nope. You got it. Shannon was going to murderize me, slowly, painfully, and with finality.

She shook my shoulder. "You said you wanted to me to make

sure you didn't sleep past three. It's three thirty. If you want me to leave you be, just say the word."

Shannon? OMG, how did Shannon find, let alone get into my hotel room ... the one with the comfy pillows and alluring smell?

I shot bolt upright. Shannon jumped backward a full yard, I surprised her so.

"I'm home," I stated for the official record. I turned to Shannon, who had the back of a hand over her mouth. "What year is—" Abort, Matt. Do not ask your suspicious, hypervigilant wife what year it is.

"Pardon?" she asked, her beautiful face hardening.

"What you's doing?" I offered up to the lone judge of my future marital success.

"Matt, when did you start talking like a hillbilly?"

I made a show of rubbing my eyes. "I'm sorry, hon. What'd you ask? I think I'm still more asleep than awake."

Her countenance eased.

"And thanks for letting me sleep a little longer. Power naps, those are the key to mental health." I tapped the side of my head.

"Power naps? Never heard of those, but if you say so, then I'm all for them. What with your history of encephalitis, I guess we can't be too cautious, now can we?"

"No, not with a history ... I had encephalitis?" I shouted.

Her face went pale. "Yes, remember, back in the spring of 1975?"

Okay, note to self. It was no longer 1975. And I had ... oh, wait. That was my cover story. It was coming back slowly. Yes, I'd woken up in a strange motel in, of all places, Reseda, California. I had no clue why I was there or what I was doing. Yes, I ran around like a chicken with its head cut off in a panic. The motel manager yelled something like *PCP* to the police she'd summoned to deal with me. As I was cooling my jets in the county lockup, I figured out that I must have been on a time dive gone wild. I concocted a story about me having encephalitis, which was why I was acting so bizarrely. I even got the ER doc to sign off on it. *Dude, I've never diagnosed that before. This is totally awesome!* he'd declared. What a moron. But it was my lucky day. Oh, yeah, and ever since, Shannon was uber-cautious about my mental state, since I was an encephalitis survivor and all.

Lord in Heaven, I was such a pathological liar.

"So, how 'bout some herbal tea?" Shannon asked graciously.

"Sounds great, but only if you make enough for two and serve it on the patio."

She screwed up one side of her mouth and furrowed her brow. "Matt, it's pouring rain outside. I'll serve it in the kitchen." With that, she turned and left. I'd dodged any number of bullets just now.

I took a series of deep breaths, then stood up. What a frigging mess. My life, it was pure chaos. My brain was the summation of thousands of Matthew Dunsrattys' lives. This me was sixty-something years old residing in a 1987 version of myself, and I just popped out of a stuck time dive randomly. I'd abandon that Matt. Oh, man. What did I know? Well, I knew Rolando murdered his family, but was that knowledge from the future Matts, or a memory this version stored based on his experience? Shit.

I headed toward my study. As I passed through the family room, I called out to let Shannon know I'd be in for tea after I check something on the internet. I logged on and check on Rolando's status. Sure enough, a few weeks after I'd met him, he butchered his family. He was locked up in the state hospital for life, just like he had been. As was the case before, he never spoke a word about his crime and no motive was discovered.

My head spun, my stomach contents suggested they were about to come up and meet me again, and I had such a headache. I guess it wasn't surprising that my simply meeting Rolando didn't alter his course. Damn, why did I bug out when I did? It wasn't voluntarily, that's for sure. I certainly had no control over how long I stayed in my past. That would have to change if I was to be effective in my new reality. Huh. Maybe I could get an advanced college degree in time diving? That way, I'd be a master of the entire process.

Encephalitis. What a dipshit.

After Shannon calmed herself down and went about her day, I had the chance to mentally regroup. Once thing was for certain. I was totally convinced that Rolando could not have done what he was convicted of. Like it or not, it was now my obligation to save his big ass. This went beyond him having done me a solid and me paying him back. The man was wrongly accused of a brutal crime against those he treasured. That was too wrong not to set right.

I had attended the Antioch Baptist Church with Rolando on Sunday, May 11. We were acquaintances, maybe even buddies. I could try to leverage that familiarity to get even closer to him, find out what he was thinking as the evil day approached. The next logical day to interact with him was the next Sunday, the eighteenth. That left a razor's-edge margin of just over three weeks to avert the crime. Well, ideally. As obviously some other person or persons did the actual killing, maybe I couldn't prevent all the slaughter. And if I was going to Reseda for a second time, I was going to have to have one hell of a story to tell Shannon. I'd told her if I got serious about a job offer, I'd take her along. If I did that, my ability to mix with Rolando and his family would be severely cramped. How did I always seem to get myself into these unsolvable dilemmas?

I had learned the hard way that in constructing a wall of lies, it was best to keep it as simple as possible. The taller the tale and the bigger the leap of faith, the more likely it'd be to blow up in your face. Oh, yeah, had a few of those in my times. Bea-u-ties. Shannon announced she was going grocery shopping. She knew better than to ask if I wanted to join in, since I absolutely never-ever did. But she yelled to me to put whatever I wanted on her list on the kitchen counter. I slipped into the room while she was elsewhere and added *sex toys* to the list. Was that juvenile of me? Duh, but it was fun.

After she was gone, I prepared to time dive back to May 15, 1975. I didn't do the mail-myself-a-letter thing. I was assuming this time dive would stick, so why bother? I also focused merely on the date, not any specific event that I recalled, mostly since I couldn't remember anything particularly distinguishing. But my time dives were changing, post incarceration and medication. Perhaps it was time to see if I could simplify the process. I mean, I invented the Rube-Goldberg method I employed. That didn't mean it was the only way to fly, right? If I was just being cocky and it went sideways, I could always fall back on the tried-and-true.

I closed my eyes, zeroed in on that Thursday evening, and when I opened my eyes, I was back in 1975 Matt's study. I sat in front of my typewriter, not knowing what I'd been doing moments before. But it was a smooth landing, so I was jazzed. There were no clues around to suggest what was going on. I listened a minute to see if Shannon was expecting me, but apparently, she wasn't. I then set my plan in motion. I went in search of my wife. Maybe she was taking a bubble bath, with scented candles and champagne? Hey, a man can dream.

I found her on her hands and knees scrubbing out the toilet in the master bedroom. Her hair was partially restrained by a mustard-yellow daisy-appointed crocheted bandanna. Oh, how very 70s of her. A rebellious wisp of hair was in her mouth. Hmm. This was pretty much the opposite on my earlier fantasy. In fact, it was down-right domestic. After a moment of grief, I asked her, "Ah, can you break away to chat?"

She turned her head to me and telegraphed me a you-have-got-to-be-shitting-me response. Then she threw, not tossed, the brush into the sudsy bucket with a catastrophic splash. She held out an arm to me. "Give me a hand up." She groaned to her feet and walked past me out the door. "Let's take this to the kitchen."

"Ah, sure," I said hesitantly. I pointed to the toilet. "You want to clean up first?"

"Don't push your luck, husband of mine."

"Gotcha." We were heading to the kitchen—now.

When I arrived, she was seated at the table with two glasses of iced tea. I noted with relief that at least she'd taken her gloves off. I sat across from her and took a sip.

"What's on your mind?" she asked tersely. She was not a fan of toilet cleaning, let that fact be known. She also knew that my threshold for feeling the need to clean them was ten or twelve light years past her threshold. So if they were going to be cleaned, she was doing the dirty work, oh yeah.

"I was speaking to one of the schools in Reseda today."

Her expression stiffened.

"They upped their offer. I'd have only a seventy-five percent teaching load and they increased the pay offer by ten percent. Now, I know we don't want to be in LA forever, but I was wondering if you and I could drive down there this weekend, you know, check the place out?"

"I was afraid of this when you mentioned this whole idea."

"I remember. And trust me, if you say the deal is dead, it's dead. But having a look-see doesn't hurt anything, does it?"

"Yes and no. Yes, it doesn't incur any debt or obligation. But no, it does up the stakes. I'm not—"

"Hey, we drive down, call it a getaway, and there's no harm, no foul."

"To beautiful downtown Reseda, the romance capital of the west coast," she critiqued.

"I kind of liked it myself," I defended.

"Yes, and you're a pig, so what does that tell me?"

"You're right," I said, switching verbal gears. "Let's stay home. You can get *all* the toilets cleaner than clean and I can relax around the house, contributing nothing, which is what I do every weekend."

"Call in sick for tomorrow, and I'm all aboard," she shot back immediately. She pointed at me. "But you're driving."

"Deal, deal, and let me leave a message on the school's recorder before you change your mind."

She took a slug of her tea. "Reseda, here we come."

The drive down was, as it always was, seven and a half hours of San Joaquin Valley dryness followed by the LA freeways. But at least Reseda was north of LA proper, so less of a journey. I thought about checking us into the motel I'd stayed in before. It was serviceable and clean. But, recalling that I had the aesthetics of a pig, I headed for a high-rise hotel I'd seen. That was a life-saving call on my part. She'd have hated the motel, and the hotel had ... you got it, a spa! Yes, Shannon booked a Friday afternoon and a Saturday morning session right there at the check-in counter. A facial, a massage, a sulfur soak, and a Brazilian wax, whatever the heck that was. Maybe I'd find out sooner or later? All that mattered was that she was in ecstasy, so it would be just that much harder for me to get into trouble. Hey, I'll take all the help I can get.

We dined at a local legend—or so I was told by the concierge—King of Crabs. He swore it was wonderful. All I could think of was a skid-row bum with an ecosystem of lice in his groin. But, again, Shannon loved the place and neither of us came away with an STD. Again, more crumple zone between me and self-inflicted disaster. I was an instant fan. On Saturday, I drove her around. I showed her the school that allegedly wanted me bad. I of course chose Saturday to take that tour, since no one at the school knew me from Adam. I elected, you see, to show her the nicest high school in the area, not one that I'd actually visited.

But Shannon was in a hurry to get back to the spa, so I was on my own most of the afternoon. We had reservations at the hotel's in-house restaurant, so it looked to be a quiet rest-of-the-day. I flashed on Rolando. He'd be just about done at his first part time job, and heading to his second. I drove to the office building and parked discreetly. Now that he knew me, I really didn't want to risk freaking him out. Sure enough, same time as last week, he pulled in and unpacked the janitor's closet. As he began to push the tools of his trade toward the elevator, he did that thing again. He suddenly stiffened, and his body seemed to be struggling mightily against some unseen foe. I was stunned.

Rolando's fit—or whatever—lasted a couple minutes. Then he went down on one knee, weak and obviously panting. I had half a mind to rush over and offer aid, but there was no way he'd believe I was randomly passing through the neighborhood. I just watched with mounting concern. A couple minutes later, he was up and headed for the elevator again. I wondered what the hell was going on. Whatever it was sure seemed massive.

Once he was out of sight, I reached for my ignition to head back to the hotel. That was when I heard tires screech. I turned to watch the black Mercedes pull away from the curb. No freaking way this was a coincidence. Two weeks, two episodes, the same Kompressor 600. I fired up the car and sped in the direction the car departed in. As I rounded the first corner, the Mercedes was gone. Crap. I'd lost them before I even got started. That was probably just as well. What was I going to do, pull them over and beat confessions out of them? But that car was on my radar now, big time.

Shannon and I had a fun night. The hotel restaurant was decent enough, the wine was inexpensive enough, and we laughed like idiots in the nearly empty dining room. Oh, and when I got frisky a little later on, I discovered exactly what a Brazilian wax was. I also found out that one didn't have sex after one until the irritation died down a bit. Oh, myyy.

The next morning, I definitely had to check in with Rolando at his church. I needed to find out what was up with those fits he was having and the black Mercedes. If necessary, I was almost ready to just ask him, instead of beating around the bush like I had been. Hmm, how was I going to sell Shannon on attending a Baptist church? She was raised Episcopalian and attended the local branch office near our place every now and then. She knew I was nowheresville when it came to religion, so my suggestion that we do would be immediately suspect.

What could I have been doing while she was at the spa that would logically explain my desire to drag her to Antioch Baptist? I had it. The choir! They were certifiably great. So I just needed a cover story for how I learned of the music there and how I was chummy with one of the regulars? I guess I could say it was Rolando who I happened to run into and he suggested it, but that wouldn't explain how I knew the family. Oh, they were out together. But what if they mentioned that I attended last week too? Man, this was getting sticky. The BS meter was getting toward the upper end of its scale.

Okay, this would have to do. I found out about it last week from Rolando, who was out with his family, and the music was superb, so I wanted to hear it again. Why hadn't I mentioned the church if it was so marvelous? Because ... this was all an elaborate lie and I was a horrible man? Probably an unwise direction to take. How about because I was hoping to surprise Shannon with the experience? Wow, that was lame *squared*. But I was a desperate man embroiled in a universe of lies. So at breakfast, I told Shannon I had a surprise for her. She smiled cherubically and asked how many carats it was. I felt my soul sink that much deeper into my self-dug tar pit of despair. Oh, no, honey, not diamonds, just more pathological lies. If I didn't burn in hell, I was complaining directly to Saint Peter.

After I said it was a drive-to surprise, not a wear-on-your-finger one, she pretended to have been joking. Yeah, a woman joking about receiving diamonds. That could happen. Note to self, Matt: If you want to live, buy the girl diamonds and buy them soon. Wait, the hotel, it had a small and probably offensively expensive jewelry shop, didn't it? Matty Boy, take the easy out. When you return to the hotel, whip out the credit card.

I drove to the church, and as I parallel-parked across the street, she eyed me with considerable circumspection.

"*This* is the surprise?" she tried to ask neutrally.

"Yes, it is," I attempted to sell. "And you are going to love it."

She lowered her eyes and looked up at me. "Honey, this isn't one of those Matt things I get so upset about, is it?"

"Well, of course not. Seriously, okay, you're breaking my balls here, so I'll tell you. This church has the best music ministry."

Her head rotated lower and her eyes strained to stay affixed to me.

"I was here last week. But no more. Come, hear, and be amazed." I dashed around the car and opened her door for her.

To her credit, Shannon took my elbow and let me escort her to the front steps. The service began in ten minutes, so I elected to mill about outside. I wanted physical flexibility to handle whatever might come up with Rolando and his wife. I gazed to the entrance. Two different men were greeters today. I scanned for Rolando, which, if you'll recall my description of him, is a trivial thing to do in any crowd. Like finding a haystack in a needle. Sure enough, there he was off to one side, speaking with some fellow, while his wife, Dorothy, was chatting with that man's missus. I decided to take the plunge there and then. I shot a hand up in the air and waved in his direction as I moved very slowly that way.

Almost immediately, Rolando noticed me and waved back. He excused himself and strode over like Paul Bunyan lumbering through a forest clearing. He snatched up my hand, wrist, and forearm and began shaking them. "Matthew, so good to see you again."

"You too, Rolando."

We both smiled like old friends reunited.

Then he spied over to Shannon. "And this must be your lovely wife, Shannon, whom you spoke of so fondly last week."

Alright, Shannon was impressed. She was bowled over by his sheer size and presence. She was doubly impressed with the warmth he showed me. She was *totally* impressed that I'd said nice things about her to a stranger.

He reached tentatively toward her, and Shannon's hand disappeared into his greeting palm.

"Honey, this is Rolando. He was kind enough to introduce me to this amazing house of worship last week."

"Rolando," she said a bit uncertainly. "Nice to meet you. I wonder why Matt didn't mention you before?" Such a suspicious wife. Of course, I'd done a lot to engender that doubting aspect of her personality.

He frowned and looked to me.

"Because this was all a surprise," I declared.

Shannon's face reflected that she got it, but Rolando, not so much. "I wanted to bring her here today to surprise her with the music ministry. So naturally—"

"Ah." He chuckled. "Now I see." He wagged a finger at me. "I have to keep an eye on you, it would appear." He continued his soft laugh up until the point that it stopped abruptly, like a car hitting a brick wall.

All present eyed him closely. Rolando ground his teeth so intensely, I feared he'd crack his jaw. He trembled and his legs threatened to buckle.

I jumped up a couple steps and scanned the street. There it was, the black Mercedes, double parked across the street. But even as I broke for it, the window rolled up and the car sped away. I doubt they even noticed my move toward them. I turned back to Rolando, and he was recovering quickly. He was panting and offering half-hearted reassurances to Dorothy. I couldn't tell, but it seemed to me like she'd never witnessed one of these spells before. She was clearly beside herself.

No one outside our little group must've noticed Rolando's episode. The crowd began to filter in, so we joined it. In the process, Rolando belatedly introduced Shannon to Dorothy. We sat next to their family once we were inside. I have to tell you that it didn't take long for Shannon to be extremely impressed by the music. She smiled, clapped along, and even swayed from side-to-side. She was an instant fan.

Understandably, throughout the service, Dorothy repeatedly asked her husband if he was alright. He repeated that he was fine and that she mustn't worry herself. But she was a wife and there was no way to curtail her period of worrying and doting.

After the service, Rolando extended an invitation for us to join them in the hall for coffee and cookies. Shannon was initially uncertain, but I told her flat out we needed to check out the cookies. No ifs, ands, or buts. After her first bite, she looked at me as if to say you were so right. I put the two women together and pulled Rolando aside.

"Man, what happened to you back there in front of the church?" I asked with concern.

He scowled, then looked concerned. "Nothing. I must have a touch of the flu or something."

"No way. You were teetering like a tree about to fall. What's up. And did you notice that big black Mercedes?"

"Mercedes?" he asked incredulously. "I didn't see a Mercedes." *You crazy bastard* flashed across his face, thankfully unspoken.

"Rolando, you can try and put Dorothy off, but I'm not your wife. I was a medic in the Marines." A total lie, of course, and a risky one, since he'd served in Vietnam. But I knew he'd respect the institution a medic represented. Sorry, Rolando, this is all for your own good.

"You were? Where'd you—"

I waved off the rest of the query. "Doesn't matter, soldier. But don't try and BS this medic." I thumped my thumb against my chest. "What happened?"

I could tell his mind was racing a million miles an hour. The poor guy was torn, but by what, I couldn't imagine. "I ... it's not something I can ... I can't say." He stiffened and looked about the room. "You know what happens when some officer hears a rumor that this one over there's losing it." He shook his head. "I'm not going down that dark road. No. No, Matthew, I'm fine. Thank you for your concern, but please do not worry after me."

Damn. I almost had him spill the beans. Whatever he's not willing to tell me must be big. It must also be something that he feels I will interpret as demonstrating that he's having a psychotic break. He doesn't want to be locked up in some VA and never see the light of day again.

I pulled out my wallet and took out one of the cards the school gave me. "Look, man, if you ever need to talk ... when you need to talk, you call me." I pointed at his nose. "You got that, soldier?"

He nodded without speaking.

Shannon took that occasion to wrap her arm over my elbow and ask what we were talking about. "Serious business, hon," I replied seriously. I pointed to Rolando's chest. "This man lives in LA. He is, and I hate to say the words, a Dodger fan. I was just trying to reverse his unfortunate brainwashed condition."

It took them a second, but finally, they both chuckled.

"Said the life-long Giants fan," Shannon accused rather than informed.

We shared another round of chuckles. Then Dorothy told Rolando it was time to go. She had a roast to put in the oven and Jesse's stomach issues were threatening to return. We all said our goodbyes, Rolando invited us back the next Sunday, and we parted company. On the way back to the car, Shannon thanked me for the surprise, said she loved the cookies, and she was smitten with Rolando and Dorothy. She did make a specific point to add that as nice as they were, moving to Reseda was still not on her horizon. Not yet at least.

We left the next morning for Northern California. Shannon was afterglowing the whole way home. And she checked out her new diamond earrings in the rearview mirror so often, I had to remind her I kind of needed the safety device too.

Me, I was brooding the entire way. What was it with the black Mercedes and Rolando's spells? I was going to find out.

EIGHT

Back home, the week of May 19, 1975 passed uneventfully. I taught at Aragon High School during the day, and Shannon and I got into major discussions about our future. Seems our jaunt to SoCal really awakened her nesting instincts. She repeated time and again how much she liked Reseda and how surprised she was seeing it with her own eyes. But, there was always a big implied *but* in her comments. She was a NorCal gal. I was deeply rooted here also. Her mom and dad, whom she reveled in being with, lived up here. If we should ever move south, our kids would rarely see their grandparents. Now, don't get me wrong. I had no interest whatsoever in a relocation to the Den of the Dodgers. Noooh waaay. My feigned interest was just a front. But I had to sell it at least a bit in order to make my trips there—oh yes, there would *be* more trips—justifiable.

My primary obligation was, and always would be, to preserve my marriage with Shannon. Helping Rolando, however altruistic, would always play a distant second fiddle. The minute this house of cards cover story collapsed, I was abandoning my efforts on his behalf immediately. I'm sorry his extended family was killed, but I'd been severely burned by excessive interventions too many times in the past to allow myself to do so again. Sorry, pal. But, so far at least, my meddling was under Shannon's radar, so I was good to continue.

All I knew were four basic facts. One, Rolando loved his family dearly. Two, he was having unexplained episodic physical symptoms. Three, there was someone in a black Mercedes that was darkly involved. Four, Rolando's family would die June 13, 1975, brutally and by all evidence, from Rolando's own hand. Setting aside my personal conviction that he could not have murdered his family, I was really left with only one logical common thread to explain those four facts. Drugs.

As hard as it was to imagine, Rolando had to be using illicit drugs. The man did work like a dog. He wouldn't be the first hard-laborer to use methamphetamine or even PCP to help him get through his days. An overdose of either could make him mentally ill enough to do the unthinkable. Also, drug dealers were felons dispensing powerful medications. They were sloppy, untrained, and, well, they were felons. They could easily have slipped Rolando something by accident or out of callous disregard that would cause him to crash off the rails.

So my working plan was to either stop Rolando from taking any street drugs, at least for the next three weeks, or to separate him from his source, who was almost certainly the person in the Benz. I was fairly certain if I just confronted a religious guy like Rolando with accusations of drug use, he'd deny it out-of-hand. But, when I pretended to be a former medic, he almost opened up to me. Wait, his almost confession was probably about his drug habit. So I could attack that angle, apply pressure for him to fess up. Stopping an obviously successful drug dealer from plying his or her trade was a much harder course to follow. But it was an option, as long as it didn't get me killed.

One step at a time, though, I reminded myself. First, I had to hope I stayed back here in 1975 and not Chutes and Ladders my ass back to 1987. Second, I had to get back to Reseda without setting off any alarms, either for Rolando or my wife. As he was a driver and hard to run into during the week, making a move on him this weekend seemed to be my wisest plan. So, how could I justify another trip down to Reseda? Job-offer related? Nah, Shannon would expect to start seeing some detailed communications between me and the school if that were the case. Also, she'd look dimly on me stringing the school along, since she had no intention of moving down south.

Hmm. What if Dorothy called me, told me Rolando was in crisis and was asking for me? That might just work. I had kept the fact that Rolando was having spells a secret from Shannon. But I could explain that away. Rolando swore me to silence. But, if I pulled this off, I couldn't use this particular lie again. That would be way too suspicious. After hatching and then abandoning a few other schemes, I settled on the call-for-help story. I just hoped my wife was still in a happy mental place from her spa treatments. She might just fight me on this one.

"So, that's it?" Shannon asked, trying to expertly blend incredulous with respectful.

"Well, yeah," I countered, making it seem like what I'd explained was as plain as day. "I had mentioned to Rolando that I worked at Aragon High. So it wasn't too much trouble for Dorothy to track me down there."

"No, I get that part. What I'm ... um, *less* clear about is why she called you. Why did Rolando ask for your help specifically? I mean, obviously, they're good people, but we just met them. If he's having some life crisis, shouldn't he contact his doctor? Maybe his family or his pastor? This seems, well, I'll just say it, far fetched."

Ooh, I hated that word, *far fetched*. When applied to a lie, as in this case, it suggested badness was to follow shortly. But, when you lie as routinely and as broadly as I have, you get real good at it. It's best to never over-defend a lie. If an aspect of one is perceived as shaky, don't suggest that your intended victim is as dumb as an ox.

"Hey, I agree. Those are all much better options if you ask me. He's also served in the Army. The VA must have a lot of support services to offer vets at some breaking point." I shook my head in confused disbelief.

"Thank you!" She moved some items on her dinner plate around. "And she left you their number, right?"

I nodded and I forced myself to choke down some food. I wanted to seem casual, natural.

"So, maybe you should call Dorothy and tell her tactfully that you're not comfortable going down to Reseda. You could offer to speak to him on the phone, maybe. That's strikes me as more along the social norm."

I pretended to ponder her wise words. "I actually did offer to call him when I spoke to her. She kind of freaked out a little. Said Rolando wasn't *so good at speaking on the phone*, whatever that means?"

"It's still an awful lot to ask of a casual acquaintance to hump it all the way down to LA," she opined, disgruntled.

"You know, I agree. I guess I just need to tell her gently but firmly that I'm not the guy to ask for help. What am I, a traveling social worker now?" I shook my head again. "It's not like we'll likely ever see them again in our lives, right." I looked away, acting as if I was trying to recall some reference. "Yeah, you know what they say. *I'm not my brother's keeper*, right?"

That was below-the-belt. I intended it to be. My Shannon was a truly wonderful human. For me to agree with her by paraphrasing Cane was about as brutal as it got.

"In fact, if you don't mind, I think I'll call her right now and tell her I can't be ... don't have any time to invest in this situation. I'll let her know the truth. I'm begging for a job down here. If I don't find one, we don't eat. Helping a stranger in no way advances my cause. Hey, baby needs shoes." We did not have a baby yet. I was being callous and shallow, thank you very much.

"Matt, I'm not sure you're getting my point here. They're *wonderful* people. If we could help, if *you* could help, we would in a heartbeat. But it's not logical that we are the first to be asked."

"No, I get it. It's inappropriate for Rolando to expect I would go over too far out of my way to help him, nice as he is. One does not enter a bank and demand money because one feels they need it more than the bank does. That's not logical." Again, I was agreeing with her, but doing so in a manner designed to inadvertently emphasize that we were a pair of lousy good Samaritans.

"And she didn't mention any specifics as to what the nature of his dire straits were?"

I chewed thoughtfully. "Not really. She just said, well, these were her exact words actually. *Rolando's a proud man. He has trouble asking for help from anyone, especially if it's for his personal pain.*"

"My, it does sound like something's wrong. Pain's a pretty strong word."

"Yes, but that's all the more reason to call in a specialist, not a high-school science teacher."

She was quiet a moment. "I wouldn't characterize it like that. They're not calling for help from a science teacher. They're calling for help from you, Matt. Someone they trust enough in a critical juncture to offer some relief. If that person happens to be new to their lives, that doesn't make their cry for help any less compelling."

"What, are you saying that maybe Rolando *does* have friends and family he could ask? But he worries that they might betray his confidence and poison the well, so to speak? I, as a trusted outsider, don't share that frightening potential, at least as Rolando sees it in his troubled mind. So I'm not that crazy a choice to call after all? *That's* what you're saying?"

"Yes, that's it exactly. You know how terrible men are at asking for help," she philosophized.

I dropped my fork with a clink. "You're not bringing up me and our drive through Winslow, Arizona, are you? Hey, anyone could've missed that sign."

She grinned playfully. "And anyone could have stopped at the gas station and asked to see a map. But it would appear some *anyones* were too macho to do so."

"That does it." I pretended to be upset. "You've played the Winslow card. I'm catching the next flight to LA."

"Well, okay. But promise me one thing."

I playfully pouted. "What?"

"If you get lost on the way to the airport, please ask for directions."

———

So, the next morning, May 23, 1975, I caught the first flight out of SFO for LAX. I had to call out sick to the high school, but I was okay with that. They weren't keeping me on in spite of a solid performance for almost the entire school year. I had no hard feelings, but neither did I have any misplaced loyalty. Since I didn't have the luxury of an invitation for Rolando's family, Friday looked to be a write-off in terms of interacting with him. But I was getting desperate, so I grasped at whatever straws blew past in the breeze. On the off chance there was an event at his church, I called Antioch Baptist as soon as the office opened. It turned out there was a blood drive there tonight from four to eight. Hmm, maybe Rolando would be there? He's been in combat, so he knew the value of ample blood supplies. I penciled it in as a possibility.

Next, I drove to his place of work, Ace Moving and Storage. Maybe I could follow him to some stop and then conceivably happen to be there myself. Yeah, needy and risky. I did not want to scare the man off by revealing that I was stalking him. I parked across the street from the facility. His truck was missing, which meant he was on a job. I waited around for a couple hours and he didn't return. I got hungry and bored, so I bailed on my dumb stake-out. I checked into my now standard motel and chilled a while. Come five, I headed to the church. It would be easy to watch the meeting hall. If he showed, I could maybe work up the nerve to go in too.

By seven thirty, I was giving up hope. Then, by gosh, Rolando did show. He cruised right past me, looking for a place to park. He was alone. I guess Dorothy stayed at home with the kids. Rolando probably showered and ate before coming to donate. I leaped from my car, determined to be inside first. That would demonstrate beyond any doubt that my being there had nothing to do with his arrival.

The hall had three blood-draw stations set up, with a fourth being broken down due to the hour. One other person was currently being bled. The room was as quiet as an empty funeral parlor. Go figure.

"Welcome!" a large woman greeted me. "I'm Sister Evelyn, please come right in." She gestured demonstrably to a chair in front of her table. Once I was situated, she continued. "Is this your first time donating here at Antioch Baptist, sir?"

"Ah, yes. I've visited a couple times. Thought I'd try and help out."

"Well, your heart is certainly in the right place, ah mister—"

"Matt. Matt Dunsratty."

"So, Mr. Dunsratty," she slid me a stack of papers, "I would like you to fill these forms out. Once you're done, a nurse will check the details, and if everything is in proper order, we can begin your collection. Why, Rolando, how are you, my friend?" she exclaimed loudly. Apparently, he was right behind me.

"And a very good evening to you, Evelyn," he returned. "It's so nice to ... Matthew?" he queried as he noticed me. "I'm most pleasantly surprised to see you here this evening." He reached out and shook my hand enthusiastically.

"Good to see you too."

Evelyn was speechless. I assumed that was a rare and transient event for her. Finally, she mustered, "You two are friends?"

"Matthew is a new friend of mine," Rolando replied proudly.

"One who I hope will become a part of our community here should the Good Lord see it fit that he moves to this area."

"Well, excuse me for rushing you gentlemen, but the hour is growing late," Evelyn directed. "Matthew, if you could complete those forms, I can get our *regular* donor Rolando squared away." She sorted through a file box and pulled his folder. "There it is. Rolando, you know the drill. Take this to the nurse. He'll get you set up."

Rolando steeled his expression and marched over to where a man in white sat. I guess he was as big a fan of blood donation as I was, which was not very much of one.

Forty-five minutes later, I was drained, taped up, and cleared by Brian, the med tech. Rubbing my arm, I headed for the exit. Rolando sat there waiting. I'd hoped he would.

"Matthew, they say we are supposed to hydrate ambitiously after this procedure. Might I entice you into sharing a beer in the pizza parlor down the street, eh, for medicinal purposes, naturally."

"Naturally," I returned with mock seriousness. "And I always follow doctor's orders."

We walked to the restaurant. The evening was pleasant and I certainly felt secure in the company of my giant friend.

"To blood donations," he toasted once our beers arrived.

"To vampires," I teased as I clicked his mug. I took a long draw. "I actually needed that," I said resoundingly as I set the mug down.

"It is the highlight of the entire ordeal, I will grant you that, my friend."

We were quiet a moment. "So, what brings you back to Reseda?" he finally asked.

"Still hammering out a potential job offer." I took a sip. "They are so anxious to secure my services, the fools keep sweetening the pot. I figured I'd come down and see if I could squeeze that much more out of them."

"Good for you," He raised his glass. "You deserve whatever you get and more."

I toasted to that. Damn, I was beginning to wish this whole job offer thing weren't so very fictitious.

"It is very good of you to participate in our blood drive," he said more seriously. "Ours is a small but vibrant community of worship. I hope you know how welcome you and Shannon would be to join us should your job pan out."

I raised my mug again. "Thank you, my friend."

I waited a few seconds before digging in. "I must say I was pleased but a bit surprised to see you donating today," I remarked neutrally.

He furrowed his brow. "Why's that?"

"With those weird spells you're having, I wondered if it were wise."

A look of panic and guilt swept across his face. "Spells?" he tried to dismiss.

"Yes, like the one you had in the hall the other day. The one you didn't care to fill me in on."

"Oh, that. Huh. I don't think it's bad enough to be called a *spell*." Then he froze. He was so distracted, I spun around to see if there was a black Mercedes in the pizza joint.

There wasn't. "You okay, man?" I pressed.

He shook something off. "No, I'm fine. I ... I react to the blood loss this way. No big deal."

"Rolando?"

"Yes?"

"You're trying to bullshit a combat medic here. I've tried to push guys' brains back in their heads. I know what I'm seeing. You had some reaction ... or maybe some *withdrawal*."

He looked down. I could tell he was ashamed to have lied. Then his eyes shot back up in anger. "Withdrawal? That's what you think you see in *me*?" He was zero-to-sixty hot. I was duly concerned.

"I've seen a thousand good men and women go into withdrawal. There's no shame in it. Rolando, I get it. Some average American kid finds himself in a hot, humid jungle where you're either bored stupid or about to die. I'm only amazed more soldiers didn't take the plunge."

His anger ebbed, at least some. "I hear you. And I know what being ten thousand miles away from home and being scared shitless does to your mind. But I don't *do* drugs." He thumped his chest. "Not then, not now, not ever."

I held out a placating hand. "Fine. I believe you. All I was saying was you experienced something serious. Drug withdrawal was one possibility. But you say you're not on drugs. I believe you. End of story."

"Thank you," he grunted.

"So what was it?"

He glanced down, then back up at me. "I can't tell you," he said tersely.

"Sure you can. I'm your friend and I'm a medic. If you can't trust me, who can you trust?"

He squirmed and looked away. "It's not about trust, man. It is *not* about trust."

"Then what is it about?" I snapped.

"Matthew, please believe me I'd tell you if I could, but I can't, so please respect that."

So close. I was so close to breaking through. It was time to max out the pressure. "You want to know what happens here, based on my experience?"

He shrugged. "Not especially."

"Well, you're going to hear it anyway." I made a show of gathering my thoughts. "When a man is trapped in an impossible situation, he reacts like an animal. That's what we are if you dig a little under the little show we put on and call it society. And when the animal in that man under more pressure than he can bear erupts like a volcano, bad things happen. I've seen good men do terrible things when they reached their breaking point before they reached out for help."

I tried to look internally conflicted, like I was dealing with some personal demon.

"There was this one poor son of a bitch stationed at Long Binh Post. I was TDY with his unit since they were down a couple medics. One morning, this guy wakes up, shaves, brushes his teeth then puts on a clean set of fatigues and a brand new Boonie. Then he walks into the command center with his M16. He has a sling around his neck with over thirty clips, eighteen rounds per clip. Son of a bitch opens up on full auto. Clip after clip after clip. He went through half his stash before someone put a bullet in the back of his head. Everyone in the CC has been shredded six times over, but he kept switching out clips." I stopped and stared at Rolando. "That, my friend, is what can happen if you keep too big a secret inside too long. You go off and people you love get killed."

Sure, I hit him hard. But, come on, I knew what he was about to do. If I was going to help him, he had to tell me what was going on.

Rolando started to cry. It was just one or two tears at first. Then he put a hand over his eyes and really let loose. Thank goodness he sobbed quietly. No one else in the restaurant noticed him coming undone. I let him weep. Turns out there was a lot of torment built up behind his emotional dam. Finally, ten minutes later, he was down to a slow enough boil that he could speak.

"Matt, he told me that if I tell *anyone*, it's going to be ten times worse. Matt, I can't let it be ten times worse. No way. You see ... you see where I'm coming from?"

Oh my God. Rolando didn't kill his family because of some mental breakdown. Someone told him to, forced him to. And whoever the monster was, he wanted Rolando to suffer horribly and in silence. He fed him a story that would guarantee he never said a word. It had to be that if Rolando didn't kill his family, the evil maniac would kill even more of them, something along those lines. But I couldn't tell Rolando I knew what I did. He'd think I was in league with this bastard; otherwise, how could I know the specifics? He was still going to have to say the words to me. Come on, Rolando!

"Okay, let's break this down logically," I said in my school-teacher voice.

Rolando nodded weakly.

"Do you know who's doing this to you?"

His head dropped like a lead balloon in the deep ocean. "I'm going to say the words to you and you're gonna hear them and then you gonna think I'm crazy and you gonna walk away. Then I'll be left with havin' told you and got nothing but worse misery for my doing so."

"Rolando, I would never do that. We're in this together, brother. I'd never bail on you." Shit, I hoped I wouldn't.

He stared me in the eyes with an intensity I will never forget. His eyes burned through my head and out the back. "The devil himself is making me do it."

Okaaay, did not see that one coming. Stay cool, Matt. "And I believe you. What's he look like when he's confronting you?" A person with a nice suit, a goat, or all red and sizzley? I guess it mattered.

"I ... I've never seen him."

Uh oh, this is getting worse. More psychiatric and less real. "Then how does he comm—"

"Inside my head," Rolando seethed. He wrapped his big hands around his skull. "He speaks in my head."

"In your head," I mumbled.

"I know what you're thinking, Matthew, but it's not like that. I had a cousin, Delford. In high school, he started hearing voices. But his aren't like mine."

"There are different kinds of voices you can have inside your head?" I asked innocently. What did I know?

"Yes. His were whispers. They said he was a bad person, That he should kill himself. They was in his head all the time, day, night, rain, shine. *Mine* are not like that. And The Voice is conversational, like he was standing right behind me talking. No accusations, just threats."

"Okay, I guess that's different. But you hear them all the time like Delford did, right?"

"No," his palms flew forward, "that's just the thing. I only hear him speak at specific times."

"A punctual devil?" I puzzled. Then I focused. "When specifically?"

"I have this part time job on Saturday afternoons. I hear him then. And before church most recent Sundays."

I was stunned. "Just those two times?"

"Well, there was this Memorial Day picnic at the church. I heard him then too. But that was the only Monday."

"This devil, he's kind of lazy," I observed.

"Matthew, please do not mock him. It can only make it worse."

"But, come on. Only weekends? What, is this, a part time haunting? That's pretty out there. And he only keeps middle-of-the-day hours. No late nights or early visits. That's ... that's not what I'd expect from an all-powerful force of evil."

"I'm tellin' you what happens. I can't explain why," he howled in frustration.

"Okay. Easy. We'll figure this out. What *specifically* does the voice say?"

Just as I asked, it hit me. Saturdays at the office building and Sundays in front of the church. The devil rode in black Mercedes to deliver his pronouncements. Why did that strike me as so out of character? He needed to be physically close to damn someone? That's not how I formerly envisioned the process. In my humble opinion, only men needed transportation to screw with someone else. My rage flared like a bonfire doused with jet fuel.

I raised a hang-on-a-second palm. "Rolando, you know I can't know, but I think we're dealing with a very mortal bad guy here. That pattern, it's just not how someone with supernatural powers would do this. No, I'm betting it's just some sick human. And I think I have a plan."

His face briefly flared with hope. Then that bright light went out and all that remained was primal fear. "Matthew, I deeply appreciate your listening and your believing me. But this ... this is too big to try and fight. Hell, even if it was some sicko, his threats, they're too horrible. I ... I can't ignore his warning."

"Rolando, this is critically important. What specifically is he telling you to do?" My gut dropped as I finished the question. I knew what it was the voice was saying, but I did not want to hear it confirmed.

"The voice tells me that I must kill every member of my family. He says I must do it this next Friday the thirteenth. Not before, not after. He says everyone I kill that day, they'll be safe. But everyone I leave alive, on the fourteenth, he's going to kill them and take their souls."

Oh - my - God. That was so much worse than I had imagined possible. Who could be that sick, that murderous, that cruel?

"So, if I don't kill my wife, he's going to *steal* her soul, Matthew. And my kids. I can't let him take my *babies'* souls. Matthew, I got no choice. And before you say it, no, I can't kill myself first. He said he hoped I did, because, and I'm quoting him here, *Then I can feast on every soul you ever loved, you fucking black pig.*"

Lord, this story only gets worse. Wait. "Wait, the devil's a racist?"

"Matthew, you haven't lived my life. In my world, if I'm not talking to a black person, I'm generally talking to a racist."

"No, Rolando, don't you see. The devil, he hates *all* humans. Not blacks or whites or green or yellows. Why would he take a racist swipe at you?"

He had to think about that one. "I don't rightly know."

"Look, give me one shot at this. Tomorrow, you go about your business. Let me see if I can't flush this asshole out and then we'll deal with him once and for all."

Rolando almost smiled. Almost. "The Army way."

"With extreme prejudice," I seconded.

NINE

I was just strolling down the street. Nothing to see here, folks. It was Saturday, May 24, in the afternoon. I was minding my own business and enjoying the fresh air. Look, there is a house finch, singing its heart out. Oh, and there is Mr. Squirrel, jumping from limb to limb. And hey, I'm approaching a 1974 black Mercedes parked in a shady patch just across from that office building. I've got nothing on my mind and four six-inch Philips screwdrivers jangling in my jacket pocket. I'm almost to the back end of the Kompressor.

As I arrived where the person of interest was parked, I grabbed the screwdrivers. I slammed one into each back tire before they could even begin to suspect something was up. I circled the front of the car, leaving the third screwdriver in the driver's front tire. By the time I was aiming at the last inflated tire, I heard shouts from inside the car. There were at least two men behind those tinted windows, one in front and one in the back. I went to the rear window, stared in, and made a circular signal for whoever was in there to roll down the window. I made certain to have an idiot's smile on my face.

The voices fell silent and the window glided silently down. There was a remarkably small, thin man in a fancy dark suit sitting alone in the back bench seat. His hands gripped a cane or umbrella, I wasn't sure which, and he had on dark glasses. A black-felt fedora topped his head, serving mostly to remind the viewer what a small head the fellow had. Evil incarnate he did not appear to be. Don Knotts going to a costume party dressed as a gangster was more like it.

"Hi, there, friend," I stated energetically, "got a minute?"

"If this is some attempt at a robbery, you will be very sorry you chose this car, my young fool," he said in a high but contempt-laden tone.

"No, no, this is not a heist. I just wanted to speak with you for a minute or two."

"The fact that you punctured my tires suggests you anticipated that I would refuse to converse with you."

"Let's just say I was hedging my bet."

"What is it you wish to speak about that is so important that you have placed your life at considerable risk?"

I tried not to lose my dumb grin. I expected some level of threat. "You know, I used to be a ventriloquist. Yeah, silly hobby, but there you have it. I was pretty good. I could throw my voice so no one could tell it was me speaking and not the dummy."

"I have no interest in your failed past. This conversation is over."

"What, you going to call the cops? Oh, wait, you don't have a cell phone because they haven't been invented yet."

His eyes flared open so much, I could tell they did in spite of his glasses. Then his face hardened like it was made of steel. "I see. You are from the future. Apparently, that makes you feel pretty cocky. Let me promise you that your confidence is sadly misplaced."

My head felt like it was hit with an ICBM. Heat, pain, blindness, and absolute confusion crashed around inside my skull. I bent over and vomited. I banged my head against the car. Then I did it again. I started to straighten up, but then I slammed my forehead against the window frame.

"No!" I shouted out of nowhere. The obsessive urge vanished as suddenly as it had started. I swayed back and forth like I was very drunk, but I straightened up again.

"Impressive," the man in the backseat exclaimed. "I would not have anticipated such an ability. Driver," he snapped, "go. Leave this location at once."

As I wobbled and was expecting to vomit again soon and very much, the car jerked from the curb. As it accelerated quickly, the slapping sound of four flat tires grew in volume. If my head wasn't so screwed up, it would have sounded comical. I partly tracked the Mercedes as if thudded left at the next corner and faded away.

What the hell just happened? One minute I'm giving the guy I suspect to be a monster some attitude, and the next I'm braining myself against his car. Then he runs away. What, was he afraid I'd cause too much damage to his damn car, so he fled the scene?

Rolando, who'd been keeping an eye on me from the underground parking lot, ran up to me. "You okay, man?"

"Yeah. Just give me a sec," I said with no conviction.

"So was that him? Was he the man putting those horrible thoughts in my head?"

I shook my head, which definitely made the queasiness worse. "Don't know. May—"

And then I was gone.

The universe inhaled me like a jet engine would a house fly. I tumbled backward toward total confusion and meaninglessness. My body flashed into nothingness and my screams were heard by no one, not even myself. Gradually, over seconds or centuries, I slowed. I couldn't see where I was going, but I knew at an instinctive level I was Gulliver-arriving at some new and fantastical way station in existence. Whatever it meant, I struggled to look behind myself. I saw lights, impossibly bright lights, streams of them, moving with intentional abandon toward some seemingly personal destination. And there were shadowy figures flying or being thrown into and across the lights. I sensed joy and I felt abject fear. Meaning began to creep into my mind ...

And then I was gone.

"Matt? Matt, sweet love, are you alright?"

I heard a woman's voice.

"Matt, do you need some help?"

No it was a girl's. Oh, my, it was Stacy. I opened my eyes. Yup, there she was, smiling down on me like an angel from Heaven. That was about when I passed out.

TEN

As I woke, I felt safe. Wow, that was an odd thing to flash on when you just stir from sleep. Oops. Then I remembered Rolando, the murderous marionette dude in the Mercedes, and my flying through the metaphysical cosmos. And Stacy. Why the hell was I feeling safe? I was trying to stop a mass killing, was attacked by a madman, and was begging to be arrested for statutory rape. I was as safe as a fat turkey the day before Thanksgiving.

I sat up and soft covers fell away. It was early evening. Or maybe dawn. The room was dark. I did a quick check physically. Fingers and toes attached and working. No pain, just a faint headache. Maybe I was hungry. Okay, I wasn't sick or injured. I scanned the room. Oh my, I was in Stacy's bedroom. I lifted the sheet. Yup, I ... I was buck naked. A quick sweep of the floor revealed no clothes. I was so dead.

As my panic threatened to cause a stroke, Stacy came in with a tray. She was wearing that ugly bathrobe some relative who secretly must hate Stacy gave her. It was fluffy and garish like an electrocuted pink poodle. Its only redeeming grace was that it was very short—butt-cheek short, if you know what I mean. The tray had a bowl of steamy soup and a bottle of Coke with a straw sticking out.

"Oh, good, you're awake. You had us worried there for a minute."

"Us?" I questioned.

"Mom and me. Us. We were worried."

"Your mom knows I'm in your bed naked?" I said aghast.

She winked at me. "Of course, silly. Who do you think took your clothes off?"

"Your mom undressed me while I was unconscious?" I said in flabbergasted aghastness.

"Matt, she's a nurse. She said she needed to examine you. She had to make certain you hadn't suffered an insect sting."

"Your mom undressed me and examined me naked looking for a *tiny* insect bite?" I ... I was pretty much anxious to die now.

"Matthew Dunsratty, my mother is a nurse. It's perfectly acceptable. She was worried about you. That's why she got out her magnifying glass."

"Your mom undressed me and examined me naked looking for a tiny insect bite with a magnifying glass? Seriously, Stace, I'm going to have to kill myself and burn my own body."

"You are so silly." She smiled playfully.

"Did she have any remarks about the quality of my circumcision?"

She giggled through her nose. "No, but if you'd like, we can discuss that over dinner. Mom said it's about done."

"Stacy, y ... y ... your mom knows I'm naked in your bed and you're here with me?"

"Matt, after the pregnancy scare we had a couple months ago, I think she's got a pretty clear picture about what's going on."

"Oh, Lord, take me now," I beseeched high Heaven.

"Come on, you fabulous man you, let's get you up."

Stacy came over and offered me her forearm. I dropped my feet to the floor and cautiously stood.

"You okay?" she asked with concern.

"Yeah, just a little dizz—"

Whoooosh. I was off again. I felt more like I was falling forward, but I was on another high-speed cosmic misadventure. I was more steady than my recent voyage-of-the-damned, but it was still unsettling.

And then I stopped. The sensation was akin to doing a belly flop into an arctic swimming pool.

I was standing on a hillock above a cold and stormy beach. The skies threatened rain, or possibly snow—it was that cold. I scanned the expanse of the sand before me. No one else was here. Not surprising given the inclement weather. The offshore waters roiled and churned. There were no ships visible, not even a stray gull. The scene had harsh beauty, but it was an appeal better appreciated when viewed from in front of a warm fire with a mug of something hot in your hands.

And, because my life sucked so very much, I had no idea why I was standing there freezing in the chaotic gusts. The scene was unfamiliar. I glanced down at my hand. It was covered in the pale, fragile skin of a very old man. Even in my original life, I'd never gotten really ancient. I was in my mid-sixties when I planned the final time dive that landed a very young Matt in the state hospital. Crap, that could mean only one thing. I had leaped into some other damn Matthew Dunsratty's life. And in this reality, I was extremely old ... and cold. Apparently, I also had abysmal taste in vacation-spot selection. No one else was here for a good reason. This place was wretched.

I decided to walk back away from the sea. Presumably, I had a car or rental close by. If I didn't, I was in trouble. My light jacket wasn't going to keep me warm for very long. Wherever I was demanded the heavy woolen clothes you see in paintings of old sea captains. Age had not led me to wisdom, it would seem. I took a few quick steps. Bad idea. This old goat's joints—each and every joint in his body—couldn't support such speed. I toppled to the rocky path. The cane I'd been holding but didn't notice added insult to injury by hitting me on the side of my head as I lay there what-the-fucking.

I will assume for the present that you have never been a decrepit old person sprawled across a wet, windy rock path. Getting up is not hard. It is right there next to impossible. I tried to push my torso off the ground. Wrong. I crumpled immediately and whacked my nose on a stone. At whatever antediluvian age I had lived to be, it was too old to do a pushup. When I'd controlled my nosebleed, I rolled onto my back, striking the rear of my head on another large stone. If there had been a pistol next to me on the ground, I'd have gone for it. After many futile combinations of bringing my knees up and struggling with my arms and stomach muscles to sit, I finally sat up. Then, after rotating around many, many times, like a dog deciding exactly where to sit, I was able to stand. My thoughts on my adventure so far: Oh, for fuck's sake.

Then I realized my walking stick was still there at the side of the path. There was no way I was able to bend and retrieve the damn thing. In spite of all indications signaling with abundant clarity that I *needed* the walking assist, it was going to stay right where it was. Did I mention how very much advanced age sucks? So I shambled in a direction that would hopefully not end up bringing me to an even worse situation than I was in already. I patted my pockets. No cell phone. Apparently, I was not only physically inept, I was a Luddite. Strong work, Matt.

After half an hour, I advanced maybe a few hundred yards. There was still nothing in sight. No telephone poles, no real roads, no cozy beachside cottages, no easy-to-get-into sedan. Nothing. What on earth was I doing here at my comically old age? It was about then I noticed the first signs of life. Off shore, just in front of a set of towering cliffs, a flock of birds glided along the air current. They were odd birds. There seemed to be just one type and they were bigger than any bird I ever recalled seeing. Oh well, they were unlikely to come rescue me, so I decided to ignore them.

Another fifteen minutes found me pitifully close to where I'd been fifteen minutes before, only now I had to pee something awful. Ah, old men and their bladders. How very unwelcome. I actually thought about unzipping right then and there, but the swirling winds promised to make me regret such a choice immediately. So on I trudged. It was then that those large birds I had been successfully ignoring forced themselves back into my attention. They were squawking something awful. I turned, looked up, and shielded my eyes. They certainly were a lot closer. And bigger. If fact, they were absurdly large. I've seen condors and eagles on wing. These had a wingspan of easily ten to twelve feet.

The entire flock started vocalizing. That was when it hit me. They weren't birds. No, just my luck, that was a flock—or pack or herd because I have no idea what you call a bunch of them—of pterodactyls. Alright, ladies and gentlemen, it is now official. My life has reached the outskirts of Impossible Land. I was a pathetically old man living in the time of dinosaurs. How ... how very unexpected ... and how undesirable. All my time dives so far had been confined to my own lifetime. Now I was hella way back in time and space and a *swoop*—because the actual name just idiotically popped into my fool head—of pterodactyls were having a dinner party and I was their special guest. Nice. Just maximally nice.

I considered walking *toward* the hungry beasts, I truly did. But I still had a few matters left unsettled. Like who the hell that marionette in the Benz was, why he was torturing Rolando, did Rolando actually butcher his family, and what the ever-loving fuck was going on in my sad excuse for a life?

I turned and attempted to move with alacrity. Of course I fell. Naturally, my forehead slammed against a rock. And since it wouldn't be a clusterfuck without it, my head began to spin, little stars taunting me before my eyes.

And *zooosh-o-matic,* I was flying like a pterodactyl. Only I was not heading toward dinner. I was headed into the intangible and the unknown. Oh, one last thing. Not only did my life suck, it now made absolutely no sense. Welcome to my nightmare.

ELEVEN

"Matthew!"

I startled alert. Whoa, very not fun. My eyes searched through a sticky fog, but I could only make out vague forms and bright lights.

"I asked you a question, young man. Were you napping, or shall we blame still more daydreaming on your part?"

There was a large dark figure looming at my side. Best I could tell, it was a floating ghost demon, but one without flames. He was the flameless kind. Go figure. Where the hell was I? I heard ... kids giggling? Man, they seemed close, all around me in fact. Hey, at least they weren't baby pterodactyls. Well, maybe, since I couldn't focus my brain, they could be. But, no, they had to be human children, maybe tweenagers? Ten or twenty in number. And no one was pecking at my eyes. Definitely not baby dactyls.

I needed to say something to the specter. Hadn't dealt with one before, but pissing one off seemed like a sure way to get myself into a big vat o' shit.

"Could you repeat the question?" I said through my dry throat.

"Yes, Matthew, I could."

Ah, a hard-ass ghost. Probably a dead classroom teacher, one who died from bursting a vein in his head because he was shouting at some student.

I reformatted my appeal. "Would you *please* repeat the question, sir?"

"Well, that's much better, Matthew. And since you asked so nicely, you will hear it again. Fredrick!" he shouted. I was sharp enough at that point to know he was calling on some poor kid, and that Fredrick was not the actual question.

"The U ... United States Government is com ... composed of three coequal legislative, executive, and judicial branches," Fredrick stammered in a falsetto.

Definitely a tweenager. Poor sod.

"Well, Matthew, time's a wasting," the demon taunted. My vision was clearing quickly. He was more a pudgy middle-aged man in a suit he bought on clearance at Sears many sizes ago.

"Ah, *yes?*" I ventured.

"I did not ask a *yes* or *no* question, son. I want you to go to the office immediately. I will call ahead to tell them they're about to receive a little hellion who thinks disrespect is neat."

"Ah, 'k. So, you want me to *escort* him there or something?" I was serious. Come on, not five minutes ago, I was a thousand years old and dinosaurs were about to eat me.

The class erupted in laughter. Hmm, I was betting that wouldn't improve my lot.

"Class, this is not funny. A young man is throwing his life away. What we see before us is a sad result of too many liberal communists in charge of our institutions of power."

What a moron. "Sir?"

"What, Matthew?"

"Communism and liberalism are widely differing political ideologies. The terms are not complementary. Liberalism is predicated on a belief in individual freedoms. Communism doesn't place any importance in individual freedoms, but rather envisions equality for all in a classless society."

"I told you to leave, young man. You're only making this much harder on yourself."

I could see normally by then. I was in a classroom with a bunch of socially tormented middle schoolers wishing to any number of deities that they were not in this class at this time. I was in junior high again, where the souls in hell are sent if they cause too much trouble. Nice.

"I'm going," I said, rising. I walked the gauntlet of stress-ridden faces toward the exit. I saw simultaneously empathy and disdain. Ah, to be a teen again. I hesitated halfway out. "Ah, which way's the office?"

"That's it, Matthew," screamed the suboptimal educator. "I am going to strongly urge the principal suspend you this time."

"Okay, I'll find my own way. Thanks."

As I walked down the hallway, I began to recognize the place. It was Herbert Hoover Junior High School, not surprisingly the very one I suffered through for the longest two years of my life. I hated myself, I hated my classmates, I generally hated my parents, and I hated Herbert Hoover with a passion of dark origins. And yes, I knew the way to the office. I was a sharper- than-average student. No genius, mind you, but I was on the smart side of the curve. If you're a clever human, junior high is not a good place to be. Given the teachers' overly broad training, their insulting salaries, and their constant exposure to hormonally-consumed meat puppets, they tended to burn out. After that, between union seniority and decades until retirement, they were pretty much able to act as they saw fit. If anyone tells you that we should all live as our inner selves, slap that person.

I still wasn't clear on what grade I was in. I think I'd just been kicked out of seventh-grade Social Studies, but I wasn't sure. Some occurrences are so forgettable that the memory of them rarely lasts until they're even over. Such was the case with elementary political science and me. I did vaguely recall the teacher had a weird last name, but for the life of me, I couldn't bring it up. I meekly opened the office door and stuck the tip of my nose in.

"Good morning, Matt," greeted the chipper secretary. Mrs. Larson? Mrs. Larkins? Betty something. She was always nice to me, which went a long way. Not that I was a trouble maker and always being sent here. I had one fight—more a shoving match—and broke a boiling flask in science class, but that was about all that was on my negative ledger. I was on the school yearbook staff, so I had some positive cred also.

"Hi," I muttered.

"Just have a seat." She pointed with her number two pencil. "Principal will be with you shortly."

"I got nothing but time," I responded. That brought her eyes up to study me in surprise. Hey, she was dealing with a summation of multiple adulthood here. I had developed a wry sense of humor many times over.

She dismissed my remark, a wise habit for a junior high secretary, and returned to her work. I sat there for ten minutes, which was fine. It was early in the period, so if this went down too quickly, I'd be returned to that rabid fool's classroom. No, I was fine right here in this well-lit, air-conditioned room with no pea brains assaulting my intellect. And no pterodactyls, at least none so far. I actually started analyzing the circumstances that led to my bizarre series of time dives. Maybe they were just time jumps, since I wasn't actively meditating to create them? But, alas, I was to catch no such breaks today.

"Mrs. Abernathy will see you now," Betty announced solemnly. In my head played the opening movement of Beethoven's Fifth, with the iconic fate motif. *Dun Dun Dun Dun!* She preceded me to the door, knocked softly, and then opened it inward for me. Betty gave me a sphinx like smile before retreating.

"Have a seat, Matt," the principal said coolly. "I'll be right with you." She was apparently doing some covert data analysis for the CIA, and it was more time sensitive than the Dunsratty Rebellion. I did leave off the quip about time on my hands. As fair as I recalled Abernathy to be, she was still the tough-as-nails woman in a man's world. You have to remember this was 1965 or 66. Women had three career choices. Nun, housewife, or teacher. But teacher did not include the upward mobility of being anyone in the administration. No, serving in those offices required a penis. Hmm, maybe she'd obtained one as a career move? No, Matt, cut the crap and focus. This is a minor brouhaha, you're a cagey force of nature, and she's anticipating a frightened kid. You got this.

I studied her desk and walls. Married, three kids at the younger end of the spectrum range. Her husband was a tall, strapping man. Yale, maybe Harvard type, the way he jutted out his chin and stood like the world would be lucky if he owned it. She graduated Cal State Hayward with a degree in Education. Pretty standard stuff. And there was a Master's degree in Psychology. Wow, now that was a kissing-your-sister certificate if ever there was one. She probably had to attend a six-week course to net that worthless piece of parchment. And there was a recent photo of her with the family at The Palace of Versailles. Very cultured.

She set down her pen and laced her fingers together atop her desk.

"Good morning, Mrs. Abernathy," I chimed in obsequiously, hoping to establish the high ground first.

"Good morning to you, Matt." She waited a three count. "I don't see you in here much."

"No, ma'am, you don't."

"And that's usually a good thing. If you and I become too well-acquainted, that's generally a bad indicator."

"I imagine it is. But it's also possible we could become friends based on my desire to learn and your role as the alpha instructor here at HH Jr. H."

One eyebrow shot up. I probably did push that a bit. Easy, Matt. But her face returned to stern-neutral. She was going to let that jab pass. She scanned a notepad. "Well, it seems you really got under Mr. Assmakis' skin this time, Matt."

I snapped my fingers loudly. "Assmakis, that's it," I stated energetically, having now recalled the jackass's name. We all called him my-ass-may-kiss, naturally.

"I beg your pardon," she demanded harshly.

Oops, not the person whose buttons I should be pushing. "Sorry, I was just agreeing with you."

"About his name or the fact that you rattled him severely?"

"Mrs. Abernathy, let me make something perfectly clear. I know you take your job very seriously. I respect that and I respect you. Of course I know the man's name. We're well into this term. My reaction was a nervous response based on my immaturity and the gravity of this situation. Nothing more, nothing less."

"Thank you, Matt, for clarifying that. You seem to have a grasp of the situation. That's actually quite helpful. Now, I've read Mr. Assmakis' report. Why don't you tell me in your words what happened during this interaction." She sat back and again knitted her fingers together.

"Thank you, Mrs. Abernathy, for allowing me to offer my version of this unfortunate misunderstanding." I waited a second to see if she had any comment. She did not. "As you may or may not know, I suffer what are called *absence seizures*, at least that's what my doctor thinks. Absence in this setting is a French word absence, pronounced like it rhymes with *makes sense*."

"I was unaware of this condition," she said apologetically. She picked up my file and began rifling it.

"It's not in my permanent record yet," I pointed out. "My parents wanted to wait until the diagnosis is firm."

"Oh, I see. Well, keep us posted and please let me know if there's anything I can do to help."

"Sure thing, Mrs. Abernathy. Anyway, in French, *absence* is meant to suggest—"

She held up a finger. "I speak French, Matthew." She pointed over her shoulder at that Master's diploma. "I studied at the Sorbonne University a few years back. I know what the word means to suggest." She smiled warmly.

"Plus impressionnant, Madame Abernathy. Je ne le savais pas," I complimented. I had missed that when I scanned the document previously. Her accomplishment *was* quite impressive.

"Mathieu, tu parles français?"

"Yes, ma'am. My grandmother was French. She lived with us when I was growing up." Man, I lied well. Actually, I'd lived in Lyon, France for six years during one of my Shannonless periods. I was trying to find myself *and* the best damn Rhone vin rouge. For the record, that'd be Chateau de Beaucastel Chateauneuf-du-Pape, IMHO.

"That's wonderful," she praised with a wide grin.

"Thank you, but I really don't want to take up more of your time than absolutely necessary. If you don't mind, I'd like to finish up my explication."

Now serious, she said, "Thank you, you are correct." She gestured her hand toward me. "Procédez."

"So, I think I was having one of my spells, but I can't actually tell. Sometimes I feel woozy after one, but sometimes not. All I know is that I was mildly disoriented and Mr. Assmakis was calling on me. He seemed to feel I was slacking off or expressing some attitude. He wanted me to answer his question to the class. Of course, I hadn't heard it, not that I recall at least, so I expressed my uncertainty. He then asked a classmate to repeat the query." I took a second to reflect. "Not sure that's an optimal format for interactive learning, but he is the seasoned teacher, not me."

I could tell she was inclined to agree with me, but checked any comment she might have offered. "Let's just stick to the facts, shall we?"

"You bet. So, the student says to me, and I believe I'm quoting him now, *The United States Government is composed of three coequal legislative, executive, and judicial branches.*"

Her brow furrowed.

"The kid's name is Fredrick something if you like to corroborate my version."

"That ... that won't be necessary. Please proceed."

"As you might imagine, I was stunned, since that's a declarative, not an question. So, wanting for all three of us to save face, I answered *yes*."

She rolled her eyes.

"Well, that set my poor teacher off. Apparently, what with all that's on a teacher's mind, he hadn't listened carefully to Fredrick's paraphrasing of his original question. All I can say is that the misunderstandings snowballed from there. I do feel quite bad about this entire incident and look forward to the chance to apologize personally to Mr. Assmakis."

There it was. Damn, she almost snickered. Man, she was good. A true professional.

"I think I have a fairly good understanding of what happened. I am troubled by just one other item on your teacher's note." She fingered the text to find the exact reference. "Yes, he said you embarrassed him by falsely ridiculing his political-knowledge base in front of the entire class. What's this to do with?"

"As they say, the road to hell is paved with good intentions. I was just trying to further a conversation, but he seems to have not appreciated my input."

"Could you be more specific?"

"Of course. Mr. Assmakis had just instructed the class that the reason I was throwing my life away was on account of there being, and I quote, *too many liberal communists in charge of our institutions of power*."

And she almost lost it. Yeah, I bet she had it up to here with his petulant rantings. She closed her eyes and I'm betting she was counting to ten silently and biting her cheek.

"Now, please don't get mad at him, Mrs. Abernathy. I'm sure he wasn't including you in that sweeping denouncement."

This time, she did snicker.

"So, as it is a poly sci class, I shared my opinion that liberalism and communism were likely antithetical and not at all similar. Rather than engage him, he seems to have taken my counterpoint as personal slight. For that, I am, again, deeply sorry."

"Alright, Matt, I think I got the full picture. Just between the two of us, I think Mr. A overreacted a bit. But just maybe you were using him as a foil for your rapier-like wit?"

"Peut-être," I confessed with a cat-eating-shit grin.

"Yes," she smiled warmly, "*perchance* you were. Here's what we are going to do. I want you to spend today in detention."

I started to object.

She raised that finger again. "Think of it as an opportunity to bone up on your French. Monsieur Delon is stuck with that ball-and-chain today. You two can maybe work on that accent of yours."

"My accent?" I said, trying to sound wounded.

"Yes, it *si rustique*. He is Parisienne. He can direct you as to the proper way of speaking French."

"And?" I pressed with a smile.

"And you apologize to Mr. A."

"That's it?"

"Well, that and I shall tell him how I hammered you and you broke and that you have a new and positive outlook on life. I shall thank him and his considerable ego for setting you back on the straight-and-narrow. You are no longer a liberal communist either."

"Why, that's very thoughtful and creative of you, Mrs. Abernathy. But you needn't go to any trouble. I'm sure Mr. A will have forgotten the entire episode by next week."

"Truer words, Matt, but I'll cover for you this time. Oh, and let us know if that diagnosis turns out to be a valid one."

"I will not forget." Actually, once I'm gone, this Matt will be clueless. Oh well, so sad. And, he doesn't speak more than three words of French. Hmm, I hope he can improvise well.

"Before I let you go, I have to comment. You seem a good deal more worldly than I recall you impressing me as being the last few times our paths crossed. What gives?"

"Well, Mrs. Abernathy, we are here to learn and grow, are we not?"

"Sure, in theory. It's usually not so noticeable in this short of a time span."

"And for that, I give all the kudos in the world to *you*, Mrs. Abernathy, and your epic achievements in middle education." I bowed my head.

"Enough! It'll take me weeks to get the smell of that load of BS out of my carpet. Go."

I stood and walked toward the door. I turned and asked, "Anything you'd like me to pass on to Betty?"

"Yes, in fact there is. Tell her she owes me a beer."

"Have I influenced some bet between you two women?" I said with false modesty.

"Yes, tell her one of my privileged little snots is actually alright. She'll understand."

Oh, this Matt was in so much trouble. Muahahaha.

TWELVE

So after that rude, and then interesting, introduction to 1965, guess
what I had to do? No, it doesn't involve retribution across time, or
setting a horrific wrong right, or even wealth and babes beyond a
teenager's wildest dreams. No, I had to return to fourth period algebra, which had started without me. Then I had to not dry heave at
the sight of the cafeteria lunch, and then I had to schlep through the
entire rest of the day. Ah, yes, youth, that which older people pine
after so ardently and often poetically. Here's an update, old farts.
Junior high school sucks.

After lunch, I was subjected to PE, where the inexcusable meal I
just choked down came back up while running laps. After recycling
my lunch and being physically humiliated by most of the other boys,
I proceeded to Spanish 1. And, yes, before you ask, I speak fluent
Castilian Spanish. Let's call it my Hemingway Phase. In three separate lives, after Shannon booted me out, I took up residence in
Pamplona, Madrid, and then, because I wanted to endure the rugged
cold, Santander. I was determined to find Papa, whatever the hell
that meant. Well, it meant I drank a lot, swore a lot, and chased skirt
even more. Did I ever "find Hemingway"? No, neither literally nor

figuratively. I did contract genital herpes and was elected mayor of a small fishing village named Almuñécar. But I don't think the two events were related and I still to this day can't explain that second one to you. The first one, yeah, I get it. You play, you pay.

The day ended with Science. That was an *et tu, Brute* moment if ever there was one. Remember that in all my past lives, I started as a high school science teacher, mostly chemistry and physics. Now, with all that knowledge and experience, I was forced to endure Kiddie Science. My teacher was nice enough, but even the first time through, I realized the gal was a major ditz. Now, with my life experience, I confirmed that she was a well-intentioned idiot. Back then, I thought maybe she was cute in a tomboy way. Now all I saw was a twenty-something woman with the body of, well, a junior high school boy very much like me. As a result, I'm going to leave off telling you the fantasy I used to have about her being my substitute PE teacher.

So, how'd my tour of mid 60s basic science go? Well, you can judge for yourself.

"Afternoon, gang," Miss Berry sang out, with hundreds of times more energy than a human should have after a full day working with teenagers. "How's everybody doin'?"

Cherisse, because tragically, that was the given name her cruel parents saddled her with, swept the room in anticipation of some response. But none there came. Hey, tired teens here. What did Cherie Berry expect?

"Did y'all do the homework I assigned? It was pretty short and darn easy."

Silence. The *Bueller? Bueller? Bueller?* kind of suffocating silence.

"Well, if you did it and have any questions, now's a super time to ask 'em."

It was as if she was alone on Gilligan's Island, the response was so absent.

"Well, cool. Y'all got it then. That's ... that's fantastic."

With my life experience, I could tell she was this close to breaking down into a crying fit from the despair that was her prison. Poor Cherie. And I'd have loved to rush to her rescue, but I had no idea if I'd done the homework or what it entailed. Hell, I almost stepped up and gave her a hug. But that was too creepy, since it would be like hugging myself. Even *I'm* not narcissistic enough to go there.

Cherie walked to the board after yet another educational defeat. She grabbed a piece of chalk and wrote half the letter "L" on the board before the chalk—that cruel, cruel mineral—snapped into multiple shards.

"Oops," she declared as she unsuccessfully tried to snag a falling chunk. She realized she still had a stub in her fingers and returned to the board. "Today, we're going to discuss a marvelous new scientific discovery. This is real science fiction in action, folks."

She proceeded to write L-A-S-S-E-R on the board. My stomach fell a little more in sympathy for the girl. This was not her decade.

"Now these lassers are powerful flashlights, like a ray gun. They can, like, shoot a hole in a sheet of metal even if the metal is on the moon."

"Miss Cherry," I said, raising my hand.

So unfamiliar was she with questions or remarks from the students that I believe she briefly entertained the notion that God was addressing her. She shot a furtive glance upward. Then she must have gathered herself. Cherie turned and saw my hand. "Yes, Michael?"

"Matthew."

"Matthew," she echoed unconvincingly.

"I believe the acronym is l-a-s-e-r, with one 'S.'"

She rested her chalk-covered hand on one hip and tapped at her chin with her free index finger.

"No, I'm pretty sure it's lasser, like doing your shoe laces."

The class stirred nervously. No one had apparently ever spoken to this woman. No one was certain what to expect if one did. Junior high schoolers are notoriously skittish, like a pack of rabbits, as you know.

"Not to seem difficult, Miss Berry, but I believe it is an acronym for Light Amplification by the Stimulated Emission of Radiation. Laser."

"Well, Mike, we'll just have to agree to disagree on this one, okay?"

"Matthew."

"Matthew what?" she puzzled.

"No, I'm Matthew, not Mike or Michael." Why I cared was beyond me, but there it was.

"Now that," she pointed at me with a stupid smile, "we can agree on."

"And, again, just for the sake of accuracy in education, the first laser that Theodore Maiman produced in his laboratory at Hughes Aircraft Company in 1960 had only a few hundred watts of power. The energy requirements for a laser to puncture a metal plate even up close is in the megawatt range."

I cannot imagine how Miss Berry's tormented mind processed my 411, but out of her mouth came, "Myles, are you trying to convince this class that Howard Hughes, one of the richest men on earth, a man who could have any woman he wanted, is trying to make a ray gun to melt steel?"

"No, no, ma'am. The *company,* not the *man,* is involved in the research. You know what? Please forget I said anything about the lasser. I am clearly thinking of something else."

"And what might that be? *Sex?* Are you fantasizing about sexual intercourse in my class? With me here?" She rested an indignant palm on her flat chest.

Wow, and to think she's not wearing a ring. Go and figure.

"No, Miss Berry, I was not fantasizing about having sexual intercourse with you here in this classroom." My, how I regretted saying it that way milliseconds after I shut my darn mouth.

But, once lofted into the atmosphere, words cannot be sucked back in. Ah, but were it possible.

"Matthew!" she screamed. Yeah, *now* she gets my damn name. "I have never been so humiliated in all my born days."

I'm betting that's a lie. I'm thinking this is a minor glitch in the radar screen tracing of her long, lonely, and loony adult life. The day of her first menstrual period, her first driving test, and her first time she ate spaghetti in public leaped to my mind as having been oh so much uglier, so much more psychologically scarring. Notice I left off that list her first kiss. Yeah, that one, I'd bet good money, was still in the *pending* column.

Cherie pounded her feet over to my side, grabbed me by the left ear, and marched me out of the classroom without another word. My classmates, naturally, were too frightened to burst out laughing. I'm sure they waited for that until we were around the first corner. Next stop—you got it—the office.

"Betty," Cherie Berry shouted, "I must see the principal at once. This young man attempted to seduce me in front of the entire class."

Of course it would have been best for me to remain absolutely still and silent. But you know what? This day was FUBAR ...

"So if I tried to seduce you in front of *half* the class, you and I would be doing the nasty as we speak?" I queried from the awkward angle my head dangled in.

Cherie pulled up on my ear, not to cause more pain but to display me more fully to Betty. Thank God Mrs. Abernathy heard the ruckus and burst through her door. She assessed the scene immediately.

"Principal Abernathy," Cherie began self-righteously, "this—"

"Cherie," she said firmly but not alarmingly, "stop right there. Remove your hand from Matt's ear this instant. Our school district has a very firm policy regarding the appropriate application of corporal punishment. This is not appropriate."

Cherie looked vexed but quickly released me. I ... I kind of added a bit to my case by collapsing onto the floor. Layering it on couldn't hurt.

"You don't understand. This young deviant openly expressed a desire to apply sexual intercourse to me—"

Now the principal's arms went up. "Cherisse, *Stop*. For the love of God, stop speaking immediately."

Cherie stepped a few paces backward and had the most tormented look on her face.

"Here's what we're going to do. I am going to take Matt into my office and find out what's going on. You, Cherisse, are going back to your classroom and continue with your lesson plan. I will send Betty to relieve you when I'm ready to speak with you. Now go."

"Okay, fine," she said with a challenge in her tone. "But who's Matt?"

"The student on the floor at your feet who had better get up très rapidement if he values his chance at continuing his education in the state."

I scrambled up.

"Fine," Cherie responded indignantly. "When might I expect to hear from you?"

"As soon as I call for you."

Cherie left in a huff. Abernathy rested a fist on either hip. "Twice in one day, Matt? Really?"

"I can explain."

"Oh, you *bet* you will." She shoved a finger in the direction of her open office door. "Move it, mister."

Once we were settled in her office, the principal took a deep breath. "First, Matt, how's your ear?"

"Oh, that? It's fine. Never better."

"I'll bet. Do you want the nurse to have a look at it?"

"No, I'm good."

"With that settled, I would like to apologize to you."

Did not see that coming. "No prob."

"You don't even know what I'm apologizing for," she said with a wry grin.

"To me, the specifics do not matter." I bound the curled up finger of my left hand into the curled up fingers of my right hand and pulled them taut. "Our relationship is strong. It can weather small storms."

"That's very big of you, and kind of creepy at the same time. No, what I was apologizing for is Miss Berry's ... unusual behavior."

"Are you referring to her latent fear of sexual contact in any form that manifests itself in the delusional interpretations of everyday interactions resulting in reactions that are greatly in excess of the actual severity of the perceived affront? Interesting point, geno-phobia or coitophobia in most cases is the tragic response to sexual trauma, all too often inflicted in childhood."

She crossed her arms and rested back in her chair. Then she smiled and gently slapped the desk top with one set of fingertips.

"What?" I pressed.

"I'm just trying to figure out where the *fuck* you're coming from, Matt."

I furrowed my brow and lowered my head. "I'll leave it to your final judgment, as you are the professional here, but are you certain it's wise to use profanity in a conversation with a minor pupil?" I made a *just sayin'* pouty face.

"Normally, absolutely. But in your case, who are we trying to kid? I'm not saying your analysis of Miss Berry is in any way true. However, no one I met at the Sorbonne ever made such a succinct and well-thought-out assessment as you just did. I am not easy to impress, but I am impressed with you." She shook her head in amused uncertainty.

"Wow. Thanks. You know, if you weren't my principal, and I wasn't like thirteen, and you weren't married to Yale here," I pointed to her family photo, "this might be the point where I ask you out for drinks after school, or coffee, if alcohol is too forward."

She leaned forward and smiled wickedly. "He went to Harvard, I'll have you know."

I shrugged. "What's the difference?"

"A lot, according to my husband."

"A lot, said the man who went to Harvard."

"Point well taken." Her smile faded. "So, back to business, if you don't mind."

My hand gestures indicated she was welcome to proceed.

"I am sorry Miss Berry went off on you. As you might have suspected, she's had some issues with her performance to date. The district felt that before we gave up on her completely, that perhaps some time under my tutelage might benefit her."

"As, my guess is, you are the sole woman principal in the district."

"Sadly, yes."

"I do wish the poor girl well, though I suspect her career path will not follow one in public education." I meant it too. She was likely a victim of something a child should never have to endure.

"So, I will ask you pro forma. Did you attempt any sexual act or imply any such act to Miss Berry?"

"First, let me say categorically no. I did not. Second, I would like to test our relationship by asking you have you taken a good look at Cherisse?"

She snickered through her nose. "That is harsh, young man."

"I call it objectivity."

Strangely, we shared a laugh.

Then she straightened up and grew serious. "Enough of this diversion. You are free to go. I will have yet another session with Miss Berry, trying to restructure how she interpreted your conversation. I would ask of you two favors." She stared at me.

I linked my curved fingers to remind her of our bond.

She rolled her eyes.

"First off, when you return to class, if Miss Berry is still your instructor, go a bit easier on her. Can you do that for me?"

"Absolutely," I reassured her. "What else?"

"Can you maybe not have your ass thrown in my office more than once per day? I mean, you're growing on me like a fungus, but I do have other duties."

I leaned an elbow on the desk. "Ay, there's the rub."

She made a flurrying movement of her head. "How so?"

"You might miss me."

She stood, rested her knuckles on the desk, and Cheshire-cat smiled. "Thus conscience does make cowards of us all."

I frowned. "Meaning?"

"I'm afraid not. Now get out of here before you miss the detention you so richly deserve."

I mimed the bond thing again, then left without further comment.

Yeah, the principal, she was alright.

THIRTEEN

You know all those films you see about boxers being beaten to a bloody pulp? Then he sits in his corner for one minute while nasty people try and fail to patch him up. Then the bell rings and he has the existential choice of safety versus rejoining the fray? Think *Raging Bull* or *Rocky*. That was me as I departed from my detention session. I had had a hard day at the office. I was buoyed by the fact that I was feeling mentally more stable. I didn't think the universe was about to spin its wheel-of-fortune with me as the flapper again. But, as the old saying goes, *You don't have to go home, but you can't stay here.* Yeah, thirteen-year-old Matt had to go home. Oh, the pain.

The sixties were a time when kids got their own butts to and from school. There were no rotating carpools or latte-drinking moms ferrying kids around in their apocalypse-ready-sized SUVs. No, you either walked to school, rode your bike, or rode the bus. We lived quite a ways away, so I was riding the big yellow bus. The problem I faced wasn't the trip, it was the arriving. Come on, I'm not just a grown man. I'm hundreds of grown men stuffed into one tormented head. And none of us wants to, are willing to, or will accept living at home under our parents' rule. But that was exactly what I was about to do.

I grew up in a very nice city. But there was one sleazy motel in town. I would much rather have braved staying there, but, realistically, I had no money. Every day my mom left a single quarter on the kitchen counter for me to buy school lunch with. That was the sum total of cash flow in my pathetic young life. Even though I happened to know that a room at the local no-tell motel went for two ninety-five a day, a dollar more if you wanted sheets, I didn't have that kind of scratch. Plus, if I wasn't home by dinner time, my mom'd start calling all the ERs, the police, the FBI, and the US Marines, in that order.

The bus dropped me off about a half mile from the house. I thanked the driver as I descended the steps. He barked at me, asking what I'd said. Apparently, one did not thank the bus drivers. I just waved to him and headed home. I did make a specific effort to drag my heels the entire way. I might be caving in, but at least my shoes were going to pay for the insult life had dealt me. As I walked up the brick path to the door, my first dilemma presented itself. Did I knock, ring the bell, or just walk in? What if I just entered and my dad like shot me, somehow recognizing I wasn't his young son? But, rationally, Dad didn't own a gun and he mentally dwelled in his own world. He wouldn't notice if a lowland silverback walked in the door instead of me. He'd reach out and muss the gorilla's fur, and ask if it wanted a snack.

I cracked the front door open and peered in cautiously. I saw and heard nothing. So far so good. My dad was an airline pilot with the seniority to choose his routes. As far as I had figured out, he was just as likely to be home as he was to not be. Mom was definitely a homemaker. By that, I do not mean she worked construction. No, that was what *housewives* were called back in the day. Come to think of it, I wonder why. Doesn't make a lot of sense.

Since I had to serve detention, I took the late bus home. That was one designed to carry students who did after-school sports and clubs. That meant it was pushing dinner time. I didn't smell anything cooking, but, then again, Mom wasn't exactly an accomplished cook. She was not above dishing out frozen or prepared foods. So scandalous! A decade earlier, she'd be put in the pillory for such dalliances. The only sound was a tabletop radio playing that bone-freezing, musically bleached Mantovani crap my parents called easy listening. Trust me, I did not find it easy to listen to.

I stepped in, closed the door softly, and began tiptoeing toward my room. It was my only potential safe haven. Halfway down the hall, right by the washer/dryer, my mom called to me from behind.

"Not so fast, buddy."

Oh, crap, the jig was up, I'd blown my cover, I was headed to hard labor in a distant prison. Slowly, I turned. Yup, that was my 1965 mom in all her glory and a yellow scalloped-collar house dress. I nearly burst out laughing.

"H ... h ... h ... hi, Mom," I managed.

She gently set a finger on her cheek. "Where's my kiss?" she asked petulantly.

Oh, God, this was turning into a night terror. First junior high—again—and now pecking my mom's cheek. Would my torment never end?

I sheepishly skulked back down the hall, she bent over just a bit, and I kissed my mother. Next stop, the bathroom and a bottle of Listerine mouthwash—lots of Listerine mouthwash.

"Did you have a nice day, honey?" she asked with no real interest.

"Yeah, sure, I'll go with that."

She furrowed her brow at me.

"Was there some problem?" she asked pointedly, now participating in our interchange.

A teacher said I tried to rape her, I flirted with the principal in French, and another teacher told me I was already a failure at life. "Nah, just a long one. What's for dinner?"

That generally worked. Teenage boys are notoriously hungry,

she was the home's designated meal preparer, and the assigned hour was approaching rapidly.

"Leftovers from last night," she said as if she were actually saying *surf and turf with a huge baked potato.* Then she displayed a smile. "You loved it, so I figured it would be alright. Dad's not back until eleven."

I loved it? Coq au vin? Raviolo al' uvo? Or maybe some culinary delight centered on SPAM? I squinted. "I can't remember what we had—"

"TV dinners, my son."

I squinted more profoundly. "We're having leftover TV dinners?"

"Dinner, *singular.* No one eats more than one of those. It ... it wouldn't be seemly."

"Ah. Gotcha. Dinner is catch-as-catch-can."

"I beg your pardon, Mattie, what did you just say ... something about catching fish for dinner?"

"Yeah, Mom, this summer when we go camping. We do that every year."

"Yes we do, and we always have a wonderful time."

Well, you and Dad do. I don't get any of the gin, so my wilderness experience differs greatly from yours. I do get green olives with those slimy red things in the middle, but they make me gag.

"I'll be in my room," I announced.

"That's the spirit," she responded, or rather the early-bird gin responded. Mom and Dad, they liked their martinis.

I went to my room, closed the door, for what little *that* was worth, and flopped on my bed. I needed to take stock. So far, I hadn't been involuntarily swept away into the time stream. That suggested I was stabilizing. Man, whatever that evil marionette did to me was powerful mojo. That brought me back to my central goal. I needed to get back to 1975 and knock that puke out. I mean *forward* to 1975. Hey, if I couldn't time dive, I could just wait around until then, finish junior high, do high school again. Where's my pistol?

But to be on the safe side, I needed to wait here a few days, build my strength back up, if that is what's even involved. Then, assuming I'm not randomly rifled elsewhere before then, I can do a formal time dive. Okay, it's Wednesday. Maybe I stay through Friday, and try then. I'd just as soon pass on the whole weekend experience with the family. I had more than enough of that already, enough to fill several lifetimes.

I only had a few allies here in the 1960s. TV, which seemed okay at the time, but watching some old shows on YouTube had revealed to me that it was almost all poorly written, poorly acted brain-toxic drivel. If you doubt me, search episodes of *Have Gun - Will Travel* or *Bonanza*. Yeah, absolute garbage. I had no real friends, and my relationship with Stacy was over eighteen months in the future. I had a few books in my room. I hadn't read *The Adventures of Tom Sawyer* in years, so I guessed I could do that. The first five volumes of the *Encyclopedia Britannica* collecting dust on the shelf held little allure. Most of what was in it was way out of date and a lot was dead wrong to begin with.

But my immediate concerns were on a smaller scale. Once Mom had "served" dinner, I could sneak back to the kitchen and load up on PBJs. That'd hold me until morning. Hey, I could always raid the liquor cabinet. Sure, that'd put me under real fast so tomorrow would get here that much sooner. Perfecto! These days, I bet a thimbleful would knock me on my ass. I spied a TV Guide in the living room. I dashed out and snagged it. What was on offer Wednesday evenings? Ah, we have your *Batman, Patty Duke, Lost in Space*, still in black and white, mind you. And *The Beverly Hillbillies*! If I avoided *The Virginian, The Big Valley*, and *Bob Hope*, I might not die of boredom. Sweet.

As early as I went to sleep, aided by an alcohol jump start, I was absolutely exhausted when my mother opened my door at 06:30 and told me it was time to rise and shine. I did rise, but I did not shine. Mom'd put a lot more effort into breakfast than she had last night's dinner. I had Eggo waffles, two glasses of Carnation Instant Breakfast, and a bowl of Wheaties. Between breakfast and the Swanson's last night, I was growing up on corporate cuisine. Child Protective Services should have been consulted. At least I was full as I hoofed it to the bus stop, my lunch quarter in my pocket. I was living large. I said hi to a few of the kids I think I was supposed to know, but mostly the ride was bumpy and painfully quiet.

I didn't know my schedule. I hardly remembered junior high, so give me a break. Yesterday, I bluffed my way along. But today, I had no initial clues of kids to follow, hoping they would know where I was supposed to go. My best bet was to find a kid who was in one of my classes yesterday and just come out and ask them. I would appear to be very uncool, but, hey, the other Matt had to live with that baggage, right, not me. A chubby kid from my science class caught my eye. Chubby kids weren't cool in the first place, so there'd be no harm asking him.

"Hey, ah, dude," I called out, flagging him down with a finger.

Kid froze like my digit was a freeze ray. Weird. I caught up to him. "Can I ask you an off-the-wall question?"

"No, you cannot have my lunch money. My mom got tired of me getting beat up for it so she prepaid for the entire year. Leave me alone." OMG, was this kid heading for an unsuccessful and disturbing adulthood.

"No, no, it's not like that. Look ... ah, what's your name? I kind of forgot."

"You forgot my name? We've been in school together since kindergarten. How could you forget?"

I waved a hand dismissively at my head. "Space cadet here, so many names. It's—" I encouraged.

"Matt."

"Yes?" I countered.

"No, my name's Matt too. How could you forget?"

"You know that's a very long story and I doubt you'd care to hear it. So, Matt, I forgot my schedule too. Do you know it?"

"It's March. How could you forget your schedule?"

"Matt, did you ever have one of those out-of-control anxiety dreams?"

"All night every night."

Why didn't that surprise me? "You know the dream where you've forgotten your schedule and wander around and you get caught and then you discover you didn't wear pants that day?"

Matt checked his Timex. "About three hours ago."

"Great. Well, it's like that. So, what do I have first period?"

"You mean after homeroom?" He said that with an implied *duh*.

"Of course." I slapped the side of my head.

"We have homeroom together. Mr. Bill's classroom."

I put my hands on my face. "*No, Mr. Bill*," I acted out from the *SNL* classic.

Needless to say, Matt didn't get the reference. Mr. Bill animations started on *SNL* in the mid-seventies.

"Okay, let's go to homeroom." I took hold of his elbow and headed up the steps.

He shook my hand off. "Please do not physical me. It makes me ... tense."

"Fine, no physicalling."

We made it to homeroom just as the bell rang. Matt pointed to my seat and walked to his. I followed him. Stunned to find me in his face again, he asked sheepishly, "What do you want?"

"My schedule?" I asked impatiently.

"You expect me to know every kid's schedules in this entire school?"

"No, just mine."

He swallowed deeply. "English, Room 103, Art, Room 401, Wood Shop, Room 322, Social Studies, Room 212, lunch, PE, in the gym, Algebra, Room 114, and finally, Science, Room 112."

"You're shitting me," I declared. "You know all that about me?"

Other Matt shrugged.

I pointed to a girl two rows over. "Third period?"

"Home Ec, Room 311."

I selected another kid randomly. "Fourth and fifth."

"Intro Math, Room 1 1 2, PE, in the gym."

"You *do* know everybody's schedule in the entire school," I said in stunned amazement.

He shrugged.

"But you protested before that you didn't."

"No, I protested that you *expected* me to know the schedules. Totally different."

I shook my head.

"I spend a lot of time in the office," he said by way of explanation.

"And do you know how to write?" I asked.

"Duh," he braved.

I tore a sheet out of his binder and slammed it down on his desktop. "Then please write my schedule down for me."

What good luck. I picked the social-outcast idiot savant who knew my schedule. One less thing to worry about, right?

"Matt, Matt Dunsratty?" I heard a high-pitched male voice query.

"Sir?" I returned.

The class laughed quietly.

Mr. Bill had a clipboard, a pen, and a foul look on his face. "When I call roll, young man, you will answer *present* or *absent*, not *sir* or *yes dude*. Otherwise, I will leave the box by your name blank and let the office sort out why you cannot remember my simple instructions."

"Oh, no, Mr. Bill." Come on, I haaad to. "Of course I know to say present but the authoritative way you call my name threw me for a loop. Sorry, you just sounded like a drill sergeant." I saluted him. "Sir."

After staring at me for many seconds, he made a mark on the roll. Maybe he checked me present. If not, hey, I got to say good morning to the principal. Win/win.

When attendance was complete, the diminutive Mr. Bill sat behind his desk and lifted a stapled set of papers. "Announcement.

Effective immediately, whoever has been flushing lit fire crackers down the toilet in the boys' room across from the office will cease and desist. Any questions?"

There were none.

"Announcement. Today is national Return-a-Book-to-the-Library Day. If you have any books eligible to be returned, please do so before the end of the school day. Any questions?"

There were none.

"Reminder. Next Wednesday is school photo make-up day. If you didn't get your picture taken in October or if you wish to possibly substitute a new one, please get a photo next Wednesday. No tank tops, tube tops, or shirts with any images or words written on them are allowed. If you wear any of these offending items of apparel, you will not get your make up photo shot. Any questions?"

There were none.

Oops, yes there was. I found I had one. My hand went up.

"Yes?" Mr. Bill asked dubiously.

"What's for lunch?"

"I beg your pardon?" he reacted, clearly stunned.

"Lunch today in the cafeteria. What's for lunch?"

"How should I know and why should I care?" he challenged.

"This is the announcements section of homeroom, right?"

"Yes."

"You know they say lunch is the third most important meal of the day. I think celebrating that fact should warrant announcing what is to be on offer."

"Then please express your opinion to the proper authorities. I have no interest."

"It's meatballs and spaghetti, Dunsratty," someone shouted out.

"Thanks," I responded with a general wave.

"Finally," an irritated Mr. Bill continued, "a correction. Last week, we announced there would be a kissing booth at the school fair, which will be held in two Saturdays in the parking lot. A kissing booth will *not* be present due to concerns that have arisen concerning communicable diseases and the social implications of having a woman in a both kissing people who have purchased tickets in order to do so. Any questions?"

My hand shot up. Seriously, I think it did so of its own volition.

"Fine, as there are none—"

Mr. Bill glanced up to see that, contrary to all past homeroom corrections, there was a question.

"Yes, Matthew, you have a question?"

"I do, sir. What if we put a man in the kissing booth also?"

He looked at me as if I'd spoken in Martian while underwater. I feared smoke would begin to rise from his open-cab-door ears. Finally, he managed to speak, although apparently in some pain as a result of that effort. "Matthew, one does not have a *man* in a kissing booth selling *kisses*. It is ... that is preposterous."

"All due respect, Mr. Bill, why is that?"

I do believe his face was white as virginal snow. "Wha ... what if a man bought a ticket and wanted to kiss the man in the booth? That's why."

"It is for a good cause, right? So what, the end justifies the means. Or, if you prefer, I quote Mr. Spock. *Logic clearly dictates that the needs of the many outweigh the needs of the few.*"

"Yes ... I mean, no. It cannot be done. And Dr. Spock never said those words."

"Well, what if a woman bought a ticket to the traditional booth and desired to kiss the pretty girl. I presume that would have been acceptable."

He started to vibrate, like there was an earthquake only below where he sat. "No, no, no. A thousand times no. At kissing booths, *men* buy tickets and they kiss *women*. Period."

"How about this," I pressed. "We put a man *and* a woman in the booth. That way, whoever buys a ticket for whatever motivation they might have, we're covered. Hell, I'll volunteer to do it."

A few kids cheered. Most tried to become invisible.

"No, we can't have a minor trafficking in kisses. We'd all be arrested under the Mann Act."

I raised a finger. "No, Mr. Bill," and yes, I said it in a real high voice, "that only applies to interstate transportation for sexual purposes. My lips will be working locally." The bell rang. "Will you consider my proposal, Mr. Bill? Bring it up in the teachers' lounge maybe?"

His head began gyrating back and forth, but in such dynamic arcs that I worried he'd break his own neck. Poor Mr. Bill. He wasn't ready for the sixties and we were halfway through them. But me, I was heading for Room 103 and my English class. I never was much into the subject, but who knew, maybe this time through, I'd fall in love with it?

I knew there would be trouble the instant I entered the room. A wash of unpleasant memories swirled to life in my head. Mr. Duvoe, his name in my mind pronounced with a hiss somewhere in there. The drama director, English teacher, and totally vile soul. Pretentious had been personified the day Mr. Duvoe was hatched. If his lips were moving, he was expressing vanity and pomposity. The man left a grease trail like a snail left one of mucus. Oh, and the girls all loved him. Many were speechless in his presence.

I was not a fan. The only reason I survived this year before was that I had the good sense to suppress my feelings and never strike out at the boob. But, come on, I had him for the next two days. I could handle this. Though I couldn't ignore his rantings, I could let them go. I was a duck's back. His words were water. Auuum.

"Matthew Dunsratty, would you please do us all the supreme honor of proceeding to the head of the class," he stated before I was entirely through the door.

Oh, this was not going to end well. There would be blood. I shuffled my feet in his direction. To give you the full picture, I should describe him. Duvoe was of average height and build. He wore an ascot. End of my description. He was a complete asshole. Come on.

He wore an ascot. I stopped just beyond arm's reach. I didn't want to strangle the life out of him reflexively.

"Come, come, everybody. To your places. We have much to do and precious little time with which to accomplish it." Then he clapped his hands in that revolting manner where only the tips of the fingers on the striking hand touch the fleshy part of the other palm.

"What did you need me for?" I asked quietly. I guess I was hoping he'd have forgotten and I could retreat. No such luck.

He rested a finger against my lips. "Shush. All will be revealed in its time."

He touched my lips. Yesterday, I had to kiss my mother, and today, this freak *touched* them. I needed new lips. A lip transplant.

"Hurry, hurry," he coaxed. "The sooner you all shall sit the sooner you all shall learn. And today's lesson, it is tres fantastique."

I scowled up at the jerk. "Vous avez maîtrisé la langue maternelle?" [You have mastered the mother tongue] I challenged.

He looked at me like my head was a round dick. "Huh?"

"J'ai pensé autant crétin," [I thought as much, cretin] I whispered back.

And just like that, his focus shifted back to ... him, naturally. "Alright. As you all are aware I have been guiding you ever so professor-like through the treacherous jungles of *Lord of the Flies*." He raised his fingers like claws and aligned them with his mouth then struck out with a roar. I was instantly nauseated.

The girls in class giggled.

"So today, I'd like us to bring together," he made a gathering gesture with his arms, "everything I've taught you. To that end, I have selected a very average-looking student to help us with our demonstration." He took my elbow like I might need support. "No offense intended, Matthew. But you are so very plain and boring."

The girls all giggled again. I was more nauseated but now a little bit pissed too.

He raised his hand up high. "For the test on this masterpiece, you will especially need to remember the characters and the symbols they represent. To that end, I have come up with *the* mnemonic of the century." He bowed deeply as he tucked his hand in his plump little belly.

The girls all went oooh. I nearly went poooh.

"So here's the deal. I will be using our volunteer, Matthew, as a model of the various characters. You will identify which character I am creating him to be, based on the qualities I will apply." He said "apply" very oddly. I was concerned.

"So, Matthew, if you will stand there." He gestured to a spot at the front of the class. I did so but with grave reservations. "First player. Now shout out the name when you get it. And Margie," he pointed to a girl with more braces than teeth, "I want you to record who got it first, because there's a *prize* for the person who gets the most."

Margie nearly fainted but took out a scrap of paper and clicked her pen to ready.

Duvoe reached into a bag on the floor, one that Santa might need back on December twenty-fourth if it'd been red. He pulled out a baseball hat with long triangles glued or stapled to the top. They pointed kind of horizontally. He placed the ridiculous thing on my head.

Gesturing to me, he asked, "Anyone?"

The room was silent.

"Okay, I thought not. Next clue." He retrieved a flashlight, turned it on, and handed it to me. I shined it toward the floor. "No, like this," he corrected and had me hold it above my head, illuminating the ceiling. "Anyone?" he prompted again.

More silence.

"Okay, now it's going to be too easy."

He pulled out a stuffed animal. It was pink and round. It was a pig. Next, he got an arrow and put in in my non-flashlight hand. "Here," he whispered to me, "stab the boar."

I poked at the stuffed pig with the rubber-tipped arrow.

"Piggy," one of the girls squealed out.

He raised a finger. "No, but close. He's hunting the beasty."

"Uuh, uuh," a boy shouted. "Democracy and boar hunting. That's *Ralph*."

Duvoe bounced on his tiptoes. "Very good, David." He quickly removed my props. Then he took a small hair thing from his pocket and pushed it against my upper lip. "Anybody?"

No one ventured a guess.

He raised my arm, like I was doing a Nazi salute.

"Hitler, he's Hitler," a girl yelled like she was meeting The Beatles. "Jack, he's mean old Jack."

"Helga wins one for the fairer sex," Duvoe proclaimed.

A few seconds later, after removing my mustache, he held an oversized cross behind me. "Stick your arms up," he instructed. "No, not that high. Like this." He rearranged my arms horizontally.

"Christ crucified," shouted some other girl. "He's Simon."

"Bethany wins a point," Duvoe crowed.

In rapid order, I had a pig's nose applied to my face, and someone guessed Piggy, and he had me chop a knife in the air and look mean, and someone got Roger. I got a headache and was fully humiliated.

"Thank you, Matthew, and thank you, class. I think you have a good handle on the characters. Now I'd—"

"Whoa," I stated loudly.

He looked to me with surprise.

"We missed a character, one I think only you can play."

He began to look uncomfortable with this twist. Smart boy.

"There's one set of characters we haven't covered, an often under-appreciated one at that. Say, class, do you want Mr. V here to help play that character?"

The class exploded in cheers.

"That settles that. I need a couple props. Everybody take five." I dashed away to the attached storage room. In a flash, I was back with my own bag of props.

"Okay, people, shout it out when you get it," I said joyously. "Mr. D, sit here." I carried his desk chair over. "Hold your arms like this." I lifted them to in front of his chest. "Go like this," I told him, showing him my hands rotating back and forth like I was driving a car. "Anyone?" I shouted.

No answer. I then reached into the bag and pulled out a quart of red poster paint. Holding it just behind his head so he couldn't see it, I removed the lid. "Anyone?" I asked again.

Nothing, but a few squirms were in evidence.

"Final clue." I poured the entire bottle over Duvoe's head. He popped up like he was unrestrained in the electric chair, sweeping his hand across his face to clear his vision.

"What the *fuck* are you doing, you little *shit?*" he screamed at the top of his voice.

"This is play acting, boss." I pointed to him. "Anybody?"

Not one sound.

"He's one of the pilots. They *died* in the crash." I swiped a finger across the top of his head. "See, blood. Dead pilots, an important yet undervalued set of adult characters in our story. Big round of applause for Mr. V."

I led the clapping. I think one or two other kids joined in, but, to be honest, I was so jazzed, I don't know for certain.

"Dunsratty," the teacher shouted, "this is inexcusable." And with that, he stormed dripping red paint from the room. The bell rang.

"Class dismissed," I stated for the record.

FOURTEEN

Call me crazy, but I was kind of anxious to get to art class. Mind you, I have *negative* artistic talent. I can't draw stick figures so that they look convincingly like sticks. But my day was going well, I was on a roll, and I was ready to see what other challenges the day might hold for me. Living as I did in an affluent district, the art department was well-endowed. We had a warehouse-sized facility with kilns, welding equipment, millions of easels, and ample staffing. Yet still I could not be taught to make a clay pot with symmetry. Clearly the fault lay not in my stars but in my hands.

As I was strolling down the hall, I tried to recall the instructor. He was a squirrelly fellow with an accent, if memory served. Maximo, Nacio? No, *Massimo*. That was it. He was Italian. I remember him as a nice enough guy, but very shy and tentative. He was also a single male who lived in San Francisco and owned three cats. They were all he ever talked about. I'll let you do the math there. He was also the only teacher I ever had who insisted his students address him by his first name. Man, that felt super weird. In fact, I don't think I ever learned his surname.

Generally, in art class, we were working in small groups or pods.

Five or six students would be doing painting, another five or six doing pottery, and so on. The teacher and some volunteers would circulate amongst the groups and offer suggestions or correct errors. I was, because the universe had a sick sense of humor, currently assigned to oil painting. We used boards, not canvases, to keep expenses down, but still, whatever costs I incurred were a complete waste. But, as long as I got a "C," I was content. Back then, if you tried and weren't a horse's ass, everyone got a "C."

"Classa," Massimo said softly with that endearing extra vowel at the end of the word, "iffa you will gette in your groups, we can begina. I'ma working with da pottery people firsta, and den I rotatea around da room clockawise. Iffa you need helpa sooner, please justa ask."

Like I said, he was a nice guy. So I found a clean paint tray and a few dry brushes. We did not use painter palettes to blend colors, but rather practical trays with wells. Massimo had said *iffa you getta good enougha, we'll see abouta tavolozza.* My project from last class was set up against a wall. I retrieved the three foot by four foot board and found an open easel. My painting was red. That's about the best description, one that presented it at its best, that I can give you. After the viewer took in the work's redness, the rest was a little bit sketchy. Our assignment was to do a still life of a couple red apples resting on a rustic platter atop a hewn wooden table.

So far, I had a red oval, sort of football-shaped, floating freely in the air. I figured apple, platter, table—one, two, three—was the way to go. I mixed up some more red because, in my opinion, I *excelled* at red. I shaded the one-tone red appleball with more red. Today's red had more yellow that the first hue, but it was close. As a result, my appleball appeared to be maybe the team colors of a color-blind foot-ball team. But, in my mind, I was making progress, so I was content.

After fifteen minutes or so, Massimo wandered over to my group. He stopped to encourage a girl named Alexi and enjoined her to *rememaber da light.* He moved to inspect the boy behind me's work, but must have accidentally glanced over at my project. Dude froze mid-step. Seriously, it was like someone'd shot him.

To his credit, he thawed quickly, and tried to appear to nonchalantly turn to check on my whateverthehellitwas. But Massimo's eyes screamed 9-1-1.

"Matta." He always added that "A" to my name. In retrospect, it was so endearing. "I see you are making very progress." Hmm, did he just omit an adjective?

"Yeah, some, I guess."

"Let'sa see." He rubbed his chin and pretended it took him time to come to some conclusion. He picked up one of the apples. "You know we are painting *apples* today, righta?"

"Sure." I nodded to the one in his hand.

"Doa you perceive whata da shape of disa apple is?" He held it before us between two fingers.

"Sure, it's apple-shaped."

"Bery good. It'sa *apple*-shaped." His finger touched the top of the apple, next to the stem that I seemed to have omitted. "We see dat the apple, it drops a tiny bita, den swells outward to a shoulder before very, very gently curving down to a narr ... narrower base. Yes?"

"Sure."

"And de base, it is not either flat like a piece a wood nor isa it pokie like you seem to suggest. It isa in reality a rough but generally a plane, no?"

"Sure." I hoped he wasn't getting the impression that I didn't get it.

"So, we gunna use dis wood as fora *practice* now," he announced, touching my board. "I want you to draws me just the two-dimensional shapea of deis apple. Usea da red you have started with, please."

With my yellowish-red, I drew a nearly perfect circle. Hey, at least it wasn't a football.

"No, no, no, no," he effused. "*Look* at de apple. It'sa not round like a soccer ball. Se, ita tapers." His fingers caressed the surface. "Try again," he instructed as patiently as he could, which was a little. Gotta give him credit again.

In my peachy red, I painted ... a football. But, in my defense, this football had less of a point at the bottom than my original one had.

"You know, Matta, I am beginning to tink you do notta have a real future in da arts. I don't usually say dat, even when itsa as apparent as de wart on a witch's nose. But I'ma tinking maybe we could have you maybe helpa with da cleaning and straightening, more than da arting."

"Sure."

"But, so nobady saysa I didn't try, let me show you what I wasa getting at."

Massimo replaced the apple on the table, then nudged it a few times for whatever reason. He took my paint tray and brush from me, almost like he was repossessing them. He started three other wells immediately in varying shapes of red, then whipped up a row of four browns. Apples aren't brown, but I decided not to tell him.

Over five minutes, he rendered a still life that took my breath away. Obviously, as a kid, I'd never have noticed. But over lifetimes, I'd come to be quite a connoisseur of fine art. Massimo was the real deal and then a whole lot more.

"Massimo," I said mouth agape, "that's stunning."

He did his shy thing. He looked down, blushed, kicked at the floor, and looked away.

"Seriously, Massimo," I reinforced, "those apples, they're so firm, so crisp. And I just know if I bit into one, it'd snap like a bullwhip, and, and the juice'd run down my cheek, but I wouldn't care because I was eating the best apple that was ever grown." I leaned in. "Massimo, these apples are erotic."

"No," he rejected.

"Yes. These apples, they *want* you to pick them up and rub them until they shine like the sun and then they want you to eat them."

Again with the shy, the looking away and blushing.

"Massimo, I'm not just saying this. You are a master painter. What the hell are you doing trying to teach talentless snotty-nosed kids and not working in your studio producing masterpieces?"

"Matta, I 'presiate your compliments. Buta, a master I'm a not." He shrugged. "I'ma nice, but I havea lot to learn."

"Massimo, go get me the last painting you finished," I told him firmly.

"Really?"

"Now. Hurry." I shooed him away.

He returned a minute later with a canvas, but I could only see the back. He removed my board and set his work on the easel. He blocked my view until he stepped behind me.

I - was - stunned - stupid. I nearly got an erection, it was so emotive and compelling. The image was of a young man walking away from the viewer. He was in front of Harrah's Casino in Lake Tahoe, just crossing the parking lot entrance walking east. It was winter. He had on worn jeans and a flannel shirt. His hands were drilled into his pockets. And he wore cowboy boots, but they were two sizes too big for him. And he did not have on a hat. Everything in the picture screamed that he was or should be wearing a hat, but he was defiantly not sporting one.

"Massimo, this painting belongs in the Louvre."

"Oh, stoppa it, Matta. Now you are just making funna me." He went to remove the painting.

I reached out and gently caught his shoulder. He turned to me with a wounded expression. "Massimo, on my mother's honor, I swear this is one of the most beautiful oils I've ever laid eyes on."

"Yeah, anda you fifteen," he spat, still hurting.

"Thirteen, but that's not the point," I replied. "Massimo, I am willing to prove to you that you are a master painter. Are you willing to risk me being correct?"

His eye lit up some. "Whata you mean?"

"Just that. I am willing to bet good money you are wasting your time here and that the world will reward you for your talent as you deserve it to. What do you say?"

"Okay. Iffa you could *prove* it, sure. But howa you gunna do dat?"

"Here's the deal. I know a guy."

"Know a guy? What's dat mean?"

"I am personal friends with an extremely rich and discerning art aficionado. He lives in San Francisco, yeah, has a suite near the top of the Mark Hopkins."

"No."

Technically, he was correct. I did not presently know Nicholas Papachristodoulopoulos III. But thirty years from now, we were great friends. Nicholas was heir to a shipping line fortune. But he hated boats, shipping containers, and docks; man, he hated docks. So he let his family run the business and he assumed the role of wealthy playboy. Nicholas, like Massimo, was a single man living in San Francisco who owned cats. Now, Nicholas didn't rave about them endlessly. But whenever I visited him, there was a set rotation of which damn cat leaped up on his lap for petting, before it lost interest and wandered away. And Nicholas was a passionate supporter of the arts, especially painting and especially oil paintings.

"Here is what I will do to prove to you, Massimo, that you are needed elsewhere. You take this painting," I pointed to the lone young man, "and two others, *any* two others, to my friend. He will look at them and he will thank the Good Lord I sent you to him."

"Justa like that?"

"Just like that. And to prove I'm serious, I'll bet all the money I have in my savings account that he does just that. If you return here with your tail between your legs, I'll pay you that much."

"Like a bet?"

"It is a bet."

"How mucha you got in da bank?" he said with piqued interest.

"About a hundred and fifty dollars."

"So, iffa he does love my work, I pay you dat much?"

"No, when he *does* love your stuff, you give me that painting." I nodded toward the lone man.

"Even iffa it'sa only worth da paint I used?"

"Or even if it's worth a quarter-million dollars," I said with a gleam in my eyes.

"Okayu, you gotta me. What I do?"

"You know the Mark Hopkins?"

"Sure."

"Go there now and tell the front desk you are there to see Nicholas Papachristodoulopoulos. They will ask if he's expecting you. You tell them no, that you were sent by his good friend and that they need to let him know you are waiting."

"And I tell hima, Matta sent me?"

"No ... that wouldn't work." Because he won't know me for decades. "Nicholas and I, we play this little game. I send him talent and he has to guess it was me that did so. When he asks who sent you, you remind him of that game. And you can tell him as a hint that I know the Queen of Hearts."

"Who da hell issa dat?"

I shrugged. "Who knows. But he'll see you. Nicholas's a sucker for a mystery. You got it?"

"Go to da Mark Hopkins. Take three paintings. Tell 'im not who you are but dat youa know da Queen of Hearts."

"Perfect. Now go."

"Nowa? I canna go now, it's a da middle of classa."

"Massimo, this is important. Stop by the office and they'll send someone to cover you. Then drive to the Hopkins. Stop in front and tell the valet you're a friend of Nicholas. They'll take care of your car. Now go!"

And he did. He wasn't exactly smiling, but he was quite intense. Funny thing, memories. Sometimes they come in waves and sometimes they come in spurts. Nicholas and I are great friends in the future, at least some futures. He still lives in the same suites in The Mark Hopkins, still has too many cats, and he lives with his husband, a guy named Jeri. I remember once hearing them mention Jeri used to go by ... you got it, *Massimo*. Why he changed it, I have no clue. But in the future, every self-respecting art museum on earth has to have a few Jeris in their collections to be considered legitimate. He's the most famous artist of his day. Oh, and you'll never guess what Jeri's nickname is. The Queen of Hearts. Small world, eh?

Knowing what I just set in motion explains another little mystery that Nicholas teases me with in the future. He's always making vague references about how I saved his life. Now, generally, you know if you save a man's life. I didn't ever recall doing so. Nicholas'd say something about when AIDS hit San Francisco with a vengeance in the 1980s, how that if he didn't have his perfect Jeri, he'd most likely have continued to mingle excessively—his words not mine—and he'd be dead. What that conversation had to do with me I never understood ... until now.

How very outstanding!

FIFTEEN

Well, second period didn't exactly go as I anticipated. But what the hell. It was fun. I wondered what Wood Shop held in store for me? That's a rhetorical question, because I know what it held in store for me. The smell of cut wood, failure at another artistic endeavor, and humiliation because the class bullies for whatever reason blossomed in Wood Shop. Maybe it was a caveman thing? Cut tree, build bowl, hit other cavemen. Oh well, how bad could it be, I said with a grim smile?

Most kids—and by kids, I mean *boys*, no girls in Wood Shop, heaven forbid—shuffled in late to shop. It was a right-of-passage or something. In fact, the only force that compelled us to enter the shop was that as the hallways cleared, the chance of getting caught without a pass increased quickly. The shop teacher was, of course, an old white man. Who else would it be? If he didn't look like your great uncle, and mumble constantly, and walk like his hips were fused and he really didn't want to get wherever he was lumbering toward in the first place, how could he teach boys to cut wood?

Mr. Maisbach. That was the old fart saddled with an endless conveyor belt of acne-faced, sullen, hormonally impaired boys who had no interest whatsoever in learning how to make a pencil box. I wonder if Mr. M regarded his employment as a form of penance for amassed past sins. If so, he must have been a bad man, because his sentence was brutal. I hope the punishment fit the crime. Then again, what did I care? He liked wood and not teenage boys. Wood liked him and not teenage boys. Teenage boys liked neither wood nor Mr. Maisbach. It was a just, if not perfect, arrangement.

"If you could take your places," he grumbled. That was the extent of his verbal abilities. He grumbled. He also slurped when his dentures slipped, but I don't count that as vocal variation since he didn't mean it to convey meaning. To us, it did, and it said nothing complimentary, but for him, it was just the ravages of time and a poor dental plan. He wouldn't have told us to take our seats, because though we had high stools, a board with the words *You Can't Sit and Cut Wood, So Don't Sit* burned into it was posted on the wall above his desk.

"I'm sorry we're getting a late start today. Some knuckle potato hid my shop shoes in the toilet. It took me forever to find them." He arched his back so he could look at us as he railed against us. "Any of you knuckle potatoes ever wear wet shop shoes?" He waited a second. "Bah. I thought not. Try it sometime if you got nothing else to do."

I didn't place that act on my Wood Shop bucket list. And as to *knuckle potatoes*. No one knew where it came from or what it was meant to convey. Presumably, it was nothing good, but none of us really cared, so its origins were a moot point.

"You need to finish your bird houses by the end of next week. If you don't finish your bird houses, how can the birds move into them? They can't, so finish them by the end of this week."

Sure, that contradicted what he'd just said, but no one cared.

"If you need help finishing the bird houses, I suppose you can tell me and I'll try to make your knuckle potato pile of poop into a proper bird house. Paint," he said like he'd just recalled the meaning of life. "You must *paint* your bird houses. If you don't paint your bird houses, then they are not finished. If they are not finished, they are not complete."

"Mr. Maisbach," some kid I remembered as a trouble maker said, "I thought birds were color blind."

"Color blind? Birds? That ridiculous. Have you ever seen a bird, young man? They have all kinds of colors. Bah!"

I saw disappointment in the brat's eyes. Mr. M hadn't taken the bait.

"So, all you knuckle potatoes get to working. If you finish your bird house, including painting it, before the end of next week, you can start on our next project."

"What's our next project," asked some kid who must have accidentally cared.

"The next project?" he replied, a tad confused. "Well, let me see. We did pencil boxes, and we did gift boxes, and we did bird houses. So I guess that leaves cutting boards. Yes. The next project is cutting boards."

I felt no better knowing that fact than I did before I knew it. In any case, we all set to looking like we were working. Mr. Maisbach sat and opened a copy of *Popular Mechanics* magazine and mentally departed the scene. I found my bird house. Mmm, best to call it a bird house in progress. They say a journey of a thousand miles begins with a single step. I had done step one with my bird house. I'd placed a round hole in a five by five piece of pine. All I needed to do was cut the rest, dove-tail the joints, glue, paint, and I was done.

I decided to see if I could just glue scraps of leftover wood to my piece. Maybe I'd make a modern-art bird house? I rummaged through the scrap pile and thought about anything else. As I did, I noticed that wise ass kid was spying around the room. Yup, he was hunting for trouble. His name was Harold Plank. Geez, with a name like that, he should have been serious about wood shop. But he was destined to fail at life and to do so as quickly as he possibly could. Last I saw him, he was the assistant night manager of a twenty-four-hour donut shop. He was in his late forties at the time.

Harry waited until one of the wimpier kids made a bathroom run. He shot over to the kid's bird house and dropped a lit firecracker into the opening. Yeah, *that* kid's bird house had six walls. Then Harry sped away. He was back to his station by the time the cracker exploded. It didn't damage the bird house much, but I could see a seam split. The kid came running out of the restroom. I guess he was accustomed to his lot in life, so, hearing an explosion, he naturally assumed he was the victim. He held up his house and promptly started crying. Yeah, he was heading for a rough life too. Maybe at least he could be night shift manager of the donut shop and boss Harry around. One could dream.

As odd as it might seem, Maisbach did not hear the explosion, but crying brought him to his feet like he was a spring-loaded toad. He scanned the room so vigorously, his jowls made a loud slapping sound. Gross. He spotted the whimpering wimp fairly quickly. "You there. What seems to be the problem?"

Kid held up his work. "Someone blew up my bird house."

"What did you say?"

"Someone blew up my bird house, sir."

He waved him over. "Let me see that."

Maisbach inspected the piece. He looked like he tasted it, he was so consumed with his inspection. "It doesn't appear to be blown up to me, son," was his final assessment.

"Well, see here." The kid fingered the ruptured seam.

"Oh, that's not blown up, son. It just needs a bit more glue. You need to put on enough to hold the joints through any weather. The birds who inhabit your structure can't very well call a repairman, or repairbird now, can they?"

The kid was confused. I was confused. Repairbirds? Were they an option for a bird house occupant?

"No, sir," the kid responded uncertainly.

"Now go put some glue on that, lad," Maisbach instructed as he shoved the boy away.

"Which lad, sir?" the squirt asked.

"Which lad what?" Maisbach questioned.

"Which lad do you wish me to put glue on?"

"None of them," he chuckled-grunted. "What good would that do? They're kids, not birdhouses." He quietly chuckle-grunted to himself.

"I'm confused, sir," the kid responded honestly.

"Go along. Work on your project." And he sat back down and started in on his magazine again.

Buoyed by his initial success, Plank waited patiently until another chance to wreak havoc presented itself. This time, he shoved two fire crackers into the unguarded house. Pop, pop. All eyes but two rocketed to the explosion. Yeah, Maisbach must have been a deaf war veteran. He ignored the sound again. This time, the boy, Adam Stranger, who had a sad, sad name to live with, marched up to Maisbach's deck and presented his now crooked bird house to him.

Eventually, Maisbach noticed Adam. "No, no, son, that will never do. Your bird house is *crooked*."

"I know. Someone blew it up."

"Not again. Didn't I tell you to just use more glue?"

"No. That was Derrick. Mine was blown up too. Just look at it."

"Now, son, no one goes around blowing up bird houses. That's silly. You probably stepped on it and now it's crooked. Go straighten it up and put more glue on it."

Glue seemed as good a solution as duct tape. Who knew?

"But I—" Adam protested.

"More *glue*," Mr. Maisbach shout-grunted and he waved his hands in the air.

A little later, Plank had to answer the call of nature. Either that or he was just bored. I went to his station and hoisted up his backpack. Rifling through it quickly, I found a string of fire crackers and a box of stick matches. I was, as most boys are, an expert when it came to fire crackers. I twisted six fuses together, so the explosions would be roughly simultaneous. I dropped the remainder of the string into my pocket. Waste not want not. I lit the fuses and tossed them into Plank's house. Then I dashed back to my station.

Bam! Nice, they went off as one. The wood was splintered on every surface and the roof was blown off completely.

Plank sprinted into the room and scanned his project. He was pissed. He held it up in one palm. "Which one of you dildos did this? Whoever you are, you're dead meat."

If anyone asks you what are the minimum number of exploding fire crackers it takes to get Mr. Maisbach's attention, tell them it takes six. Before Plank was done threatening, the teacher was at his side. "What have you done to your bird house, son?" he asked angrily.

"Not me, you old fool, it was fire crackers. Some dildo put fire crackers into my bird house and blew it up."

Now that was a lot for the senior teacher to process. He'd been called a fool. This student was making a dildo. And there was that claim about blown-up things again. Where had he heard that one before? Oh, bother, he couldn't recall.

"Now, son, you and I are going to have words," he began to wind up. "First off, you may not call me a fool. Only Mrs. Maisbach enjoys that privilege. Second off, this is not a dildo. It's a broken bird house. You didn't put enough *glue* on the darn thing. What is it with you knuckle potatoes and glue." He mimed squirting glue in a downward direction. "Use a lot of glue. It's cheap, you know?" Then an afterthought must have struck him. "How dare you try to make a wooden dildo in my shop class. Do you have any idea how inappropriate wood is in fabricating one of those?" He actually thumped Plank on the side of his head. "Think it through, boy. You're going to get splinters up there where the sun don't shine."

"No, you old fool. I am not making a *dildo*. I was calling the other *boys* dildos. That's a blown-up bird house." He pointed at the shattered wood.

Maisbach started thinking deeply. He looked at the boy, then the floor, then the boy. "Did you just call me an old fool?"

"Ah, no. I said you were not to be fooled, sir."

"Coward," I shouted.

All eyes swung to me.

"Pardon?" Maisbach asked.

"I called Plank there a coward, Mr. Maisbach. He called you a fool twice, then lied about it to your face because he's a coward. He comes from a family of cowards," I accused hotly.

"Is that a fact?" Maisbach asked Plank point blank.

"No, Dunsratty's just being a dildo," Plank snarled.

"You ... you really seem to have a troubling fixation with sexual toys, son. Should you and I go see the school nurse?"

"No. I'm fine. Dunsratty blew up my project, that's all."

The teacher turned to me. "Did you blow up his birdhouse, son?"

I fingered my chest. "Me? How could I even do that?"

"Well, did someone blow up his work?"

"No, sir. It was the birds, sir," I reported as seriously as I could.

"Say what?" he grunted.

"Mr. Maisbach, did you hear that?" I asked him.

"Hear what?"

"Someone knocked at the door."

"Really? I didn't hear it." He turned and limped away as quickly as he probably could.

Once he was as far away as he would be, I lit the rest of the string of fire crackers and tossed them to the floor. They went off before Maisbach was back. As he entered the shop, he gestured over his shoulder. "No one was there. Did I hear explosions in here?"

"Yes, sir," I replied solemnly. "It was the birds. They're back. They're dive-bombing our bird houses."

"Why, that's absurd," he declared.

"Sir, you've heard the reports about blown-up bird houses, right?"

"Something to that effect, yes."

"The SPCA thinks it's something the birds are eating, maybe bad berries, sir, but maybe it's climate change and DDT and everything bad we've done to Mother Earth. But there are reports all over of them dive-bombing objects that offend them. Surely you've read about that in your evening paper, sir?" I pleaded with the man.

"We get the *morning* paper at my house," he clarified.

"Well, maybe that explains it. But I'm afraid the birds have selected the shop as their next target. Pardon my French, but the damn avians are very systematic. They took out home economics right in the middle of poached eggs, Mr. Maisbach. Poached eggs! I ask you, how are those girls ever going to catch a man if they can't poach eggs? As much as it pains me to say the words, sir, in the interest of student safety, I feel we should stage a tactical retreat from the wood shop until we can get trained bird handlers in here."

"Don't you think that's overreacting just a bit?" he challenged.

"Your call, Mr. Maisbach. I'd just hate to see someone lose an eye if that could have been avoided."

"Losing an eye is serious business, son," he replied with resounding gravity. "Just to be safe, let's exit the shop in an orderly—"

He stopped talking when he was nearly knocked on his large behind by a torrent of boys running, yelling and screaming, from the room.

Class dismissed.

SIXTEEN

So far, I have to say I was rather enjoying my return to junior high school. Not what I would have anticipated. You know how older people are always pining about their lost youth and how if they had a time machine, they'd return to high school in a hot second? Well, I never thought like that. Partly, I'm sure it has to do with my career as a high school teacher. I'm exposed on a daily basis to the empty-headed, mind-numbing conversations that go on between the kids. They are a bunch of children with children's issues and children's intellects, or lack of therein. I always envisioned returning a person to high school with their adult mind in their youthful body to be a standard punishment in one of the circles of hell. Remember that when I used to time dive back into my high school years, I only planted a thought in that otherwise empty head of mine. I didn't have to stay and *be* teenage Matt. This was different. Then again, in two days, I hadn't done a lot of socializing with my contemporaries. The only girl I sort of asked out was the principal. But I was here and would remain for a day or two more. Then I'd leave with no regrets.

My next period was Social Studies. Yeah, that's the one taught by that lunatic Assmakis, the asshmahole who sent me to the office yesterday. Crap. I hope he got laid last night. Maybe that'd improve his mood, though both those ideas, that he'd ever get laid and that his mood was improvable, were ludicrous. Ah well, at least today I had my wits about me. As I walked to class, I began to notice a shadow coming up to me from behind. I turned my head. Plank, the bully from shop class. He was making a beeline for yours truly. So much for limited interactions with the locals.

I assumed his bully-from-behind SOP would be to grab my shoulder, whip me around, and start in on me, verbally and physically. Hey, I was a high school teacher. That's how kids thought and acted. From the angle he was approaching, I had to guess if he'd go for my right or left shoulder. My bet was on my right. I slid my left hand, palm up, on top of my right shoulder while keeping up a steady pace. Bullies are like bulls. Plank wouldn't notice once his rage was at full steam.

Sure enough, he grabbed for my shoulder but actually got my hand. I closed on his hand and spun around so I had his arm behind his back in half a flash. I twisted it hard to double him over and began frog-marching him forward to maintain control over him. He wasn't much bigger, but I'd just as soon keep him at a disadvantage.

"Well, good morning again, wooden plank," I taunted. "Miss me already?" You know that scene in *Back to the Future III* where Marty inadvertently calls Biff *Mad Dog*? Yeah, Plank hated the wooden nickname about as much.

He pivoted hard to his left to escape my grip. "What the fuck you doing, you dildo?" he snarled.

"You know what, Woody, I agree with Maisbach. Your obsession with the steely dan suggests some latent sexual issues."

"Like-I-care-you-dildo-let-me-go," he spat back.

"Not until you say you're sorry," I said calmly.

"Sorry? Sorry for what—"

"You dildo," I finished his thought for him. "Plank, come on, sorry for you being born. For you being such a failed human. For you being so *you*."

"Screw you, dildo."

His obsession was getting on my last nerve. "Hey, Woodsman without an axe, let's make a deal. I let you go if you never say the word dildo again in your life. Deal?"

"Once you let go, I'm pounding the shit out of you, dildo."

"Giving me what motivation for releasing you?"

"Because when you do, I'm pounding the shit out of you, dildo."

"Toothpick donor, my verbal pearls are lost on your swininess."

What was I going to do with ... ah! There was Hall Monitor Bob. Bob was not a security guard or a cop. He was a hall monitor. Bob's qualifications were that he was huge – brick shit house huge—and that he was able to walk the halls in order to monitor them. By the way, I never discovered if HM Bob had a surname.

I needed to time this just right, but what the hell? Plank couldn't see Bob, since I had him bent over nose-to-floor. I angled us to approach Bob from his six o'clock. When we were a couple yards behind the big man, I shouted, "No, friend Plank, do not hit me." Then I released his arm.

Like a consummate idiot, Plank straightened up, spun, and lunged at me with a raised fist. I grinned at him but stood perfectly still. One second Plank's arm was flying forward to strike me, and the next his entire body was whooshing away from me. Nice!

"Hey, kid," Bob thundered. "Cut that out."

You know those perfect moments in your life? The first time you climax when making love to a woman? The vista from the top of Half Dome in Yosemite the first time you scale it? The birth of your child? Yeah, I have an add-to for you. The time Plank spun in a blind rage and thumped HM Bob squarely on the jaw. It ... the memory of that moment will bring a tear to my eyes until the day I die.

Of course I doubt Bob felt a thing. If he had, let me assure you that the blow was not the first punch Bob had taken, but it was the lightest. His eyes did, however, turn red as I watched. Plank went stiff and said *oh shit*. Bob responded with *oh shit your skinny ass*. Then, I kid you not, HM Bob pressed Plank up against the ceiling. Was Bob extra tall with gorilla arms? Was the roof atypically low? I have no idea, but the image was sublime. Oh for a cell phone.

To his eternal credit, HM Bob did not proceed to violently dismember Plank. He held him pinned against a fire sprinkler for thirty seconds, then lowered him so they were face-to-face. "You gonna calm the fuck down, kid?" Bob inquired calmly.

"Y ... yy ... yes, sir." There grew a long wet streak down both of Plank's pant legs.

"Do not call me sir," HM Bob growled. "I *work* for a living."

Ah, Bob must be retired military, some level of NCO. I thanked him for his service in my head.

Bob then quite literally dragged Plank behind him in the direction of the office. I sincerely hoped for Plank's sake that was their destination. Plank was a moron and a leech on society, but he was just a kid. There would be ample opportunities for his ass to be kicked by actual tough guys once he reached adulthood.

Then again, what did I care? I didn't want to be late to Social Studies, now did I?

The crowd observing Plank's comeuppance was dispersing. I joined in and made for class, which was a building away. As I mingled with the kids, a cute little girl whose name escaped me pulled up beside me.

"Were you afraid?" she asked, doe-eyed.

"Beg pardon?" I replied, surprised to have been addressed.

"By Plank, when he attacked you. Were you afraid?"

We entered the class but pulled to one side to stop and converse.

"Of Plank? No. He's more bark than bite."

She blinked repeatedly. "He bit you?"

"No. I mean to say, hey, what's your name? In all this excitement, I seemed to have forgotten it."

She seemed flattered. I'd forgotten her name in the heat of battle. That had to be almost romantic if you were a teenage girl.

"Lilita," she said breathily.

I snapped my fingers loudly and pointed at her. "That's it," I confirmed. "Gosh, thanks for helping me in my recovery from my recent trauma. You didn't have to, but you did. Thanks."

Hey, what? Sure, I was eighteen months from my relationship with Stacy, but I wasn't dead either. Lilita was really cute and the weekend was approaching. Cut this lonely teenage boy some slack.

"Oh, you're welcome," she responded in a whisper.

I extended an arm toward the classroom. "Shall we?"

"Oh, yes," she replied like I was ushering her into her new palace.

We found our seats. As I said, junior high was not nearly as bad as I seemed to remember it.

"Last session, we were discussing the three components of the American government," Assmakis began, already droning, promising to be snoozerific as usual. "Matthew, why don't you remind us of those three separate but equal bodies."

Okay, that was how it was to start. A direct assault. Well, bring it on, fool. "The executive, the legislative and the judicial."

"Wrong as usual," he snapped back instantly. "They are the Executive *Branch*, the Legislative *Branch*, and the Judicial *Branch*. If you had remained in class as opposed to being defiant, you might have learned that critical element of citizenship."

Grr, I let that shit-bird distinction pass. This contest was still early days.

"And what, Matthew, do we consider the highest law of the land?" he asked, strutting at the front of the class.

"Social Studies teachers?"

My nervous classmates, sensing the tension between Assmakis and me, laughed quietly.

"Ah, humor, Matthew," he derided. "How expected. Now, quickly, the highest law?"

"The Constitution."

He glared at me. "Are you certain?"

"Yes. How about you?"

"What is that supposed to mean?" he lashed out.

"I'm just curious if you're confident in your answer. Is it now a crime to ask a teacher if they're certain of their facts?"

"No, I suppose it's not," he granted reluctantly. "Along the same lines, what document did our Constitution replace?"

"The Articles of Confederation."

"Alright. And—"

"What year was that, sir?" I tossed back.

"I beg your pardon?"

"What year was the present Constitution adopted?"

"Are you challenging me to a duel of *wits*, child?" he asked indignantly.

"Call it what you will. You ask a question, I ask a question. We test each other's knowledge in a friendly contest. Does not the Socratic method work both ways?"

"A smart aleck, eh? Sure. This should be fun," he stated confidently. "So, as the teacher, I shall ask—"

"Uh, hang on. The initial question is already on the table. What year was the present Constitution adopted?"

"I see your trick. I state the correct answer and you agree. You don't need to know the answer. I am no fool, Matthew."

"If it's trust you lack, trust you will have." I ripped several sheets out of my binder. "Both questioner and questionee write their best answer." I scanned the room. "You," I pointed at a big kid who played a lot of sports. "Jumbo, you be the judge."

Assmakis pursed his lips, but quickly said, "Sure. I love being right." He came and sat next to me. "Let's do this."

"The Constitution was adopted in—" I made a show of writing my answer.

Assmakis hesitated, then scribbled something.

Jumbo extended a hand to both of us and scanned the paper. "Matt says 1789. Mr. Assmakis' paper says 1777."

I held up the textbook. "Would you like me to look it up?"

"No, that's alright. I ... I must have been thinking of some other document."

"One point for Matt," Jumbo declared.

"Alright, Matthew, what is the full name of the document the Constitution replaced?"

We both wrote something and handed it to Jumbo.

"You both have The Articles of Confederation and Perpetual Union. No points awarded."

Assmakis actually stomped a foot.

"What date did the Constitutional Congress declare independence from Great Britain?" I asked quickly.

"Oops, we have a disagreement," Jumbo said as he read our responses. "I'm afraid you lose, Matt. It was July fourth, not the second."

I raised a finger. "No, they *approved* the document on the fourth. They voted for independence on the *second*."

Jumbo furrowed his brow. "You sure?"

"No, he's correct. It's a trick question," Assmakis conceded.

"Alright then, Matt two, teacher zero."

"There were several differences between the Articles and the Constitution. Write one down," the teacher instructed.

"Matt has here," Jumbo said seeming to stick on the big words, "the declaration of a tripartite government. Ah, is that correct, Mr. Assmakis?"

"Yes it is," he replied sourly.

"Same question," I challenged. "Write another difference down."

Again Jumbo studied the paper he'd been given. "The power to raise taxes? What do you say, Matt?"

"Correct."

"Okay, still two zip," Jumbo summarized.

"Same question," Assmakis asked angrily. "Write another down."

"Is the power of the central government to raise an army count?" Jumbo directed to the teacher.

"Yes, it does," Assmakis hissed.

"Same question, back atcha," I stated confidently. "Give me another."

I wrote while Assmakis sweated. He began pacing. After a minute, Jumbo said he needed the teacher's paper.

"I can't think of another," Assmakis snapped with venom.

I handed Jumbo my paper.

His eyes widened. "Mr. Assmakis, will you accept the Constitution focused on power shifting from the states to the central government?"

He glared at me. Oh, my, if looks could wound. "Yes, I shall accept that response. Well played, Matthew. I have no idea how you cheated, but you did so well enough to pull this charade off." He studied Jumbo critically. "You were in league with him, weren't you, Mr. Peterson?"

Jumbo thought a second and said, "Yes, I was."

"Ah ha!" Assmakis screamed, rifling a finger at me. "I knew it. You will pay for this, the both of you. Oh, yes, you will pay dearly."

"Ah ... Mr. Assmakis?" Jumbo asked tentatively. "I'm not sure why Matt and me being in summer league baseball together last year should be such a big deal?"

"He asked if we were in league together," I said to Jumbo loudly enough for the janitor outside and down the hall to hear clearly. "As in pranking him, not playing ball."

Jumbo thought about my words a second, then burst out laughing. "You're freaking nuts, My Ass May Kiss."

That was when the teacher formally lost control of the session. Poor devil.

Not.

SEVENTEEN

I'd forgotten what an appetite you could work up by learning. Through the commotion in Social Studies, we couldn't hear the bell, but we left when it seemed time. I waited to see if Lilita would hook up with me, but she did not. Ah well, the day was young and I was fairly certain we had Science class together later on.

I fell into the fairly long line waiting for grub. I recognized some of the kids around me, but I didn't think we were on talking terms, so I mostly avoided eye contact and looked elsewhere. As I entered the cafeteria proper, I smelled what I presumed to be lunch. I have to say the aroma was dissimilar to those I've been allured by in trattorias across Italy. Someone alert the media, right? I grabbed a tray and slid it closer to the serving area. Pretty soon, it was my turn. I offered the lunch lady my empty five-compartment tray. She plopped a lump of pasta on the big hole, threw the tongs back into the metal serving dish, and hooked a ladle of sauce. With a backhand slam, she plastered the upper right corner of the pasta-berg with redness. She then reached for the next kid's tray. Apparently, I was dismissed to the lettuce-covered-with-something-wet station.

"Excuse me?" I said cheerfully.

It took a second, but lunch lady realized a child had addressed her. She looked at me like I was a lesser thing than the food she had just served me. "What?" she barked as she rested her knuckles on the counter and looked all the world like she was about to spit tobacco juice to the floor. Maybe her teeth were just loose.

"Hi, how's your day going so far?" I made pleasant conversation.

"Fair to middling until you opened your damn mouth."

"Ah. Well, I was just wondering."

"Thanks for sharing."

"This is supposed to be meatballs and spaghetti, correct?"

"No, it *is* meatballs and spaghetti, your Highness."

"There you have it," I agreed pleasantly. Pleasant was my middle name at that moment. "If you'll look at my tray, you'll see spaghetti and red sauce, perchance a marinara, though the chunks hint at a Bolognese."

"I understand the part you said in American and none of the rest. What's your point? This line is getting longer than my hemorrhoids, kid."

"Well, when listed as meatballs and spaghetti, I anticipated *meatballs*, as the first ingredient listed would be the star of the dish."

"I hate you, but please go on," she grunted.

"Were you in the military before your employment here ... ah, Constance?" I asked as I spied her name tag.

"Retired Army. Slopped troops from Fort Benning to hell and back. Now could you get to your point, short stuff?"

"There are no meatballs on my plate." I pointed to the plate for clarity.

"Life's tough, then ya get no meatballs. Move along 'for I give you a meatball backwards."

Instead of asking if that meant what I thought she intended it to mean, I simply asked, "Could I please have at *least* the volume of meatballs as I have of pasta, please?"

"Mr. Childs," she shouted like an air-raid siren. "This kid's trying to break my balls."

Charles Childs was a nice man. He was one of the English and History teachers. He was also a tall man with a low voice and bad breath. In other words, he was an authority figure. He also happened to be on duty in the cafeteria that day.

He stepped over to my side directly. "Matt, is there a problem?" he asked sternly. If you teach junior high, you always open strong.

"Kid's bustin' my ass about the lack of meatballs. Chuck, I'm a lunch lady, not personal chef."

"Is that so, Matt?" he confirmed sternly.

"Ah, yeah. Sign says meatballs and spaghetti and I got no meat-balls." I shrugged.

I could tell Childs was torn. On one hand, I was morally in the right. On the other hand, he was supposed to crack the whip. He pointed to the far corner. "Step into my office."

I and my deficient tray accompanied him into the corner. "Matt," he began more conversationally, "I hear you, but, as a favor to me, could we move past this? You eat what Connie served you, you don't get detention, and I can zone out again for the next ten blessed minutes. Can we do that?"

"Sure, Mr. Childs, since you ask so nicely. I was thinking of becoming a vegan anyway, so I'm good."

"Fine, Matt," he said, patting my shoulder. "I'll see you later."

"Sure thing, sir. Have a nice mental hygiene break."

He squinted one eye at me, then realized he didn't actually care what I said and walked away.

I did push my way back to the wet lettuce and hard bread stations. Hey, I'd laid down my quarter. These guys owed me food. I sat alone and ate very little. As I suspected, the red sauce was neither marinara *nor* Bolognese. It was ketchup. But that was understand-able. I was living in the USA.

After lunch, I had PE. Yesterday, the coach—remember, no one *teaches* PE, no, they apparently *coach* it—said we'd be doing boxing today. That sounded about as much fun as getting my face pounded in because, given my skills, they were one-and-the-same.

After I'd changed into my shorts and tee shirt, I was heading over the slight rise that led to the gym. Between me and said gym stood Mrs. Last Name Begins with L first name Betty, looking every bit as uncomfortable outside the office as I would have expected her to be. She was clearly glaring at me, the central cause of her present disquiet.

"Good afternoon," I greeted her.

"Don't start with me, Matt. Mrs. Abernathy said I'm to bring you by force of will or force of body to her office before you cause more trouble."

"Me," I pointed to myself, "cause trouble? Perish the thought."

"Don't want to hear it. Taking guff from you is above my paygrade. Let's go."

And go we did. The office was quite a walk, but I was unable to talk any intel out of her. She was a determined office secretary, I'll grant her that.

She pointed to my recent seat once we entered the office. "Sit. Do not move. Do not talk."

"May I—"

"No," she said with finality. She fingered her intercom and then sat numbly at her desk.

A few minutes later, the principal's office door opened. Mrs. Abernathy appeared in the portal. She raised a hand and, with a single digit, beckoned me to come.

"Sit down, Matt," she said with exhaustion. She thudded into her wooden chair.

"Rough day at the office?" I asked gently.

She eyed me with contempt. "I don't know, Matt. You tell me. Here's my day so far. I come to work. I forgot my travel mug of coffee, so it does not begin auspiciously."

"I can only imagine."

"I get here, and everything is wonderful until after homeroom, mind you. Before the bell for first period has stopped ringing, Mr. Bill waltzes into my office without so much as a knock. He's beside himself, ranting about men in kissing booths kissing boys in kissing booths who are kissing women in kissing booths."

"How bizarre. Why was he fixated on kissing booths?"

"I do not yet know. He left to see, and I quote, *my team of psychiatrists*, end quote. He seemed to indicate he would get back to me after extensive consultation with *the team*."

"That is an unusual start to any day, I must agree."

"You wouldn't happen to know anything about kissing booths now, would you, Matt?"

"No. I've seen one once, but never had the nerve to purchase a ticket."

"Ah. Thanks. So, back to my day. No sooner had the ambulance carrying Mr. Bill left, than Mr. Duvoe stomps in here covered in red paint. Me, I'm relieved when he told me it was red paint. At first, I assumed it was blood."

"That would be worse, I suppose," I concurred.

"Scared the living shit out of me, I'll tell you that for nothing."

"Sorry?" I sort of squeaked.

"It took me fifteen minutes to calm him down enough to get part of the story. He claimed you assaulted him with that paint."

"Assaulted? Is that what they're calling classroom teaching nowadays?" I protested.

"Let's hear it," she demanded.

I explained that the man had spent almost the entire class belittling and criticizing me, and that when it came to turn-about-is-fair-play, he proved to be a sore loser. I knew she was on my side, because he was being a major league dick.

"And did he come around to see the error of his ways?" I asked.

"No. He left for the day. Said he was calling in mentally ill."

I raised my hand. "I second the diagnosis."

"He said he'd be back after I paid to dry clean his ascot." She tried not to, but she started laughing. "The tool wears an ascot to junior high?"

"Someone didn't tell him," I observed.

"Anyway, after that, my day got really weird."

"On top of all that?" I said with disbelief.

"One of my favorite people here, Massimo Puccini, comes in clutching three paintings like they were his kids he just pulled from a burning building. He says he has to leave because, and again I quote, *Matta says I'ma master.*"

"He is very talented. You know, you really should get him to sell you a few oils."

"I asked him when he was planning on returning. Guess what he told me?"

"I ... I have no—"

She held up a palm. "He said, *probably after forever isa over.*"

I shrugged. "Maybe that's a saying in Italian?" I speculated.

"I don't know. Never did get into Italian much." Then she studied me. "How's your Italian?"

I wiggled my open hand in the air. "Mezza mezza."

"I thought as much," she huffed. "Then comes third period. I'm thinking my day has to be over the hump, but no. Guess what happened next?"

"You won the lottery?"

"No, but almost as good. Mr. Maisbach rushes into my office. He has a metal bucket on his head and the man's animated."

"No?"

"Yes. He starts yelling about mutant birds taking out home ec class and then declaring war on the wood shop. He said, *Mary—* that's my first name in case you didn't know – *Mary, they're going for the eyes this time.*"

"You paint quite the picture."

"Please, I'm still not over Massimo yet. Anyway, it takes a bunch of us to calm him down before he strokes out. I asked what it would take to get him to go back and resume class. He says, and here I am quoting again, *we need to call in top bird people.*"

I snickered.

"Yeah, laugh it up," she taunted playfully. "I'm frankly confused as hell. I'm wondering if he means top people who are expert at all things bird or if he means, you know," she flaps her arms, "bird people."

"Maybe both?" I shared.

"And fourth period put those first three to shame. Mr. Assmakis storms—and I mean *storms*—into my office. He's madder than a cat in a Jacuzzi. He says you and Jumbo conspired to humiliate him. He said you twisted the meaning of the Articles of Confederation to suit your deviant needs. Matt, I don't even recall exactly what the Article of Confederation are. But to hear you twisted them just to make Assmakis look bad, why that's beyond the pale."

"When's he due back?"

"He wouldn't commit. Said he's better than you and better than this ship-of-fools school excuse for a school. He'd let me know."

"Ship-of-fools school? He must have been upset."

"And speaking of upset, guess who is also upset?"

"At this juncture, I'd hate to speculate."

"Me. I'm upset. You know why?"

"Might I have a clue?"

"I spent three years getting the district to let me trial a program where big strapping guys are on campus to help with discipline."

"This wouldn't have to do with HM Bob?" I queried tentatively.

"HM?"

"Hall monitor."

"Yes, it would. Just before fourth period, Bob drags this kid in, urine streaking the floors of my office, kid crying like he's about to meet his maker, and Bob's got an announcement. He says he still has strong feelings toward his career in professional wrestling. Yeah, he's already booked himself two bouts for tomorrow at the Cow Palace. He says he walked away from the big show too soon."

"We certainly can't begrudge a man his dreams."

"Well, I do, because he was the only one without a criminal record to apply for the position."

"So he's unlikely to be replaced in the short run?"

"Not hardly."

"Unskilled laborers without baggage can be so hard to secure," I commiserated with her.

"Speaking of which, I was wondering, do you like meatballs and spaghetti?"

"Are you hedging around asking me out on a date?"

"No, I'm just trying to figure out why one of our lunch ladies threw a bowl of salad on her supervisor's head and left for parts unknown as soon as lunch service was over."

"Her name wouldn't be *Constance*, would it?"

"You're a regular fortune teller, Dunsratty. You should leave school and join the circus."

"I'm sure you're overestimating my talents."

"No, I'm serious. Please leave school and join the circus. I have twenty-seven years until I retire. I can't take this. But with you touring the seedier venues of America, I might just make it."

"I'll discuss your suggestion with my parents."

"That's all I can officially ask."

We were quiet a minute.

"So is there anything specifically I can do for you today, Mary?"

"Not one damn thing, Matt. Not one damn thing. You may have pushed the limits more than wisdom might suggest is healthy, but I can't really *blame* you for anything." She straightened up. "But here's what we're going to do."

"I am all ears."

"You are going to walk off campus. Cut your next classes."

"I am?"

"You are."

"What if the principal finds out?"

"She won't."

"And just how many classes should I cut, Mary?"

"Matt, I'm going out on a very long, very shaky limb here."

"Be careful."

"Are you familiar with the terms astral projection, spirit walking, or out-of-body experiences?"

"Yes, I am," I replied cautiously. This lady was good.

"G.N. Tyrrell wrote about them as long ago as the forties. Green and Monroe have tried to bring them into the science mainstream. They have been largely dismissed, but the concepts are out there. We studied them at the Sorbonne."

"And this has to do with my cutting class because—"

"Because you are not Matthew Dunsratty."

"I assure you that I am. I swear that I am, in fact, on my mother's grave."

She paled. "Your mother's not dead."

"Maybe not to you. Maybe not to the me you address. But I wish only to make the point that I am serious when I say that I *am* Matthew Dunsratty."

"Look. Matt, I don't want to sink into a semantic cesspool. You are not the teenager I met at back to school night a few months ago. That person was a dumb kid. You are a very cagey adult. I can't prove it and I can't explain it. But I *can* control it."

I sat mute.

"Look, Matt, I rather like the you I'm speaking with. But I am a junior high school principal. I have to protect these kids. Letting an adult predator in a child's body run free through my halls is not an option."

"What if that adult is not a predator?"

"There cannot be too many reasons for a man to project himself into a child's body. Most of them that come to my mind are bad reasons."

"I fully agree. Let me be honest beyond the bounds our trust should likely be tested. If I were an adult in a child's body, the last place I'd want to be is in junior high."

"But society demands it of you? Your parents expect you to stumble off to school each and every day. Same old same old."

"So what would this adult in child's clothing do? Run away and join the circus?"

She grinned. "No. He'd do whatever the hell he wanted to that didn't include attending junior high."

"And what would he tell his parents? His teachers?"

"He'd tell them nothing. He'd ride the bus to school each day and he'd cut all his classes. If he spent more than ten seconds on campus, he'd be arrested."

"Arrested for?"

"I'd make up something nasty. Trust me."

"I do trust you, Mary."

"Good." She reached into her drawer. "Here's two hundred dollars. Use it to occupy yourself while you're cutting class."

"Two hundred dollars is a lot of money in 1965. I can't take this."

"I can't have you on campus. Either you and I work this out or I'm forced to call in the cops."

"And tell them what?"

"Something that would land you in jail for a very long time," she said with grim conviction.

I nodded. "Here's what I can live with. I'll take your money on two conditions."

"I am not negotiating here."

"And I admire you for your integrity. But you'll like my plan."

"I'm listening."

"Go to the art room. Massimo gave me a painting. It's of a lonely man in winter up by Harrah's Tahoe."

"Yes?"

"I won it off him in a bet. Anyway, take the painting home. It's yours. But condition two is that you not sell it for at least ten years. By then, I guarantee you it will be worth a fortune."

"I can handle fortunes," she said with a grin.

"One other thing. A word."

"A word?"

"Yes. Remember it. Amazon."

"The river?"

"No the online retailer."

"What's online?"

"Spoiler alert." I smiled. "But keep half an eye on the stock market. When you see Amazon pop up, buy all that you can."

"And what will happen if I do?"

"You will be a very happy woman."

She stood, hand extended. "I think you'd better leave before I stop asking you to."

"You are wiser than you pretend not to be, Mary, and kinder than I deserve."

"Hey, we all got issues, Matt."

"Like where you're going to find a new bouncer as hall monitor?"

"Amen I say to you. Lord send me a bouncer and make him a big sucker."

We laughed a moment, and then I left.

EIGHTEEN

So it was Friday morning in 1965, I was strolling away from my former junior high with a couple C-notes in my pocket and no plans for the day. Footloose and fancy free, as they say. As long as I didn't run into either my parents or a truant officer (if they, like pink unicorns, even actually existed). Dad had flown out last night, so it was most unlikely I'd be outed. I was still tripping on being the first student in the history of education to be told by his principal to cut class on a semi-permanent basis. If I could bottle this mojo, I could be rich.

My school was reasonably close to our downtown, so I moseyed off in that direction. Today would be the day I planned my time dive to get back to 1975. I needed to confront the evil marionette and save Rolando's family. After what that creep did to me, I knew I'd have to be very careful and not underestimate his strength. My only ally was surprise. My mission was not going to be easy, but I was committed to taking that ass-candy down. And knowing for certain why Rolando had done the unimaginable motivated me that much more. He'd been randomly selected for horrific treatment based on the color of his skin and the whim of a monster.

I went to a diner I was fond of and ordered a second breakfast. I could tell the waitress was dying to ask me why I wasn't in school and where my parents were, but, in the end, the fact that she worked for tips outweighed her natural concern. Once I was finished eating and was ready to set to planning, I really missed the concept of an internet wi-fi connection to a smart phone. It would've made my task so much easier. I had to settle for pencil and paper. So last century.

Based on my recent experiences with time diving, especially the offensively directed ones I was subject to, I decided to try to streamline the process. I would make my attempt while being simply quiet and alone, as opposed to in a meditative state. Hey, if that failed, I could always do it the old-fashioned way. I had nothing but time.

Rolando had confided in me, so I didn't need to be as secretive as I had been. I also knew that Friday 13th was approaching fast in that timeline. I could try attacking the bad guy before I did the first time, but that might lead to confusion or a time paradox. I might have to aim for him after he sent me on my present journey. Since I was absent from the period, it would be safe to reenter the time stream just a little after I was thrown out of it. He'd be all that more surprised the quicker I showed back up. He'd also likely still be near where I'd last seen him, since he had four flat tires and I knew what turn he took at the next corner. After some deliberation, I had a fairly good if not-too-detailed scheme. I paid my tab, with a nice tip to validate the waitress's discretion, and I walked to the nearby city park. They had a wonderful Japanese garden, the perfect place to launch my assault on 1975 from.

I found a great spot, nestled up against some pines and red-leafed maples. The tiny stream dripping into a small pond filled the air with water sounds. I sat on one of the many benches and relaxed a few minutes. Then I closed my eyes. I focused on the suburban office building, that Saturday, May 24, 1975. Rolando was at his second part time job. I was there, waiting for the black Mercedes to show. I had decided to take an enormous risk. Well, I should just say it, it was a stupid, excessive risk. But I was getting desperate. I was going to enter that timeline while there was another version of Matthew Dunsratty already there. Clearly, I couldn't double-possess one body. I was going all in. I was aiming to take over Rolando's body. Yeah, dumb, stupid, idiotic, reckless, and untested.

I was hoping that if I didn't "stick" in Rolando's body, I'd just bounce back to these Japanese gardens. Then I'd have to try to jump into that Matt when some other me wasn't taking up temporary residence. Man, was this all a mind fuck. Gone were the simple days of planting a thought in a past version of myself. This was full-contact time travel. I just hoped I'd survive. There were so many ways this could go south, I forced myself not to dwell on them. Negative thoughts were poison to time diving.

I reached out to Rolando in the basement where he was prepping for work. I remember he went to push his mop bucket backwards, and he must have caught his foot on something because he tripped. I wanted to aim for a very specific point in time since this was all so new.

I closed my eyes, reached out, and "saw" Rolando tripping. I "moved" toward him. I could feel his shock as he started to ...

Ooowwwowoo. I did not feel too well. I was nauseated and falling and confused and I hit the ground at an odd angle and I thought of that girl, My-Duyen, I kissed at the church social in Vietnam when I was stationed there, and my shoulder hurt.

I opened my eyes. I was lying on the ground. Okay, I made it. I was in Rolando's head. And I was sticking. This ... this was going to ... what time was it? I checked my watch. 5:33. Cool, just ...

"Get the hell out of my head," screamed through my mind.

That was weird. I didn't think that thought. If this got any ...

"I told you to leave me *alone*. I'm a God-fearing man and I won't abide the likes of you in my head. Be gone, devil."

Oops. That had to be Rolando thinking those thoughts in "our" head. This had never happened before. Whenever I popped in, the other Matt Dunsratty either went dormant or went away somewhere. I was never certain. But never did he remain active. I sure hoped ...

"Matthew Dunsratty?" he screamed. "Is that you in my head? Matthew, are you the one tormenting me, trying to make me ...

"No, no, Rolando. Hang on. I can explain."

"Why you're in my head trying to take control of my body? There's no way you going to explain away that. Now get out and never—"

"Stop, Roll-Row. Hear me out. I had—"

"How'd you know my pappa called me Roll-Row? Are you eating my memories?"

"Rolando, calm the fuck down. I can—"

"Do *not* think profanity inside my head, you heathen. Take it back."

"Take what back?"

"That curse word."

"How'm I supposed to—"

"Just take it back!"

"Okay, there, I took it back. Now listen—"

"No, *you* listen. I told you too much and I'm about to snap from the pressure, so now I'm hearing your voice in my head just like my cousin, Delford. I'm going crazy and it's you that will torment me. This is unfair."

"Seriously, listen to me. I don't have much time."

"Do you possibly mean to say *we* don't have much time? Because it seems there are at least two of us in here."

"I don't. We don't. Fill in the blank later. Listen—"

"No, *you* listen. I see now that you are in league—"

"Stop right there. I am not in league with anyone, human or supernatural. Let me talk and then if you're still mad, well, we'll see what happens then."

I checked my ... our watch. Wait, it was still 5:33. Did I break the watch falling or was our "conversation" transpiring really, really quickly? We were inside the same brain apparently. Why didn't I ever get an easy day anymore?

Rolando hadn't fired back, so I dove right in. But this was going to be a bitc ... hard one to explain. He didn't know I was visiting from the future. In fact, my memories were probably as open to him as his were to me. That could be a ...

"You were never in the *military*. You lying sack of *shit*," he wailed.

"Hey, what happened to no profanity in here?"

"*You* happened to no profanity in here. And you're some vampire from the future. What, you here to cheer your boss on?"

"Wow, you're making this harder than it needs to be. I am from the—"

"We met in a mental hospital. What the ever-loving fuck, Dunsratty? Now I got two crazy men in my head. Lordy, Lordy, what am I gunna do?"

"No, I'm not crazy. I was in the mental hospital on a technicality."

"Yeah, you technically *killed* a boy with a toy sword 'cause you thought he was dipping his bucket in your well."

"Stop. We need to rescue me and stop that damn psychopath."

"Who it turns out are one and the same man."

"Don't be clever. We don't have time for clever."

"I will be the one who determines what we will and will not do in my own brain, Dunsratty. My house, my rules. Oh, wait, this is now officially too much. You think you saved John Lennon's life? This proves you're nutty as my auntie's fruitcake. John Lennon is alive and well. Hell, he just did a gig with Elton John at Madison Square Garden. Matthew, they don't let dead people sing at Madison Square Garden. I rest my case."

"You done whining yet?"

"I am *not* whining."

"That's what everyone else calls what you're doing. Now, do you want to kill your family or do you want me to try and stop that from happening?"

"I ... I told you. I been warned. I can't take a chance, not with their immortal souls."

"But if we can stop him, you don't have to kill anyone." I checked the Timex. Still 5:33. Just wow.

"What, you got a hot date?"

"Beg pardon?"

"You keep checking the time."

"Rolando, we gotta book."

"Wait, where you're from book means hurry? That's just wrong."

"Okay. I'm done. I'm just going to sit here on the cement until you start acting like an adult."

I started to rotate my torso so I could sit up. Halfway through, Rolando countermanded my order and we flopped back hard on the ground.

"Ow," we said simultaneously.

"I hope that hurt," I sniped.

"You know it hurt, so why you hoping?"

"So now you're going to fight me just because I want us to sit?"

"My body—"

"Don't even finish that thought. Look, I'm not the one who is soon to kill those I love the most and spend the rest of my life in a locked ward. You want that life, then you got it."

"Just like that?"

"Just like that what?" I was getting really frustrated.

"Just like that, after all the trouble you've gone to, to help me and mine, you just gonna bail on me?"

"I am because you won't let me sit up."

"Fine, if that's what it takes so you'll stop me from being a mass murderer, we'll get up."

We awkwardly and slowly jerked to a standing position.

"There, you happy now?" he taunted.

"No, I'm not happy. But I am committed to fixing this, so let's do this."

"Just for now, and mostly 'cause you're a medically diagnosed psychopath, I'll go along with you. But I reserve the right to own my own head at any point I see fit."

"Did I mention harder than it needs to be?"

"What's next, Matthew?"

I checked our watch. Damn, still 5:33. But the second hand had moved a little. "In about ten minutes, the me out there will put screwdrivers into—"

"I know, I know. Stuck the hell in here with your memories."

"We need to stop that car after it makes the turn. I'm afraid the little mean guy may disappear for good since I blew his cover. It may be now or never in terms of stopping him."

"And what do you propose we do?"

"Not sure exactly."

"Which makes me feel so much better about my family's future."

"We need to stop a moving car and incapacitate the two occupants. You got any ideas?" I asked him.

"C4."

"Yes, good plan, except we got no C4."

"You asked."

"Okay. Here we go. Does the building have one of those CO_2 fire extinguishers? The ones that make all the fog?"

"Yeah, they have a few."

"Let's go get one." I leaned back—whatever that means—and let Rolando dash up the stairs and grab a cylinder.

"Now what?" he asked.

"Now we need to stop that car."

"We can put mine in front of it, block its way."

"Nah, he'll just back up and go the other way."

"Then I say C4."

"Wait. We could block the street with a car or something, then trap the Mercedes with your car."

"There's a building under construction right past the corner. We can pull down the temporary cyclone fence."

"Good idea," I complimented. "You go ... No, cancel the divide and conquer. Let's get your car and circle around the block the other way."

Within five minutes, we had temporary fencing littering the street. Now, if no one else chanced to come along and move it, the Mercedes would be forced to stop. We parked our car—come on, share and share alike when in one brain—just past the corner. This might work.

We sat in Rolando's car with the windows down. Pretty soon, we heard the shouting from when I confronted the mean little guy. Then we heard the distinctive sound of flat tires thumping toward us as fast as they were able to move. Instead of fishtailing around the corner, the Mercedes plodded in an bumpy arc. The driver saw the barrier sooner than I would have liked, but fortunately, flat tires don't stop on a dime. They advanced just enough. We slammed on the gas pedal and leaped just behind their bumper.

The Mercedes slammed into reverse, but stopped almost immediately when they struck the side of our car. We grabbed the extinguisher and sprang out the door. We knew what side the bad guy was sitting on, so we immediately shattered that safety glass window. Boom, it cascaded down perfectly. We flipped the cylinder around, pointed the nozzle at the man with the look of surprise on his rat face, and pulled the handle up with all we were worth. He was enveloped in a freezing cloud of carbon dioxide. We emptied the container.

As the thick mist cleared, we could hear the driver gasping and coughing. But the little man was gone. I checked the far door. It was still closed and locked. We tore open the driver's door, anticipating the man would be in the passenger seat. It was empty. That door was closed. Both windows on the far side of the car were closed tight.

We grabbed the driver harshly and dragged him into the street.

Remember, we were in Rolando's body. We were good at dragging stuff. "Where is he?"

He coughed and squirmed but quickly realized he was not escaping our hold.

"I will ask you once more, and then I will break your neck. Where is he?"

"Gone," he gasped.

"We know that," I snarled.

He shot me a look of concern. Perhaps his captor had a dual personality. That could not be good news.

"Where is he? Where'd he go?"

"Look, pal, he could be anywhere. When Biblico's scared, there's no telling where he'll disappear to."

"That's his name," I yelled and Rolando shook the driver.

"Yeah." Then he looked at us much differently. "You don't know who Biblico Hoxha is?" he asked in stunned disbelief.

"No, why should we?" I challenged.

"Stupid fuck. May God have mercy on your soul, because Biblico sure as hell won't."

Rolando pulled the driver to his feet. "Where does Biblico live?"

"Anywhere he wants to."

Rolando laid upon the driver a look that no human ever wants to see directed at them. It was pure hatred and absolute intensity. "Do you know what that man was doing to me?"

He shook his head slowly. "No. No way. I drive him around. That's all. He makes weird-ass stops, but he tells me nothing."

"You swear it?" he said in a manner that prevented the driver to lie due to its ferocity.

"On my mother's grave. I'm just his driver, well, a driver licensed to carry a concealed-weapon driver."

Rolando held out our massive palm. The driver gingerly retrieved a forty-five automatic and passed it over handle first.

Rolando released him. "Do you know how to run?"

"Yes."

"Then impress me."

The driver sprinted away in spite of his fancy dress shoes. I was impressed. I think Rolando was too, but his part of our mind was white hot, so I wasn't sure.

"Now what?" he said sternly.

"Now I go find Biblico Hoxha, and once I do, I kill him."

"Didn't do so well on your initial attempt, Dunsratty," he observed flatly.

"Then I am bound to do a better job next time."

"Let us pray you do."

"Look, you see he's not the devil, right?"

"Is it the fact that he disappeared from a closed vehicle that should be tipping me off?"

"Good point. But don't let him win. Here's what I want you to do. Rent a cabin way in the middle of nowhere. On Wednesday, June 11, take your entire family there. Call it a vacation, call it a retreat, call it an orgy. Just get yourself and your loved ones out of harm's way. Stay there as long as you can, and then, when you're back home, be triple careful. I will get this Biblico character. And even if I don't, sooner or later, he'll forget about you."

"What if he's not the type of man to forget?"

"Then you'll be triple ready when he comes for you. At least this way, your family stands a fighting chance."

Rolando was quiet for half an eternity.

"This I will do. I will vote for life. Thank you, Matthew Dunsratty."

"My pleasure. But, say?"

"What?"

"You think you'll be lonely when I vacate your head, with just one person inside?"

"There is no chance of that, you spook." He began to chuckle.

I closed our eyes and thought of home ...

NINETEEN

I opened my eyes and had to smile. I was home. The one that was always in my heart and on my mind. I lovingly took in the room. There was the uncomfortable French revival sofa with its creepy silk. And there was the china cabinet with what I'd always complained about were the useless and unused dishes that were wedding gifts and had been put in service maybe four times in forty years. And there it was, the piecé de résistance, our wedding picture. Shannon was resplendent in her long, flowing dress, her sumptuous bouquet cuddled tenderly to her waist. She was so young and so beautiful. Girl hadn't changed a bit since. Oh, and there I was in a penguin suit looking like the stuffed Christmas goose.

I stood from the living room floor and turned to the mirror. Yes! I was in my mid-sixties, fat in a bloated sort of way, and had a third of a head of gray hair. I started to tear up. I was a FOM again. Fat old man here and proud of it. In my mind, I was sticking my tongue out at Thomas Wolfe. Yeah, buddy, forget your novel *You Can't Go Home Again*. Matthew Dunsratty just did!

Now, I know I need to take a second and explain. Why would any sane man *wish* to be old, have ED, turn women's heads, but only in the opposite direction, and be one dash up the stairs away from a heart attack? Because, my friend, I was back to Ground Zero. This was where my very long and very problematic journey began. In my perpetual mind's eye, this was who I was. When I was chatting with Mary Abernathy, I saw *this* person speaking to her. When I made love to my wife the night Moe Howard died, it was this Matt that benefited from the moment. Seriously, if I could choose, I'd rather think of myself as the thin, relatively fit Matt of my mid-twenties. But no, I was Matt the FOM.

I wasn't sure what the day or time was, but I had a sudden impulse to see my Shannon. I'd been gone so long and I missed her more than reason suggested I should. The Shannon who was hopefully somewhere within these walls was the one I thought about for all my years in the mental hospital. Though I was a kid and in a relationship with Stacy when incarcerated, it was this woman who was my heart's lone desire.

I heard a thud coming from the kitchen. Like a kid running down the stairs on Christmas morning, I rushed toward the sound. For once in over half a century, Matt Dunsratty had hope. I stopped at the doorway and dared to search the kitchen.

There she was, my vision of bliss, my Shannon. She was scrubbing a pot like it was personal. She must have heard my approach, because she craned her neck to look back at me. "You volunteering to dry, big guy, or are you just admiring the view?"

I started to speak, to reply, to say something. But all I could do was break down in tears. I began to sob and gasp in fits. Life was so, so good.

"Matt," Shannon asked in a panic, "are you alright?" She rushed to me, dripping sudsy water the whole way. She even dropped her Brillo pad on the floor. She took my shoulders. "What's the matter, Matt?" she prompted.

"Nothing," I said through my ecstasy. "Everything's perfect."

She guided me toward the kitchenette and sat me down. "Sure it is, honey, but grown men don't usually cry their eyes out because everything's peachy perfect." She slid into the seat across from mine.

I reached out and patted the backs of her hands. "But most grown men don't have you, my perfect wife."

Shannon got a puzzled look, then gestured over her shoulder toward the sink. "I'm not going to have time to finish this up, am I?"

"Take all the time in the world, my love. I'll just sit here and bask in the glory that is—"

She stood, reached back, and untied her apron. "Nope, not going to have time to finish, am I? Ah, well, they'll still be dirty when we're done."

You know what? By the time I was done kissing, stroking, and loving my wife, I bet that pot had grown so impatient, it did clean itself and jump onto the drying rack. It might have even found its way back under the range.

Shannon levered up on an elbow, the sheets dropping away to reveal her torso. She tapped the tip of my nose. "So you going to explain what that was all about, you dirty old man?"

I thought of some quip, some snarky Matt thing to say. But instead I stroked her breast and kissed her arm. "It was about being married to the best woman to ever walk this Earth."

She rolled her eyes. "Oh, no. We're done here. You're not sweet-talking yourself into a double header. I have scores of chores and endless errands. You'll just have to hold that thought until tonight."

I ran the back of a finger alongside her eye. "How about late this afternoon?"

"No, Mr. Dunsratty, this is not a negotiation." She bunched up the sheet to cover her front and bounded out of bed. "We'll see how lucky you get tonight. Land sakes, a man of advancing years has a blip in his hormones and a woman's supposed to drop everything and be his personal Playboy bunny. It's not fair, Matt. It's just not fair." You know those bunched up sheets didn't cover up a thing as viewed from behind.

As I showered and rediscovered where my clothes were,

Shannon did return to the kitchen. As opposed to my desires, that pot was still in the sink and, at least per Shannon's standards, still dirty. By the time I was presentable, the kitchen was spick and span, the coffee was fresh, and Shannon had on a clean apron. We shared unimportant conversation, half a pot of coffee, and it was sublime. I could not recall ever being happier, which was counterintuitive based on the years I'd spent wandering this globe and sampling freely of its delights.

Shannon finally announced she had a hair appointment and had to leave. I walked her to the garage, waved to her as she backed out, and stared at her sedan until it turned a far corner. Then I sighed deeply and wandered back into the kitchen. I freshened up my cup and sat down with an old man's grunt. I had a lot of planning to do. Given my dangerous, nearly fatal interactions with Biblico, I needed information. I needed a lot of information. Who was this evil mini-man? What was the basis of his powers? How could I defeat him? Lots of major questions. And, more for the worse than the better, the only possible source of answers I had was one odd and capricious old fart, Maurice Augustin, my erstwhile instructor of transcendental meditation. You remember him. He was the huge guy who taught the very first TM class I ever attended at the community center before this whole shitstorm hit town. He wore a cape and a goofy hat, like Cyrano De Bergerac's, minus the feather. 'Nuf said about his taste in clothes.

After a few classes, which I was enjoying immensely, he up and told me, *We are all bestowed with a force of nature, a spirit, a soul if you will, of variable power. My concern with you, Mr. Dunsratty, is the level of your aura, its raw power. The changes I have sensed in you, why, they are truly remarkable. So you must quit.*

I was so stunned, it was comical. I was good at this, a rare power, in fact, so I needed to quit? That made as much sense as foam-rubber crutches. But, he went on to tell me something that stuck with me and that seemed to apply now. *A different time, perhaps a different place of life, it might all be different. Primal talent like yours could be molded and honed. But this is now and we are who we are in these particular versions of our lives. So I must and I will bid you adieu.*

Even back then, that last warning set me to wondering if he wasn't some super meditator who could time dive like I self-taught myself to be. Reflecting on his words and having met Biblico made it imperative for me to find Maurice and squeeze out all the information I could get from him. Hopefully, locating him would not be difficult. Getting him to share, meh, probably not so much. But he was my only lead.

I started by going to the community center website. Sure enough, Intro to TM was still listed. Instructor, M. Augustin. Classes had begun several weeks ago and were still ongoing, Mondays, Wednesdays, and Fridays at ten. I checked the computer clock. 08:45. Perfect. Now what the hell day was it? A quick click revealed Wednesday. Bingomatic, I was in business! I got ready and found my car and my keys—remember, I hadn't been this me for decades—and was on the road in a flash.

The center wasn't far, so I arrived way early. That was fine by me. I did not want to miss Maurice. If I caught him early enough, maybe I could be done with him by the time the class began. One could have too much of Maurice, trust me on this. At a quarter to, the first student arrived. By 10:10, almost twenty were milling about, but there was no Maurice sighting. That was odd. He was quite punctual before. I always figured he wanted every moment he could get talking at a captive audience.

Finally, when it was obvious enough that he was late, I approached a man about my age. "Say, did Maurice call you and say he would be late?"

He shook his head. "Didn't call me." He scanned the room. "Hey, Bill, did Professor Augustin call you about being late?"

I actually started to protest to the man that Maurice was an instructor, not a professor, but I let it go. Making a sore point would not advance my cause in any manner.

"Nope, he didn't contact me."

A young woman raised her hand. "Ditto. Not a word."

The man I'd asked said, "Well, let's give him a few more minutes and then call it a day."

Most people inclined to respond nodded positively. Ten minutes later, there was still no sign of Big M. A few students grumbled that enough was enough and left. Within five minutes, I was the only one left. It sure seemed odd the class wasn't notified. I decided to go the community center office and find out what was up. There had to be one, right? You can't have an organization without an organizational structure.

The admin office turned out to be nearby on the same floor of what once had to have been an elementary school. As demographics move about or age, elementary schools are frequent victims of loss of a child-base to warrant their continued existence. I stepped into an industrially stark room with few redeeming qualities. Metal furniture, no pictures on the walls and no carpets on the floor. A solitary fan spinning with absolutely no conviction was the only relief for the eye. A man in his late thirties sat at a desk near the front of the space. He typed away at his computer with even less conviction than the fan exhibited. I was struck with the thought that I might just have entered perdition's waiting room, the scene was so bereft of life, so deficient in hope.

I stood there a minute and received no acknowledgment from the pseudo-busy office worker. When he had successfully pissed me off sufficiently, I called out, "May I ask you a question?"

The man nodded his head toward me, but a bit to my right. I followed that apparent direction to discover a plastic waiting-line ticket dispenser. The number "12" dangled from the device. Above it on the wall was a red-LED sign that read—you guessed it—Now Serving Number 11. He absolu-a-fucking-lutely had to be kidding. Then again, I needed help and he seemed perfectly willing to ignore me until he left for lunch, so I pulled number 12. I was hoping he wasn't going to insist I take a seat while I waited.

I stood there looking as calm as I could for another minute. Hey,

I needed a potential favor. Mr. Personality was in the driver's seat. Finally, he walked silently to the reception counter and fingered a switch hidden underneath the surface. The number being served changed to 12. It was my lucky number.

He rested one hand on the counter and wordlessly extended the other palm up. I set the winning ticket in his hand. Thoreau, of whom I've never been much of a fan, famously said, *The mass of men live lives of quiet desperation.* The guy I faced was the mass' point man.

"May I help you?" he said in a lifeless tone that sent shivers through my bone marrow.

"I'm hoping so. I'm in the meditation class." I thumbed over a shoulder. "It's supposed to meet in Room 3 at ten."

His eyes moaned as they drifted up to the clock on the wall. It read 10:22. They then arced back down listlessly to rest on my chin. "Yes," he stated in a tone that suggested he'd died several weeks ago, but since he was so inconsequential no one had noticed, hence he was still on duty.

"The instructor has not shown up yet," I informed him.

Up moaned the eyes to the IBM Standard Issue Wall Clock, and then redescended to my chin. "Maybe he or she is late."

"*He* is late. I was wondering if he called in to let you know?"

"Let me check the phone log."

I nearly shouted that I'd rather he not, because I knew it was going to be too painful to witness. But, again, I needed his help, so I decided not to alarm the zombie secretary. He shambled along the counter to a clipboard attached to it by a chain. He fingered the page, moved his finger up and down, then shambled back to where I stood.

"No calls today."

I had been correct. That spectacle was too painful to have observed. "Well, I have a critically important message to deliver to Maurice Augustin. May I please have his address so I might deliver it at once?"

To my amazement, his eyes blinked several times. Maybe he was alive and cogitating? "Who is the person of whom you speak?"

"Ah, my bad. Maurice Augustin is the meditation instructor who is missing."

"You said he was late. Now you say he's missing. Which is it, please?"

"*Late*, of course. Sorry to have used English so abstractly."

"Apology accepted."

"So, if I might have Maurice's address, I'll be on my way and out of your ha ... I'll be able to allow you to return to work."

His lips began to move. Then he gestured toward the portrait of an old white man slung so low on the far wall I hadn't noticed it before. I have to confess I was taking no meaning from his response yet. And, no, there was no label identifying the elderly fellow.

"We are not a ... a ... al ... allowed to give out personnel personal inform ... m ... mation."

Oh, dear. He was a robot and I'd just short circuited it.

"But I have critical information, information he asked me to deliver to him as soon as possible. For all I know, lives may be on the line, er, at risk here."

"Mr. Pecker said I am not to give out sensitive information."

Oh, my. Was he referring to his private's commander or a human supervisor? Did I wish to go there?

"I beg your pardon. Who is Mr. Pecker?" I needed help, so enter the pit of the insane I must.

"Mr. Pecker is my supervisor."

"Is he here?" I asked hopefully.

"He is on break."

This might be a good development. "When is he due back?"

"After his break."

Hmm. Not too helpful.

"When did he go on his break?"

The man, whose name I still hadn't been offered, calmed visibly.

He returned to the clipboard and slid a finger down the sheet. "Nine ten this morning."

Remember it was 10:22 when I entered? It was later now. Mr. Pecker seems to be a dick. He left ten minutes after the office opened and was yet to return from break. With little positions come little men.

I studied the poor wretch. *I wish you would be more helpful,* I thought to myself angrily.

It was like I flicked him between the eyes with the back of a finger. His head jerked back and his eyes fluttered. Then he was the same old dull stiff. Most odd, I reflected. I wonder ...

"Jump," I thought at him.

Nothing. Maybe I was the one losing his mind here.

"*Jump!*" I screamed at him mentally, picturing myself to be a Bengal tiger.

Damn, the fool jumped. He didn't jump very high, but his feet likely left the floor. Oh my goodness. Maybe I could do to people what Biblico was doing to Rolando? That would be ... intense.

Well, let us just find out. "*I want to give this man Maurice Augustin's address,*" I commanded psionically.

He rocked on his heels, but otherwise showed no response.

"*Give him Augustin's address or he will never stop tormenting me,*" I urged.

Ah, Glenn with two "Ns" took one glance toward the computer terminal on the counter. I was getting closer.

"*If Mr. Pecker finds out I did not give this nice man the address, he will fire me.*"

That was motivation enough. Glenn shambled to the computer, tapped some keys, and then found a scrap of paper. He wrote on it and handed the slip to me. There was an address written down. I prayed it was Maurice's, but who knew?

"Thanks, Glenn," I said in my softest dad voice. "You have done the entire world a favor. I am so proud of you. When Mr. Pecker returns (probably around four fifty), tell him you did a wonderful job today."

Glenn smiled, kind of like a rock might if rocks could smile. Then his face grew stern. "I am sorry. Mr. Pecker says I cannot give out personal information."

Perfect, Glenn had already forgotten he had. I couldn't say for certain yet, but I think I was loving my new superpower.

It was a remarkably long drive to Maurice's place. He practically lived in another area code. Why he traveled all this way to teach a dumb class was beyond me. Were there no TM needs nearer to his home? Forty-five minutes later, I rolled past a very nondescript apartment building that matched the address Glenn had provided. I was able to park right out front. I would find my car easily too, because it was the only one with a complete paint job and no missing parts. Maurice was slumming it quite a bit, wasn't he?

Needless to say, his building did not offer security amenities. I walked to the elevator, found it was "Under Repair," so I took the stairs three flights up. 303 *A* was my target. I passed 300 A, then B, 301 A, et cetera, until I stood nose-to-door with 303 A. There was a combination view port/doorbell screwed and duct-taped to the door. I guess community center education did not pay so well. I depressed the button, because, when in Rome, do as the Romans do. The place was depressed, so I depressed. It was more broken than it appeared on the surface to be, which was actually hard to imagine, given how bad it looked.

I knocked. It occurred to me that he would likely recognize me, so I placed a thumb over the viewport. Thirty seconds later, I knocked louder. Right before I started kicking at the damn door, it opened. There stood Maurice. Without the fancy hat, I saw he suffered from a spindly baldness. Without his cap, he was still as tall, but he was positively gaunt. And he smelled like the apartment frowned on water usage. I felt a twinge of regret for the guy.

"Yes? How is it I might *'elp* you, my good man?" he said with his familiar flair and French accent, which, now that I spoke French, seemed it was from an indistinct regionality.

"Maurice, you don't recognize me?" I said as I walked past him.

Big mistake. All the outward clues of decay and disrepair I had tried to disregard suddenly affronted me physically. Maurice lived in absolute squalor. If he owned more stuff, I'd say he was a hoarder. But all he was was a pig with crap everywhere. His sofa had more holes than it did sofa and that was his only stick of furniture.

"Do I know you?" he asked suspiciously.

"Enough to throw me out of your dumb-ass class you do."

"Which class is that?"

"The one at the Hernando de Soto Community Center, the one you blew off today."

He squinted at me. "I fail to recall you."

Okay, he was toeing my last nerve. I leaned toward him. *"Remember me!"* I shouted at him in my head.

He barely reacted, but he did. His shoulders tensed just a bit.

"Matthew Dunsratty," he stated in the form of an accusation.

"You do remember me."

He shook his big head. "No, I do not."

I furrowed my brow. "But you remembered my name."

"No, I did not. You just *pissed* it into my head while I was unprepared. Do not ever do that again."

"Just now, when I ordered you to remember me, you caught my name?"

It was his turn to brow furrow. "Of course I did, you regressed moron," he reviled me.

"Wow, this head connection shit is more powerful than I thought it was."

Maurice walked over and sat down, studying me the entire time. "I do think I am recalling you now. Yes, you were in one of my classes and you showed potential, but I was disinclined to scrape you from the slime you resided in. But ... but that was not here."

"Of course it was. I mean, it was at the place you taught the class."

"No, my deluded companion. That was many years ago and many dimensions ago."

"No," I responded uncertainly. "It was, two, maybe three years ago."

That was when he started laughing like a drunken hyena.

"Move over," I snapped loud enough for him to hear over his embarrassing display. I sat next to him.

A few minutes later, he was all tuckered out. "You about done?" I probed angrily.

"Yes, I believe so I am." He chuckled a few more times however, the son of a gun.

"Are you going to tell me the hilarious joke?" I snarked.

"I am afraid it is you, Matthew. The universe seems to have taken a particular dislike to you." He sniffed grossly. "Not that I can blame it. Do you not see?"

"No, apparently not. So, spill it."

"You have become a Lord of Time. You have danced upon the circuits of temporality. And yet you think you are merely leaping from here-to-there, now-until-then." He chuckled again.

"Lord of Time? That sounds a lot like *Doctor Who* science fiction," I accused.

He scowled. "Where do you suppose they borrowed the name from? Hints they'd heard of us, my good man."

What a lunatic. But I had bigger fish to fry. "So why don't you tell me what it is I'm actually doing?" I said with as much sarcasm as I could, which was actually one hell of a lot.

"You are doing as many have done before you. You are transiting in time, yes, but not necessarily linearly."

"Not necessarily linearly. What the hell does that mean?"

"It means not linearly by necessity. Come now, surely you under-stand that there are many universes out there, and each may be remarkably similar to another or frighteningly distinct?"

"I've heard of the theory."

"Why, you simpleton, you have *traveled* the theory."

"By returning to my past?"

"By returning to *a* past. Sometimes we return to our pasts and futures. Sometimes we return to other pasts and futures."

"Bullshit."

"No, no, it is true. Some of us can control our movements some of the time, but it is not always an option."

"But yet you just happen to know you and I last met on Mars a gazillion years ago?"

He shook his head. "I have never been to Mars, though I hear it has its appeal. No, you and I met in a place similar to this but perhaps fifty or sixty linear years ago."

"Look, you halfwit. When we met, I was in my mid-sixties, and you were no spring chicken either. So that makes us, what, one hundred and twenty now?"

He considered me like I was an ant crawling up his forearm. "Do I look one hundred and twenty years of age to you?"

I scanned the room. "Maybe."

"Ah, you are referring to my disguise. What do you *tink* of it? Superb, no?"

"If you're trying to pretend you're a hobo who decided to take a break from the road and establish himself as an unwashed lunatic, then yes."

He grinned. "I rather thought so myself."

"Ah, Maurice?"

"Yes, Matthew?"

"Who the hell would you be hiding from?" I looked around again. "Someone who wants to steal all of this from you?"

"No. Do not be ridiculous. The disguise is so that no one would tink to come looking for me."

"Like Biblico Hoxha?" I asked with a cat-eating-shit grin.

Oh, yeah, that got his attention. What little color he had drained from his face and his lower lip began to tremble. "You know of Bib ... of *him?*"

"Know him? I sprayed him with a fire extinguisher until he evaporated."

Maurice's eyes nearly bulged from his head. "You crossed swords with Bib ... with him and lived to tell the tale?"

"Yes. And why is it that you and his driver *tink* that's such a big deal?"

"Mon Dieu! Tell me you are *agrandissant.*"

"No, plain and simple truth telling."

"And you conversed with Bib ... *him* and Otto?"

"If Otto's the driver, yes on both counts."

"I was correct about your potential. Very few people cross Bib ... *him* and live to brag of it."

"And Otto?"

He shrugged. "An adequate chauffeur, lacking in deference, however."

"Why is it you won't even say Biblico's name?"

"If you knew him as I do, you would not either. He is a monster, an apparition from hell."

"This I believe. He was brainwashing a friend of mine into executing his family."

Maurice nodded. "Sounds like him. He draws pleasure from places others would refuse to imagine."

"And he's dangerous?"

"Is he dangerous? Matthew, would you put a live cobra's head into your mouth and close your lips around it?"

"Ah, no."

"Well, you'd be safer doing that than being in the same *city* as that abomination."

"So you two are not palsies?"

Again he shrugged. "Once, a very long time ago indeed, we were cordial."

"But you had a falling out?"

He wagged his head side to side. "If you call World War I a falling out, then yes."

"Wow, that's fantastic. You two served together in WWI?"

He scowled at me. "No, *cretin*. I tried unsuccessfully to stop him. Biblico Hoxha *caused* World War I."

TWENTY

June 27, 1914, the office of Dragutin Dimitrijević chief of the Serbian military intelligence.

Dimitrijević rolled the cigar between his lips as he struck the match, savoring its taste and the conversation that was to follow. Life was good. He puffed the flame into the cigar with an intensity that suggested it was the fire and not the smoke that flared his passions. Once the tip was more conflagration than tobacco, he tossed the match to the floor.

"Gentlemen," he began in a cheerful, almost sing-song voice, "it is time we got down to the business at hand."

Major Vojislav Tankosić pushed off of his armrests and stiffened his back further, if such additional tension was possible. Of the three men in the cabal present, he was the least convinced, the one who clung to the greatest uncertainty. "I suppose that is another example of your gallows humor alluding to the fact that we are members of the Black Hand?"

Dimitrijević lovingly admired the tip of his cigar. "You see,

Major Malobabić, your friend here is smarter than you give him credit for. He's most perceptive, in fact."

Rade Malobabić was a hot-headed true believer whose life at that juncture was fully dedicated to a Serbia free of Austro-Hungarian domination. That he had to put up with his sniveling acquaintance Tankosić was almost more than he could bear. That he had to kowtow to the imperious Dimitrijević was worse by geometric proportions. The man was pure evil. Yes, he gave lip service to the cause, but his attitude betrayed him to be nothing more than a casual on-looker, a soulless killer simply looking for his next victim. Soon, Rade would put a bullet in the forehead of the infamous colonel, codenamed Apis.

"I know that we have greater goals to accomplish than the insulting of my fellow officer," Rade protested harshly.

Dimitrijević slowly shifted his focus from his cigar to that last remark. "Come now, major, surely you would agree with me that a touch of humor is an excellent oil to smooth the operations of any complex machine."

"Let us discuss niceties at a less critical point in our project," Rade hissed.

"Our project?" Dimitrijević questioned with humor in his tone. "You call the coldblooded murder of a man and his beloved wife a *project*? What have your morals declined to, my dear Rade?"

"We are killing a cancer. We are assassinating dominators, defilers, not human beings," Rade raged. "Expunging from this world Archduke Franz Ferdinand and his piglet wife Sophie can be considered as nothing other than an act of public kindness."

"That, my good man, depends entirely upon whom you direct that remark toward," Dimitrijević observed darkly.

"I move we advance this discussion beyond a fencing match," Tankosić pleaded. He sounded to the other men gaspingly similar to a sheep bleating.

"Very well," the colonel agreed, resting his cigar in an ashtray.

"Have you two seen to the provisioning of our team of juvenile assassins?"

Rade cringed visibly, his face flushing crimson.

"What?" Dimitrijević protested, "they are but children, these seven boys."

"Princip, Mehmedbašić, Čubrilović, Čabrinović, Popović, and Grabež were hand-selected by Danilo Ilić. They are *not* children. They are committed patriots willing to die for a cause greater than themselves," Rade declared scornfully.

"Again with the verbal sparring," Tankosić whined. "I've had it up to here."

"Fine, fine," Dimitrijević soothed. "All I really care to know is if our team has been properly outfitted and supplied. They require pistols and bombs to complete their mission, along with cyanide tablets to ensure the secrecy of this organization." He gestured casually to a large bottle on his desk. "I have here the cyanide that the young men will use to ensure they are not captured alive. See that each gets his fair share."

"It will be distributed," Rade replied tersely. "It is fresh cyanide, yes?"

"No, you fool, I'm giving them outdated poison so that when they take it they will vomit and not die miserably, thus when they are tortured, they can expose this entire group of conspirators."

It took all of Rade's strength not to draw his sidearm at that very moment. But he remained still and silent, aside from the ragged breaths he pulled in.

"And of the weapons?" the colonel pressed.

"They have been smuggled in and distributed," Tankosić responded nervously.

"Finally, the operatives all know the route the archduke's car will take to and returning from the various destinations?"

"Yes," Rade replied through clenched teeth. "I have tasked Danilo Ilić with the placements of our assets and their constant supervision."

"Hmm, I would have chosen the Princip boy. He seems the most competent and passionate. But I guess we shall see," Dimitrijević mused critically.

"We shall see indeed, colonel," Rade seethed.

"Then our meeting is complete," Dimitrijević announced harshly.

"What, without a toast to the success of our endeavor?" the imbecilic Tankosić questioned.

"Yes, without antiquated superstitions and the worshiping of trees or mythical beast, Tankosić," the colonel dismissed. "Now get out, the both of you," he commanded.

The majors left, but not without Rade having to restrain himself, yet again, from killing Secret Agent Apis, the stunning discredit to his species.

Once the door was closed behind them, a solitary figure emerged from behind a partition pushing a diminutive figure in a wheelchair. "So, are we about ready, sir?"

"Yes. Let me escape this revolting pissant's head and then we can go out and witness the fruits of our labors," Dimitrijević said in an odd tone as he stood. He walked to the side of the man in the wheelchair and set his hand alongside the compact head. The colonel's eyes fluttered shut and his shoulders dropped.

Dragutin Dimitrijević stumbled backwards, barely averting a nasty fall. He started hyperventilating and his heart threatened to leap from his body. Resting a hand on his chest, he frantically took in his office, where he'd been sitting what seemed like only seconds ago, awaiting the arrival of his co-conspirators. But now he was standing and there were two complete strangers studying him impassively.

"Who the devil are you?" he managed to ask through his gasping.

The little man in the wheelchair stood and walked confidently to Dimitrijević's desk. He picked up a lit cigar the colonel did not remember lighting, and admired it lovingly. Then the near-dwarf took a heavy set of puffs. "There you are, my precious," he soothed. "It is time to go."

"B ... but I asked who you were," Dimitrijević demanded a bit more steadily.

"Yes, I recall that you did," Biblico replied sarcastically. "Think of us as ghosts." He turned to his assistant. "Leave the chair."

"*Sir!*" Otto snapped back.

As Biblico was striding away, he called over his shoulder, "I would wish you a good day, Colonel Dimitrijević, but, as much as I enjoy irony, with what you are about to endure ... I shall allow you one last moment of peace."

On the morning of June 28, 1914, Danilo Ilić placed his assassins along the predicted route of the hated Franz Ferdinand's motorcade. He then slipped back and forth between them, offering words of encouragement and demands for bravery. Though nervous, Ilić was excited to be involved in what he considered to be the first blow for liberty for his beloved homeland. He wished he'd been allowed more time to drill his young team more, but he trusted in their fervor to make up for any deficiencies they might have in their training.

The motorcade passed the first assassin, Mehmedbašić. Ilić had placed him in front of the garden of the Mostar Cafe and armed him with a bomb. For reasons that were never determined, young Mehmedbašić failed to act, and the car passed unchallenged. Vaso Čubrilović was stationed next to Mehmedbašić. He was equipped with both a pistol and a bomb. Again, fate seemed to intervene on Ferdinand's behalf. Čubrilović too failed, without known justification, to attack.

As the motorcade proceeded blithely, Nedeljko Čabrinović lay in wait on the opposite side of the street from the two failed assassins, near the Miljacka River. He clutched his bomb so tightly, he worried he might set it off prematurely. At 10:10 AM, as Ferdinand's car passed in front of his position, Čabrinović sprang to life and hurled his explosives. The bomb bounced off the folded back convertible cover and dropped to the street. Čabrinović cursed his fate and himself. The bomb was activated with a timed detonator. By the time it went off, it was under the next car in the procession. That car was destroyed and scores of bystanders injured, but Ferdinand and his team were safe and now on high alert.

A dejected Čabrinović swallowed his cyanide pill and jumped into the Miljacka river, determined to never be taken alive. To his later chagrin, Cabrinović's suicide attempts failed pathetically. The cyanide was, as Biblico had declared openly, old and weak. It only induced vomiting in the young nationalist. Again, as if fate had taken sides in the struggle, the river Miljacka was only a foot deep due to a particularly hot and dry summer. Čabrinović was dragged out of the river by the police, upon which he was promptly beaten to within an inch of his life by the vengeful crowd.

The frightened procession sped away toward the Town Hall, leaving the disabled car behind. Popović, Princip, and Grabež also failed to attack as the motorcade rocketed past their stations on the scheduled route. What had seemed like such a good plan was melting away like an iceberg in tropical waters.

After coming to grips with the fact that the first assassination attempt was in ruins, Princip had the brass cojones to still wish to complete his mission. He pondered if there was a position on the archduke's return journey where the man might still be vulnerable. With few good options, Princip decided to position himself in front of the nearby Schiller's Delicatessen, near the Latin Bridge. It was a logical path of egress for the Ferdinand's party to employ.

To his elation, he witnessed the panicked flight of the returning royalty. The first and second cars of the archduke's motorcade suddenly turned right into a side street. The archduke's driver spun his wheel to follow their route. That was when fate officially switched sides. The local governor, a man named Potiorek, who accompanied the imperial couple, shouted at the driver to stop. They were going the wrong way he warned. The driver stopped and attempted to put the car into reverse gear. The engine sputtered into a stall almost in front of where Princip was standing. The assassin stepped up to the footboard of the car, and shot Franz Ferdinand and Sophie at point-blank range. They were both dead within the hour.

All of the assassins were eventually caught, brought to trial, and punished harshly. Biblico Hoxha was last seen on the early afternoon of June 28, 1914, enjoying a plate of ćevapčići sausages and pickled vegetables al fresco in front of Moritz Schiller's Delicatessen. His manservant, for the record, stood behind Biblico facing the street, hands behind his back.

On July 28, 1914, due to a breakdown in redress negotiations for the assassinations, the Austro-Hungarian Empire declared war on Serbia. Those two brutal deaths, along with the tinderbox politics of Europe at that time, led unalterably to the commencement of World War I.

TWENTY-ONE

I was getting a lot of revelations out of Maurice, but he was a reluctant and inconsistent teacher. Go figure. At first, I think he wanted to show off his superior knowledge and background. But his fascination with self-congratulations faded quickly. After a couple hours, he had pretty much clammed up. After a couple hours, I was about ready to vomit. Between his disheveled appearance, his lack of hygiene, and his absolutely depressing apartment, I was ready for a total-body dry cleaning.

"Maurice," I finally had to ask him, "if I'm to believe you're this wizard of time, how can I square that with the fact that you live like a cockroach? Wouldn't a man with limitless time and wealth live in Monaco and be driven in a car no one can pronounce?"

"I told you, this is my disguise. It is so very effective, is it not?"

"You call it a disguise, I call it bad life choices," I corrected.

"Ah, but you are wrong. To survive in a world with Bib ... men and women such as that, one must be very difficult to locate."

"There's more than one Biblico? I mean, there're others like him?"

"To be certain." He was quietly reflective for a spell. "With power such as ours, corruption is an easy trap to become ensnared in."

"So what you're telling me is bad people like Biblico are actively hunting not-bad people like you?"

He stared at me harshly. "I see you employed the term not-bad, as opposed to good, when referring to me. That is most hurtful."

"Maurice, I barely know you. Are you good, bad, or medium-rare indifferent? I don't know."

"Fair enough, I suppose. But to answer your query, no, they only infrequently hurt others of our kind. But if they chance across one of us," he clicked his cheeks, "that is a dangerous situation to exist in."

"Are we a threat to them or are they all just that depraved?"

He pooched his lower lip pensively. "Tous les deux. Both."

"So what do we do about the bad apples?"

Maurice gestured to his slovenly home. "We avoid them."

"I think I'd rather duke it out with them, mano-a-mano."

He raised a finger. "Be flippant about it now. But when you are at the mercy of one of them, you will wish to have felt differently."

I thumbed my chest. "Hey, I took on Biblico and came out vertical."

He angled his head and clicked his tongue. "Almost unheard of." Then a thought struck him. "The second time you took him by surprise and he retreated. But the first time, you say he hit you with some force, and you were cast into the circuits of time."

"If that's what it was, yes."

He was very puzzled. "Where did you go initially?"

"To my teenage body. I was—"

"No, no. What did you *first* experience after he struck you?"

I had to think back. "Yes," I whispered absently. "I backed into some place. I immediately thought *way station*. There were brilliant lights and shadowy figures. It was frightening and reassuring, both."

He was shaking his head, a deep frown on his face. "And then?"

"And then I wasn't there. I was slammed into my teenage body."

He sat up. "Think carefully. Did you think of this teenage form, or wish to be in that body?"

Hmm. I didn't recall any such desire. "Nah, I was just there."

"*Humph!*"

"Humph? What the hell does humph mean?"

"It means your journey was most peculiar."

"I'll say. Light, dark, evil, blessing, all in one—"

"No, my simple friend. It is peculiar that you survived."

"Oh," was all I could muster. That was an unwelcome revelation.

"Biblico cast you into the Nexus," Maurice explained in a serious tone. "It is presumably where he sends all those he intends never to encounter again."

"Nexus? What nexus?"

"The Nexus of Time."

"Ah, that sounds heavy."

"If by heavy you mean to say significant, you are understating."

"Have you been to the Nexus?"

He reaction was like I'd asked him if he enjoyed and partook of piglet porn. "No, obviously I have not," he snapped.

"What?"

"Matthew, one does not leave the Nexus of Time. That is why Bib ... *he* sends his enemies there."

Palm to chest, I shot back, "I returned."

"Yes, and that is unprecedented, as far as I know."

"Well, if we're what you call Lords of Time, why should the Nexus of Time be toxic to us?"

"It is not *hostile* to us. You do not take my point. The Nexus *desires* us. Those who stray too close are captured by the forces that exist there."

"The shadowy figures," I stated.

"Presumably. And the fear and misery you sensed."

"B ... but, if that's true, how the hell did I escape?"

Maurice looked at me and breathed deeply for way longer than I liked. "Because you are apparently a new force amongst our ranks,

Matthew. New, strong, and thus an even greater threat to Biblico and his ilk."

I snapped my fingers at his face. "Hey, at least I got you to say his name."

"Yes, you did. Our present situation is just that dire."

TWENTY-TWO

Impossibly cold, whistling streams swept under the closed doors of the massive stone room. The raging heat from the fireplaces did little to deter the bite of such frigid tendrils. If one was more than a few yards away from the nearest source of comfort, their presence was undetectable. The woman seated alone at a desk wore fur over her layers of wool that covered her silk undergarments, yet her skin was as frigid as the grave. She did not care, and barely noticed. Sixteenth century Galicia, Spain was as cold as Viking hell in the winter, and those seasons there were inhumanly long. But the Condesa de Altamira lived in the Fortress of Altamira, and that fortress stood in Brión. Katherine Bayer cared nothing for *noblesse oblige,* but some rules could not be broken. She was in the guise of Doña Isabel Sofía González y Saavedera. As such, she must cohabitate with her genetic throwback of a spouse just long enough for the gossip mongers in the royal court to focus their perverse attention elsewhere. "Just long enough" being the operative phrase.

She picked up the inkhorn and rubbed it to keep the ink from freezing before her letters were complete. Then she dipped her quill and returned to writing. So much nonsense, all this communication and mindless well-wishing. It was enough to make the peasantry look desirable if it weren't for the starvation, the farm animals in the house, and the fleas. Katherine positively detested fleas. She made a mental note to be away from this cold, regrettable place when the next plague rolled around.

A soft knock sounded off the gigantic wooden doors of the main entry to the room. Did whoever disturbed her really think such a timid request could be heard over these infernal winds?

"Come," she shouted impatiently.

The door parted with a dry screech and the head butler stepped limply through. He stood awaiting further acknowledgment.

"Yes, Señor Morquecho?" she asked tersely.

"There is a gentleman to see you, My Lady."

"At this hour? This is unthinkable. Send him away."

"If I might, My—"

"And with the Count away hunting, a male visitor at any hour is *out* of the question," she decreed.

"If My Lady would hear me out. The gentleman in question is already *inside*. He appeared in his ..., er, *usual* location a few minutes ago."

Kathrine's face hardened. "The root cellar?" she asked with scorn.

"Yes, My Lady, the root-cellar man has arrived. He now awaits an audience with you just outside this door." The butler bowed slightly.

"Oh, bother," she snapped. "Well, show him in. And bring some hot tea. Chamomile should do nicely."

"As you wish." He clacked his boot heels together and bowed slightly again. He stepped back into the hall and offered the cellar man an ushering gesture. "The Contessa will see you now."

"It's about bloody time," the diminutive man groused as he slipped by the butler.

"Biblico, so nice to see you again," she greeted with a false smile.

"It's too damn cold to keep me waiting or to lie to my face."

"I suppose it is, my old friend," she agreed coolly.

Without being asked, Biblico dragged a heavy chair to the hearth and sat down. He proceeded to pound his feet loudly and rub his hands frantically.

"I do not believe it is cold enough to warrant such a display," she tsked.

"I'm small and wearing normal-person clothing." He cast her a backward glance. "You have several foxes and two sheep covering you."

"In other words, I came prepared," she stated triumphantly.

"I came in a hurry," he said angrily.

"Don't tell me one of our rivals got the drop on you, Biblico. Such a turn of fortune would be such upsetting news this close to bedtime."

"It was a new player and he tricked me."

Katherine's eyes widened upon hearing that update. "A new player? Are you certain?"

Biblico stood, turned to face her, and spread his arms wide.

"Thus the heavy dusting of white power," she deduced with a wry smile.

"I had to abort my position while immersed in fire extinguisher spray. I thought it might be mustard gas at first."

"So you panicked and came home to mama."

That drew her a nasty scowl. "Let us leave my mother out of this convivial discussion. You know I seem to trigger here when the situation surprises me. What with our history, it's—"

"Our history is precisely the issue. While I am *here,* I am the dutiful and pious wife of a count. Our past is something that simply must remain in the future."

"You, dutiful and pious? The people of these times are rubes and marry their cousins, but they can't be that stupid."

"Mind your tongue, *visitor,* lest I forget my hospitality and ask one of my knights to skewer you. Speaking of flunkies, where's Otto?

Did he have a falling out with you as I did?" Katherine could barely keep from laughing.

"Hardly. We aren't engaged. Hence, if *he* were to betray me as you did, he wouldn't last long enough to say the word *sorry.*"

"I must keep that in mind when we first meet. What, it was 1856, wasn't it? Paris?"

"I'm not in the mood to spar with you, Kat. Damn, why hasn't that useless butler brought me anything warm yet?"

"Perhaps I asked him to drag his heels," she replied coyly.

"If I catch a cold, I swear I'll pass it along to you before I kick the bucket." For once, a small grin formed at the sides of his mouth.

"Always the giver," she teased. She looked up when the butler knocked. "Come."

The servant silently set and poured the tea, then slipped out without having spoken a word.

"So what are you planning to do about this new player?" Katherine asked after Biblico had taken a few sips of tea.

"Try to kill him and soon."

"Try to kill him? Why on earth have you not dispensed with him already?"

"I tried," he mumbled.

"Beg pardon?" she returned.

"I said I tried. There, are you happy?"

She pouted. "Not in the least. There's someone out there whom you tried to kill yet he still haunts this plane? What positive could I *possibly* find in that distressing news?"

"That maybe he will be able to kill me," he speculated gruffly.

"A world without Biblico? Shame on you for saying those awful words," she responded in mock protest.

"I cast him to the Nexus."

"Aanndd?" she said, drawing the word out.

"He came back and sucker-punched me with a fire extinguisher."

Katherine Bayer, the famous Iron Bitch of Munich, dropped her tea cup to the floor, where it shattered into countless shards.

"Yes, I thought you'd appreciate the gravity of that summary," Biblico said with a sneer.

"Are ... are you *certain* you cast him all the way into the Nexus?" she said weakly in utter disbelief.

"I've never heard of anyone being cast *partway* into it. Have you?"

"Not that I can recall," she said absently. Then she focused. "But you said he blasted you with a fire extinguisher. Perhaps that distracted you enough—"

"The extinguisher was *after* his return from the Nexus, *weeks* after."

"Oh, my."

"Oh, my indeed," he agreed sarcastically.

"And who is this new player? Do I know him?" she asked, still clearly distracted.

"No, he's actually new on the scene. Name's Matthew Dunsratty."

"Dunsratty? I've never heard a name like that." she asked in disbelief.

"Yes, the idiot's name is as unexpected as is his power." He looked down briefly. "I think he's one of Maurice's boys."

The back of her hand went to cover her mouth. "Maurice fathered a *child?*"

"No, please, Kat, this is the real world here. No, I mean he's one of St. Augustin's *disciples.*"

"Why do you suspect this?"

He shrugged. "A hunch mostly. It was his clunky manner, his lack of shielding. Something just smelled of your old master's loose-wristed hand."

"Wait a moment," she snapped. "You said you cast him into the Nexus. Now you say he was not shielding his mind? Come on, Bibbles, it cannot be both. Unless you've lost your touch completely, he was *either* heavily shielded or he did *not* survive the Nexus."

"I know," he replied pensively. "If you'd told me the same thing before these vexing events took place, I'd have called you a lunatic."

She grinned. "You've called me worse."

"Deservedly so," he agreed with a wicked smirk.

She was quiet a spell. "So are you suggesting that this Matthew fellow is so powerful that he resisted your assault in spite of his being untrained?"

Biblico sipped at his tea, deep in thought. Finally, he set down his cup. "I suppose this was inevitable. We evolved from nothing. I suppose that process cannot be stopped."

"Oh, my goodness. I never thought I would live to see the day when Biblico Hoxha was uncertain."

He sighed profoundly. "Not uncertain, my dear. Frightened out of my wits."

TWENTY-THREE

It turned out, as I had predicted so many years before, Maurice wasn't much of a teacher. We talked, sitting there on his dilapidated couch, for a few hours. Then he was done. He stood, arched his back, and, because he was a weirdo's weirdo, did some quick knee bends and toe touches.

"Matthew, I am afraid I must call this little rapprochement to an end. I am fatigued of it."

"Whoa, Moe, I still have a million questions for you," I demanded.

"Then, *pardonez moi,* you will leave here with a million unanswered questions."

"What if I don't leave? You think you can make me?"

He eyed me like an old sardine can discovered under a chair. "Whether I can or not will not be at question." He slipped into his bedroom and returned promptly wearing another ludicrous hat. This one was a *bourrelet.* You may not know the term, but you've seen them in old paintings. It's a padded irregularly round puffy beret with a cornette, or scarf, dangling from the back. They looked geeky back when they were the height of fashion. Today, they just

scream that the head it rested upon contained a severely impaired brain.

Maurice gave me a slight head bow and stepped quickly toward the front door. I was just able to pop over and block his exit. I spread my arms wide and backed into the door. "Where are you going?"

He pulled out a gold fob watch, clicked it open and then snapped shut. "If you must know, Monaco."

"I was kidding about that earlier," I admitted.

"Be that as it might, I retain a small apartment there. I feel I have just enough time to go there and become properly cleaned up." His eyes drifted away to the far distance. "And perhaps enjoy a bit of the *bon ton* while I'm there."

"Just enough time? Before what?"

"Before the demon you have summoned from hell catches up with me."

"What, you hallucinate that Biblico is currently scouring the planet to find you?"

He retrieved a gaudy cane resting by the door. "No, he is currently scouring the globe to find *you*. I merely wish to distance myself from what promises to be an ugly incident when that occurs."

"So you head to Monaco to get cleaned up, and then what? He can't find you there when he's finished with me?"

"Of course he can. He would. But I shall be upon the wind by the time he arrives." Maurice spied me with one half-closed eye. "You know *he* is quite good friends with the prince?"

"Biblico? With prince ... prince whatshisname?"

"Prince whatshisname?" he tsk-tsked me. "You Americans are so provincial."

"Maurice, you can't just leave me."

"Why cannot I?" he asked, truly puzzled.

"Because I'm a babe in the woods here. I'm a sitting duck. You choose the idiom. You have to stay and help me. If you don't, you might as well kill me yourself, you'd be so guilty."

"Matthew, one last lesson," he said with a flare of his cane. "In order to feel *guilty*, one must be subject to remorse for their actions. Please understand I feel nothing of the kind. Fate has placed you where it has placed you. If Biblico is to be the hammer and you the nail," he threw his arms up, "who am I to say this arrangement is incorrect?"

"You're a coward and a cheesy one at that," I snapped.

"How is it do you imagine I have made it to my very ripe old age? By seeking defeat at the hands of my enemies?"

A thought that had been bothering me tapped me on the shoulder, requesting to be asked. "Why did you blow off your TM class today? Was that for the same reason?"

He poked his flappy lips out and angled his head. "Very good, Matthew. Yes, I sensed something not good was there, so I took the day off."

"You sensed me there?" I asked uncertainly.

"Not you, just something better avoided. As I said, I did not reach this maturity allowing chance alone to govern my actions." He peered past me, out into the hall.

Shit, this was the end. Dude was leaving me high and dry. "Okay, one more question and then I'll step aside."

"Hmm," he intoned.

"An easy one. Just how old are you? How old do we get? We're ... we're not immortal, are we?"

He bobbed his head as he considered my query. "In a manner *yes*, and in a manner *no*. I myself have no concept of how old I am, how many lives I have lived."

"Ballpark guess."

"Six ... seven centuries perhaps."

"Moe, how the hell do you expect me to believe that? You don't look a day over seventy-five."

That brought a nasty look. "Matthew, when one of us approaches what would be the end of a mortal's existence, we are free to and generally do transfer ourselves permanently back into an earlier version of ourselves."

"You ... we, we relive our lives?" I asked incredulously.

"No, no. We live the life we are living in that body."

"Well, wait, what happens to the person in that body, that copy of you?"

He shrugged. "Who cares?"

"Well, the person you eject, that's who. And, *Maurice*, that son of a bitch is almost certainly another vampire version of you who stole that body for the umpteenth time several years before."

"I repeat, who is there to object?" Then he set his cane on the side of my shoulder. "Now please step aside."

Reluctantly, I did. Maurice grinned thinly and walked out. Since I'd already had way too much of this dump, I almost immediately followed him out.

Maurice was gone. Vanished. No way he could have moved that quickly.

This was getting way too weird. I wanted my money back and I wanted to go the fuck home. But it seemed I didn't have a home. Maybe I never did? All I had was the next place I could run to.

Matthew Dunsratty, welcome officially to the world of the Lords of Time. Now get a move on before someone punches your ticket.

TWENTY-FOUR

I got in my car and started driving home. I was in an impenetrable fog. I remembered the precise feeling I'd had when I flushed my life down the toilet the first time. Ultimately, my relentless self-destructive behavior landed me in an insane asylum for decades, with no family, and that no one I ever cared for even knew I was alive. And here I was, the King of Morons, starting the process up all over again. The ironic part was that I was less in control. Hell, I honestly did not know what I was doing. Just ask Maurice.

Maybe what I did long ago was a normal stage in the maturation of a Lord of Time? By the way, I'd only learned that term an hour ago, but already I detested it. How pretentious. How self-aggrandizing. How lame. If we called ourselves time lords, I could hang with that. That way had panache. I considered calling myself simple a LOT. But that was even more painful. *Say, what do you do for a living, Matt,* I would be asked. *Oh, I'm a LOT,* I would respond. Yeah, not gonna happen. I was a time diver. End of story. Maurice could—and probably did—wear a crown of laurels or thorns for all I cared, but not me.

I was very nearly home when I slammed on the brakes. I actually surprised myself, and the minivan that had been following too closely. She nearly hit me. What, I asked myself then and there, the fuck was I doing? If I went back to my house with my wife, not only was I inviting Biblico to find me, I was placing her in extreme danger. If I was only risking my hide, I could live with that. But I could not put my dear wife in jeopardy. Never.

But I knew in my heart-of-hearts that I already had. I'd placed every Shannon in every timeverse at risk. And every Stacy and Nick and every child I ever did or did not have. Biblico was two things. A perfect monster and an old hand at payback. Capturing and torturing my loved ones was Revenge 101. He knew that I'd come to their rescue if I learned of their peril. And if I didn't the first few times he tried to force me to confront him, he'd wreak holy hell on my friend, just to let me know what would happen the next time I didn't respond to his summons.

As a wave of nausea enveloped my body, I realized there was one and only one solution to my present crisis. I needed to kill Biblico before he killed me. There was no way out except via coldblooded, first-degree murder. If I shied away from the reality, he certainly wouldn't, and I'd end up dead along with a lot of those dear to me.

Oh, crap, now that insight just sucked the big dick. From what Maurice had revealed to me, I had only two options as to how I could kill Biblico. One was in a manner so sudden and so foolproof, he wouldn't have an instant to escape to a former body. And the other was to murder a baby. Yeah, I'd have to eliminate the possibility that Biblico could leap to a very young form of himself like they all apparently do when faced with a catastrophe.

And I thought killing Francis as a young teenager was horribly bad. Now I was *hoping* for infanticide. Maybe ... maybe I should *find* Biblico and let him off me. I sure as hell deserved it. And I would welcome the relief. That man was so lucky, him being a sociopath and all.

But for as much as Biblico knew about hunting down a time diver, I knew by comparison almost nothing. I could search the ethnicity of his name. But even if that was his real name and I located his homeland, it was going to be full of young boys. King Herod ordered the Massacre of the Innocents in his lust to eliminate Jesus. I knew before I even finished the thought that I was not capable of such an atrocity. So was unearthing Biblico's origins worth the effort?

The honking horns and the colorful insults drivers that squeezed past me issued woke me up to the fact that I was still stopped in the middle of the street. I started driving ... away. No destination, just *away*. I finally stopped at a library. I searched the internet for any information on Biblico Hoxha. Guess how many hits I got? Yes, zero. And searching his last name wasn't much more enlightening. The surname was Albanian of all things. However, it turns out it is an extremely common name in Albania.

Looking up Biblico itself only revealed weirdness. There is no name *Biblico* anywhere. The only hits I got were similar to the one I found in the Royal Galician Academy. In Spanish, it means *related to the bible*. Trust me on this. There is perfectly nothing biblical about the man, except maybe for something out of *Revelations* and the End Times. So I was left with what, a Galician Albanian? I was so freaked out, I actually searched that term. The only results were translation sites for Galician into Albanian. I'm thinking those sites were only lightly trafficked.

I sat there staring at the computer screen for quite a while. How long? Well until a dowdy librarian sheepishly tapped me on the shoulder to say she was about to lock up and would I please leave. That's how long. I apologized profusely and almost offered her a tip. But I realized that would come off as either my soliciting her or JPN —just plain nuts. I left quickly.

You really have to understand how much I hated myself for the way I conducted that first life of mine, how horrifically I treated Shannon over and over again. But I could feel it. I was standing on the edge of the Marianas Trench, holding my breath. With both hands, I was grasping on to a ten-million-pound weight. And I was about to jump with it over the edge. Down I would go, fast and completely unprepared. I was going to have to ditch my current Shannon. Leave like I was abducted by aliens. But her first guesses as to why I'd split would be younger-woman-with-larger-breasts, I was a louse, and younger-woman-with-larger-breasts. Let us agree she would not recall me fondly.

If I did the impossible and killed Biblico, I doubted I'd ever be able to return to my old happy places. No, in order to accomplish what I had to, it needed to be a burn-all-bridges, take-no-prisoners, scorched-earth assault. Was I confident I could succeed? Seriously, you even ask? No way. David slew Goliath. Sure, that was a long shot. But the kid was good with a sling and Goliath was a very big target. I was so screwed, it was impossible to be as screwed as I was, but I was.

The only slim lead I had on Biblico was that he was spending time in 1975 Reseda, California tormenting poor Rolando. So that was where I needed to be. Naturally, any pretense or insane explanations to the Shannon of that period as to why I was basically living in Reseda would be out-the-window ineffective. So why bother? I'd save us both some degree of pain and just do it. If she decided to come search for me and an explanation, I'd be forced to blow her off. Yeah, for better or worse, we once swore. Let's just put that to the Matthew Dunsratty test, shall we?

I'd alerted Biblico to my presence. Even someone as coldhearted and smug as he would likely not allow me to confront him there again. So I would have to take him on in the weeks prior to our two meetings, back when he was stalking Rolando before I arrived on the scene. That would be risky. I hadn't established trust with Rolando in that period. Then again, this wasn't really about Rolando anymore. Biblico messed with him and he was going to do what he was going to do. No, this was only about me and the marionette.

What could I realistically do to Biblico? Blow him up? Sure, if I knew thing one about blowing people up, which I didn't. Propose marriage to him and have him die of fright? Hmm, not the most solid of plans. Plus, whatever I did was going to be extremely illegal. If I *did* kill Biblico, and presumably Otto too, I sure as hell didn't want to get caught and sent to the gas chamber. And if I did attempt to kill them and failed and ended up in prison, well, I'd be a sitting dead duck. That could not happen. So all I needed to do was go to Master Criminal School, hopefully an accelerated course. Right.

What did I know about us time divers? Hmm, I did know one thing. I wondered if Biblico knew it too. Hey, let's find out, little buddy!

TWENTY-FIVE

All excellent criminal schemes require money—lots of money. Ergo, I needed lots of money, and I needed it back in 1975. The Matt and Shannon of that period didn't have two nickels to rub together, so that easy-way fix was out. Not a problem. I had conceived of a work-around.

My final act as old fart Matt Dunsratty was going to be one of the riskiest stunts I'd ever pulled, or tried to, I should say, because I was way out on a limb with this one. I wanted to be *a* Matt of 1975, but I did not want to be *the* Matt of 1975 who had an established life back then, the one whose body I had used previously. The main reason for this preference was social attachments. If I was a free-agent Matt, there'd be no Shannon looking for me, or her attorneys. I wouldn't have to establish cover stories, like calling in ill to the school or coordinate using that Matt's money and ID.

So how was I proposing to be a *second* young adult Matt in 1975? I was going to copy a page from Biblico's book. Hey, he was an evil master, but he was a *master*. When I shot him with that fire extinguisher, he did something I was stunned to observe. He disappeared. From talking subsequently with Maurice, it became clear to me that us LOTs (hate the term) could not only do what I had done —inhabit a past edition of our body—but we could cast our *body* through time, presumably forward or backward. That was how Biblico escaped me after I'd doused him. While I was expecting the mist to clear and then find a pissed-off cold, wet rat, he'd departed the scene.

Where was I to find a copy of 1975 Matt to, eh, *borrow?* Why, in 1975, of course. Actually, my plan was to nab one from 1976, just to be safe. I wanted the Matt of the 1975 timeline, where Rolando either did or did not kill his family and the one who confronted Biblico, to remain as he had been. So, in a two-part time dive adventure, I was going to leap into a 1976 Matt and then jump that Matt, *body and all*, back to the 2020s, where I was presently. Insane, right? There'd be the old fart me here, and the younger one too, with the old fart me's brain in his head. We could meet, share an ice cream sundae, make a secret handshake, whatever. The psycho twist was that we'd both share the same knowledge set. Clones differing only in age, so to speak.

All I needed to do was to make that 1976 Matt time dive, body and soul, and hopefully clothes and wallet, into the 2020s. If I failed with this critical component, I'd need a new plan. By the way, I had no clue as to what other plan there might be. This had to work. Also, you may wonder what the hell happens when the 1976 version of Matt disappears without a trace. The answer is: I don't care. Remember, this is all-out war, me versus Biblico. I was not going to worry at all over what happened in that timeline. My attitude was too bad, so sad.

I was in a cheap motel, the cash-only kind of place, so as to remain off everyone's radar. I dimmed the light, *singular*, and sat in the chair, also *singular*. I thought back to a moment in 1976, America's bicentennial year, that I recalled vividly. I pushed my mind backward in time and focused on that Matt ...

... I was white-knuckle gripping the steel bar. Shannon, seated to my right, did the same, but she also had her eyes clamped shut. She was so darn cute. The roller coaster car click/clunked itself up to the top of the lift hill and began its slow right-hand turn to its first big drop, where the bottom dropped out. Oh, and the bottom was about to drop off but good. We were on the Screamin' Eagle on its first day of public operation, April 10, 1976. The wooden roller coaster was located at Six Flags St. Louis. We were there as part of the park's America's Bicentennial celebration. For those curious, *Guinness World Records* listed the coaster as the largest one in existence at one hundred ten feet high and attaining a maximum speed of sixty-two miles per hour. Yowzer!

The car swooped into that first dip, then charged through a series of gut-wrenching hill-and-valley shots, before making its first left-hand turn. We picked up speed. I felt like an F-15 fighter pilot. Knowing, as I did, that we were destined to survive the ride, I was more welcoming of the experience. It was super intense. Up, down, right, left, I was buffeted, my teeth rattled, but the urine remained in my bladder. I took a moment to clear my head ...

Soon, the car rocketed into the covered braking section, just before it crept back to the loading platform. Once the car came to a complete stop, I imagine Shannon turned her head to tell me what a scary ride that had been.

I can only imagine the real-life scream of terror she made when she found the seat next to her was empty.

The next thing I knew, I was standing on wobbling legs looking into the face of old fart Matt. My eyes flared open and I threw a bear hug around my other self. We hopped and bounced in a circle, looking like father-and-son idiots. What a pair. But, against all odds, I was there as a younger version of myself. Most importantly, I did have my clothes on. If these jumps were like in the *Terminator* movies where I couldn't take anything with me, well, that'd be a problem. A big problem.

We calmed down quickly. We both knew equally well we had a lot to do. I, the 1976 Matt, needed to time dive back to a specific time in the past. The old fart Matt had his work cut out for him too. It was double go-time.

APPENDIX
How To Catch A Small Rodent

Step One—Seed Money

I opened Google and typed in the search parameters: *US paper money 1960s.* It took me a while to find the right shop that seemed to stock what I needed. I entered its address in my Google Maps and all-too-gladly left my fleabag motel.

I parked directly in front of Gilbertson's Coin and Gold. My, what an unpretentious-appearing business. Middle spot in a strip mall thirty years out of fashion, heavy bars across the windows and doors with an industrial pull down metal door suspended overhead. And not one lick of color. Just suburban decay and brute-force security. I went to the front door and pulled. Nothing. I pushed. Nothing. I checked the business hours printed on the glass. They were supposed to be open. Then I saw the crooked sign hanging taped to the inside of the door. *PRESS BUZZER TO ENTER.* I checked. There was a buzzer, labeled BUZZER no less. I pushed it.

From the back of the store, a sixtyish-looking round man walked out of the stockroom. He studied me like he was on safari in Africa and I was possibly a water buffalo. Then he reached under the counter and buzzed me in. Warm and fuzzy was not the business philosophy of Gilbertson's Coin and Gold, that much was clear.

I strolled toward the back, eyeing the coins and other collectibles in the display cases. Surprisingly to me, the glass was spotless, in spite of the fixture's apparent age. When I reached the solitary figure, he grunted, "Help ya?" in some New York accent. I never could keep those straight.

"Good morning," I countered.

"'F you say so. Look, you're new, so I'll asks again. What can I help ya wit?"

A man of few and mispronounced words. Okay, we were not destined to be BFFs.

"I'm in the market to purchase some older US bills."

He pinched up one side of his face. "How old and what denominations? Anyting special, like misprints or Hamiltons?"

"No, just 1950s and early 60s lower denomination bills."

Now both sides of his face were pinched down. "Please tell me youz lookin' for uncirculated?"

"No, not particular—"

"Oh, crap. Anoder *Back to the Future* nut job." He ran his hand over his bald head. "Like I gots notin better to do dan baby nurse one a youz guys."

"I ... I beg your pardon?" I asked, truly stunned.

"So, who you? Doc Brown or Marty McFly?"

"Name's Matthew Dunsratty," I objected.

"Ya, sure, when da lights is on. But what about in your *head?*"

"Excuse me, we seem to have arrived at a disconnect. Please explain yourself."

"Look, youz fellas come in here two, three times a month. Ya wants old bills but not de uncirculated kind. You want dem so youz can put 'em in a briefcase full of bills for when you travel in your time machines. But none a youz buys shinola so I got no use for ya."

He did lack business tact. In fact, he lacked any tact. "I'll humor you to ask why it is we ... I mean, *they* ... never buy anything?"

He held up a finger. "Wait here a sec." He disappeared into the back and quickly emerged with an ancient metal cashbox. He opened it and randomly pulled out a bill.

"Here, tell me, what's dis?" He stuck the note under my nose.

"A ten-dollar bill."

"Right." He inspected it. "It's a 1958 ten spot printed in Philly, and it's a mess, right?"

"It looks well-loved."

"Here's where you conspiracy theory time nuts leave da building, literally. How much you guess it's wurt? Ballpark me."

"More than ten dollars."

"Hey, you go to da head a da class. Yeah, it's a ten spot, so it's wurt ten bucks at da crappy burger stand across da street. So if youz wants to buy it, it'd cost you at least ten dollars. Plus, I got to make a profit and old money can be valuable. So, contrary to what youz Doc Browns tink, it ain't wall paper material."

"Thank you for explaining the business model. I am not, even though it is none of your damn business, a *Back to the Future* wackjob. I'm an aging adult who wishes to purchase back a part of his youth."

He shook his head. "Ya, dats what you guys *all* say. But ya still don't buy nothin' on account a being a nut don't pay too powerfully well."

"Here is my offer," I stated, able to control my temper because I didn't have time to do this again elsewhere. I held up my Visa card. "I would like to purchase three-thousand dollars' worth of old US currency from the 50s and early 60s, anything prior to 1967. It can be in any condition. I would also like a roll of dimes, same time constraints."

"A roll a dimes? Dat's a new one."

"Pay phones back then needed a dime," I stated matter-of-factly.

"I thawt ya said ya weren't a *Back to the Future* nut?"

"I'm not. But I've always said it's better to be prepared than sorry."

He waved a very dismissive hand. "Gimme ten minutes and I'll have ya order, if ya still here, dat is."

He tucked his box under his arms and went into the back again. "Darz cameras 'erywhere," he shouted as he disappeared.

Sure enough, about ten minutes later, he returned with the

same box. He opened it and carefully set the money on the counter. "Look, pal, I tried to be square wit' ya. I put togeder all the crappy bills I had, plus a few not-so-crappy ones cause datz all I had. You see before ya tree hundred eighty-five dollars in negotiable US currency, mostly ones and tens, wit' a few twenties trown in."

"Three thousand dollars for three hundred? Is that the going rate?"

"More or less. Like I said, dis is money we're talkin 'bout here. And it's appreciated."

"Fine, I'll take it. Can you wrap it up?"

"Youz can keep da box." He ran my card then stuffed the money into the cashbox. Then he reached into his pocket and held up a roll of dimes. "Dez are on me. Crappy dimes ain't wort' much."

"Thank you very much."

He buzzed me out and my adventure got underway.

Step Two—Seed Money Sprouts

I took a deep breath and pushed through the doorway of the Whistle Stop Club. It was what's colorfully called a tippling house. More cynical people call it a dive bar. The place is located, big surprise, by the commuter train stop just south of downtown where I grew up. There is a tobacco shop on one side of it and a magazine store with a distinctly adult focus on the other. In an affluent suburb, those three establishments constituted our skid row. Gotta have one, right?

At age thirteen, I wasn't entering Whistle Stop Club to drink or to, God forbid, socialize. I was calling for business purposes. I scanned the room. Dingy by any alcoholic's standards, it smelled of old beer and cigarettes, and, at eleven in the morning, was inexcusably full. I drew another deep breath, regretted that immediately, and walked over to the lone bartender. You'll never guess what he looked like. Late forties, fat, bald, with big hairy arms, and an apron that once was white. His scowl showed through his unkept mustache like a unwelcoming beacon to one and all.

He was swiping at the bar with a gray towel. "Kid, you not supposed to be in here. Dares laws about this shi ... stuff."

"I'm looking for Fast Eddie," I said as calmly as I could.

"Kids ain't supposed to be asking for Fast Eddie either." His scowl expanded.

"I hear my name, Alphonso?" a greasy little man at a wooden booth called out.

"Kid here, who ain't supposed to be here's asking for you."

The man who it seemed was Fast Eddie waved me over. There was a completely disheveled and spent-looking man sitting across from Eddie. "Do I know you, son?"

"No, sir."

"You here 'cause your pa sent you?"

"No, sir."

"Well then, I am now intrigued. Please sit." He gestured to the other side of the booth. "Al, can we get a boiler maker and a Coke over here. No ice in the glass, please, but a cherry'd be nice." To me, he furrowed his brow. "You like maraschino cherries, kid?"

I hated them. "Sure. Who doesn't?"

"This gentleman is a friend of mine, Miles, no last name." He tossed the back of a hand in waste-of-space's general direction.

Fairly quickly, a shot of whiskey, a mug of beer, a glass, and a bottle of Coke were on the table. Eddie dropped the shot glass into his beer and sloshed half the mug down in one gulp. I trickled my Coke into the glass. Fortunately, cola is dark. The streaks on the glass vanished.

"So what can I do you for, kid?" he asked as he reflected upon his drink.

"I'd like to place a bet, sir," I said respectfully.

"Paaha," he blurted wetly. "You think I make *book* or something, kid? You know that profession is strictly illegal, right?"

"Word gets around, sir." Actually, I knew Fast Eddie, aka Edward

Frank Demana, was a bookie because I reviewed his arrest record when he got sloppy in 1974.

"If you say so. What's your name, kid?" he asked as he picked up his mug.

"Matt," I pointed to Miles, "same last name as his."

Eddie laughed as he wiped his mouth with the back of a sleeve. "Same last name. That's perfect, kid," he responded. "So, if you were to place a bet, what might it be on?"

"Maybe hopscotch at school," Miles slurred and giggled. It was an unflattering combination.

"San Francisco Giants baseball, sir," I replied steadily.

"You a Giants fan, kid?" Eddie all but shouted. "Well, good for you. They're a good team this year, may go all the way. Me, I like it when a local team gets hot." He grinned knowingly at Miles.

"Good for bee's wax," Miles proclaimed sloppily.

"So, sports betting is a complicated institution, kid," Eddie said professorially. "You got any idea how baseball bets work?"

"Yes, sir. My older brother explained it to me before he went off to Vietnam."

"What's the difference between a moneyline bet and a runline bet?" he asked pointedly.

I shrugged. "In baseball, a moneyline bet is a bet on the winning team regardless of the score. The runline is baseball's version of a point spread. Simple."

"Hey, kid knows his shit," Miles blurted out.

"Language, Miles, please," Eddie implored.

"Sorry, kid," Miles said with no conviction.

"Okay, if I were to take a bet from you, kid, what kind of funds are we talking about here? I run a business, not a fan club."

"To start with, a hundred a game." I shrugged again. "If I get lucky, who knows?"

Miles whistled. "Kid's got dough."

"Miles, can it," he snapped. "A hundred's a lot of money for a kid, kid. How'm I gunna know you're good for it?"

"Isn't that what running a book *means?*" I asked as innocently as I could.

"Sure, for my regular clientele."

"How about this? The first few times, I put my end up front. If I win, I return and you pay it all back to me."

"You thought this through, kid," he complimented.

"So you'll do it?"

"Sure, why not. As long as you don't try and stiff me or your mom don't come in here with her rolling pin."

"With her rolling pin." Miles chuckled.

"Okay. I'd like to place a bet. You want a runline?"

"It's standard operating for me, kid."

"Cool." I reached into my coat pocket and slid five twenties across to him. "A hundred on the Giants versus the Cubs tomorrow."

"Sure thing," Eddie said, scooping up the cash. "A C-note on the Giants April 14 to beat the Cubs and the spread. Sound about right?"

"Sure. Do I get a receipt or something?" I honestly wasn't certain.

"No, kid, that's another reason they call me a bookie. I write stuff down. If you win, come back day after tomorrow and I'll have your money."

"Thanks." I extended my hand across the table.

"Good luck, kid," Fast Eddie proclaimed as we shook on it.

The Giants lost badly to the Cubs on the fourteenth. Of course I knew that. But I figured it would help to lose my first bet with Fast Eddie. I didn't want to seem superhuman, at least not yet. I didn't return to Whistle Stop until May second. There weren't any games I was keen on betting until then, and I had a master plan.

"Hey," Fast Eddie shouted the second I entered the bar, "there's my little trooper. How's it going, kid?"

"Fine. How about you?"

"Couldn't be better. Hey, I figured you didn't come around 'cause losing that hundred stung too much."

233

"Nah, I just been busy. So, how about another hundred on SF over the Dodgers tomorrow?"

"You sure?" he said with something akin to parental concern.

"Yeah, of course." I patted my pocket. "Got the money right here."

He held up his hands quickly. "Don't do shit like that in a place like this, kid. No, you're good. I have you down for a hundred tomorrow. Runline's not bad. Maybe it's your turn, hey?"

"Time'll tell," I replied with a grin.

"Yes it will," he agreed as we shook.

The Giants stomped the Dodgers May third. I dutifully returned to the bar on the fourth and Eddie handed me an envelope. Then the asshole mussed up my hair. "You're a winner now for sure, kid. You got another bet to place?"

"Yes. Two hundred dollars says they beat the Cardinals on May seventh."

"Stepping it up a notch, eh?"

"Scared money never wins."

"No, kid, it sure as hell don't."

And so it went. May eighth, I bet three hundred Giants over St. Louis, then five hundred on the Giants over the Pirates May eleventh. I tossed Eddie a bone by losing with a bet on the next day, another five hundred. I didn't want to scare him off. May fourteenth, I upped it to five hundred on a losing bet where the Mets won. May eighteenth, I placed a "dime" on LA covering the runline in their loss to the Giants. In betting circles, a dime is a thousand dollars. When Eddie handed me the envelope, I was up around three thousand dollars. Eddie, ever the drunken businessman, shook it off to beginner's luck and challenged that he'd get me next time. He was incorrect.

May nineteenth, I showed up at my usual eleven o'clock time.

"Hey, there's my little Giants fan," Eddie extolled. "You here to further defend their honor?"

"No, I have a hunch on a different sport," I replied modestly.

"Do tell? What has caught your young eye?"

"The Ali fight."

He didn't see that coming. His head jerked back a bit. "The one day after tomorrow?"

"That's the one."

He shook his head. "You're the boss, but I don't recommend that one too much. Ali's a heavy favorite in the chump-of-the-month bout. Even if you pick him and he wins, you're not much ahead."

"I agree. That's why I want to make a round and outcome bet."

He squinted deeply. "Do you even know what that means?"

"Sure. I want to bet on the round Ali wins and how he does it."

"Your call, kid, but those are tough bets. You only wanna bet mad money that way."

"I got a hunch."

"So, tell me."

"Ali by knockout in the sixth round."

He gave me a very suspicious look. "And how much we talking here?"

"Ten thousand dollars."

"No way I'm letting you bet ten Gs on a round bet, kid. That's crazy."

"Eddie, if you're worried, I'll put up my end like I did before."

He furrowed his brow. "You ain't taken me for that kind of money, kid, at least not yet."

"Hey, you're the boss. But if you're afraid I'll welch, I'm happy to make this easier for you."

He breathed deeply. "No, I trust you, kid. We've always been square with each other." He pointed to my eyes. "But just you remember I told you this was a *very* bad idea."

On May 21, 1966, Muhammad Ali retained his world Heavyweight title with a sixth-round knockout win over a thoroughly beaten Henry Cooper, in a London match. I was up around eighteen thousand big ones and had the common sense to never cross the threshold of the Whistle Stop Club to place another bet. No need to tempt either fate or Eddie's code of ethics.

. . .

Step Three—Securing Those Funds

I walked into the Fourth Street branch of Union Bank carrying a medium-sized suitcase. Union was a small bank, but one which I knew would be around for decades. Small and safe, that met my criteria. I was there right at opening, so there were no lines. I stepped up to the nearest teller.

"Good morning, young man," a middle-aged woman in a completely nondescript dress greeted me unconvincingly. Her lipstick was heavier on the right side and didn't match her outfit. Did I smell old gin on her breath? Never mind, Matt. It didn't matter.

"Good morning," I returned perfunctorily. "I'd like to open an account."

She looked up from something she was scribbling and batted her eyes. "A savings account?"

"Are you the person who will be opening the account for me?"

"Why no, dear, one of the bank officers must do that."

"Then I'll discuss the particulars with him or her."

It was as if I'd said *I want to drink your blood,* she was so stunned. "There are no female bank officers." I could hear the cringe in her voice. I'm certain she'd already labeled me as a commie sympathizer. She recovered quickly. Gin helps one do that. "If you have a seat on that bench, I'll let one of the men know you're waiting."

"Thank you. And sorry."

She rattled her head. "Sorry? For what?"

"That there aren't any female officers."

"This is America in 1967, my dear. It is what it is."

"Ah," I replied. I picked up my suitcase and went to wait.

Fifteen minutes later, a man who'd been filing his nails stopped doing so, took his feet off his desk, smoothed his pants, winked at a passing teller, and then meandered over to where I sat. I knew him to be, as Daffy Duck says, *despicable.* I'd done my homework. It was blatantly obvious looking at him that he was a small man in many ways. About four inches shorter than me, the attention span of a gnat, and his worldview was microscopic. Brad was the second cousin to the branch president, otherwise he'd have never been hired and, if he had been, by now, he'd be long gone.

He thumped me too hard on the shoulder. "Hey there, sport, I hear you want to set up a savings account." He only then noticed I was alone. "Where's Mom?"

"She's yours too?" I replied cryptically.

He then actually looked at me for the first time. "What'd you say, son?"

"*My* mother was *your* mother too." I looked down. "I always knew she kept secrets, God rest her soul."

"Whoa, horsey. I think we've gotten off to a major misunderstanding. My mother is Mildred Snodgrass. She's alive and well in Sunshine City, Florida. I was asking where *your* mother was?"

"She's dead, sir," I responded matter-of-factly. "I thought you might have gleaned that fact from my last statement."

"Look, kid, I'm sorry as hell about your mother. But I was using a figure of speech. Get over yourself."

"I'll try, Brad."

"Good, er, wait, how'd you know my name? I haven't introduced myself yet."

"And therein lies a fascinating story. Perhaps we could go somewhere a bit less public and I'll amaze you with it."

"Kid," he said, putting a hand on his hip, "are you on drugs?"

"You mean like the cocaine you use most days, Brad?"

His eyes nearly exploded out of his head. "Why, how dare you, you little—"

"Brad, don't finish that thought. It'll end poorly." I scanned the room and then returned my eyes to him. "Do you notice anything funny about the eyes of everyone in here?"

Brad peered up furtively. "They're staring at us."

"Hence why I mentioned *less public* prior to your cocaine use."

"Say, are you trying to blackmail me, ya little shit?"

237

"Let's go to the privacy room and find out, shall we, Brad? Or is it okay if I call you Wet Stallion Steve out here?"

Hmm. I perhaps pushed that revelation. Brad paled, for sure. Then his legs wiggled like Jell-O. But he'd have hit the deck if I hadn't jumped up and supported the poor bastard. Ohh yuck, I had to touch him.

"Let's take this to my office," Brad said between pants, and pointed toward a series of closed doors.

We entered a generic office used to entertain major clients in. I set Brad in the chair behind the desk and scurried around to sit opposite him.

"Do you need a glass of water?" I asked attentively.

"Water won't cut it, kid."

"Gin? I could go to your desk like the teller Mrs. Miller I spoke with earlier does and bring you the bottle." I placed a sad expression on my face. "By the way, it's a cultural shame she has to service you so she can keep her job. Just sayin'."

"I'm good, you vile child. What do you want from me?"

"Like I told your sex slave, I wish to open an account." I raised my upward tilted palms to display simplicity itself.

Brad stood and knuckled the desk. "One more wise ass word out of your mouth and I'll beat the living shit out of you." He sat back down.

"Wet Stallion ... ah, may I *call* you Wet Stallion?" I proceeded without awaiting his response. "Another outburst like that and I do two things. I pull my pants and underwear down and I run from this room screaming *fag attack*. Any questions?"

"What kind of account?"

"Checking," I replied with a grin.

"I know you're not eighteen and I know your parents ... er, *parent* isn't here. So I'm sorry, what you're asking me to do is illegal under federal law. You can try and convince anyone I'm screwing a divorced teller. I'll admit to that freely. As to the other thing, I say prove it or get the fuck out of my face."

"So you have no familiarity with the Ritch Street Baths up in the Castro?"

Dude nearly fell out of his chair. Nice.

"But in all honesty, I don't need to blackmail you for being a sexual deviant. No, if you are unwilling to help me this morning, my next stop will be the FBI offices in San Francisco. I will mention to them two words. Intercontinental Shipping." I rested back and stared at the puke.

Brad stewed a good long while. Then, from somewhere, he found his testicles. "You're in way over your head, kid. Do you know who owns IS?"

"It's a front for the Vitali syndicate, if my sources are correct."

That tipped the scales in Brad's mind. "Who the fuck are you? Nobody knows about me and Intercontinental Shipping, and sure as hell *nobody* knows about the Vitalis. You got a death wish, kid, and someone's going to grant it to you."

"Brad," I said soothingly, "I'd like you to calm down. You're making this much harder than it needs to be. I'm worried that you might have a stroke, the way you're stressing. Sit. Have a drink."

I opened the suitcase I had set on the floor by my side and retrieved a bottle of Beefeaters and a single tumbler. I poured his a double and slid him the glass. He looked at it with longing, then at me with spite. He grabbed the glass and threw the gin down. He slammed the glass down. "More," he demanded.

"First business. Then I'll leave you the bottle."

He took a second, then nodded in agreement. "Okay. Here's the deal. I do not know what you're talking about with the Mafia and with that name you made up, but if it'll get you out of here, I will do what it takes."

"Good answer, Brad."

"So, I presume that suitcase is full of cash." He nodded toward it on the floor.

"Yes." I set it on the table and clicked it open. Inside was nineteen thousand dollars in various denominations.

"Holy shit, I was being sarcastic."

"Turns out you were also correct."

"If that's more than ten thousand dollars, the bank ... it starts paying really close attention."

I opened my arms wide. "Not a problem, Brad. I have nothing to hide."

"Well, I do. When they see I opened an account for a kid, we'll both be down shit creek."

"The expression is *up* shit creek, Brad, and that's not going to happen. I am, after all, eighteen years old."

"No—" Then he stopped himself.

"Because that's what the record will show."

"I'm going to need to get a couple things to open the account. I'll be right back."

He was gone a couple minutes. I wasn't worried he'd call the cops or bolt. He was still hoping to save his ass and his job. I should have mentioned earlier, but I don't want you to think I'm some Elliot Ness, Dick Tracy crime solver. Just like with Fast Eddie, I learned about Brad and his dealings from the newspaper reports. Yeah, he was convicted of racketeering, money laundering, and embezzlement three years from now. His sexual dalliances came up in his sensational trial. Oh, how the public loves a juicy story. He was a hot topic for weeks. Then he "fell" and broke his neck in the showers of Leavenworth Federal Penitentiary two weeks after his incarceration there. Seemed the Vitalis liked their loose ends tidied up.

He huffed back into the room and set a few items down. "Here, fill this out." He slid me a deposit card. That's where one listed their name and other necessary information. I filled it out.

"Here's the tough part," he sighed. "We are required to get a positive ID, your Social Security number, and a valid mailing address. You can't just list a bunch of bullshit because they can and do correlate this information. Sooner or later, the government will be knocking on your door asking a lot of embarrassing questions."

That wasn't a problem. I'd planned ahead. Plus, identity theft was quite easy back in the day. Birth and death notifications were a matter of public record. Copies of birth certificates were easy to obtain by mail. And you could apply for a social security number by mail, no visit or ID needed aside from your birth certificate. With a little work at the library and a few postage stamps, I had become Lance Kapowski, with a valid social security number and everything. Sorry, Lance, this was important. I'll try to make it up to you, a statue or an endowment maybe.

Once I was done filling everything out, Brad eyeballed it and grunted. "Okay, *Mr. Kapowski*, age eighteen, I think that's about it. But, you know you're an idiot. Anyone who really wants to can track your ass down." He shook the documents in his hand. "We got your address right here."

"Obviously, you didn't inspect the information I provided very carefully."

He furrowed his brow, scanned the paper, and then slammed it down on the desk. "That's *my* home address."

"Yes, it is. So if anyone comes a knocking, don't be surprised."

"I know what you're thinking. You plan on kiting your laundered money around from place to place and you think no one'll be the wiser. But prison is full of people who thought they could get away with it."

"Let's place that concern under the column *Let Me Worry About It*." He was correct. But I only needed the funds for a few years and my information was all valid. Once anyone noticed Lance was actually dead or that I never filed IRS documents, I'd be done with the money and impossible to hunt down.

"Okay, your funeral." He harrumphed. "I'd love to be there when they start shoveling in the dirt."

"One last thing."

"What?"

"I'll need at least twenty counter checks."

"We usually only issue—" Then he realized there was no usual in this transaction. He left and returned with twenty checks that had the account information, but the name and address areas were blank.

"You know no one in their right mind's going to accept one of these from you, right?"

"Please place that under the same column as the last one." I grinned. "Now, if you just call the manager in and both of you verify the amount of my deposit, I'll be on my way."

"You want me to have my *boss* inspect this bogus paperwork? You are stupid, kid."

"Are you familiar with the expression *hidden in plain sight?*"

He nodded.

"Think of it like that. Plus, you don't think I'd trust you and your sex toy to count it, do you?"

"I really fucking hate you, Lance."

"The feeling is mutual, Wet Stallion." This grin was larger than last one.

Step Four—Grow Those Dollars

"Good morning, young man?" the pretty lady sitting behind the reception desk at Merrill Lynch greeted me. She was the very picture of a dressed-for-success 1967 woman looking for a rising-star broker to marry. She had a tight beehive atop her head, a silk blouse with one of those ridiculous bow ties in front, thick coral lipstick, and a conservative wool sport coat on. I'd bet good money she wore a pencil skirt beneath that desk. "How can I help you this morning?"

"I'm here to open an account," I stated confidently. "And a very good morning to you," I rotated the name plate on the counter, "Dennis Allen."

She flushed a cute shade of red. "Dear me, I haven't switched them yet, have I?" She pulled Dennis' down and slid hers in place.

"And a very good morning to you, Betsy Clark." I got a concerned look. "It's okay if I call you Betsy, right?"

She frowned. "Why wouldn't it be? That's my name."

"I was just concerned management here might have chosen that shortened form for you, you know, a sexist thing."

She considered me like I was slowly materializing from a mist. "In fact, the branch president did just that. But I don't mind, really."

"Well, good for you, Elizabeth." I pointed at her. "You need to draw a line with these men. But if they've not gone a bridge too far, it's all good, I say."

"*Thank* you," she said curiously. "Now, do you have an appointment to set up your first account?"

"No, I do not. But the day is young and I'm a patient fellow."

"What a refreshing attitude times two, ah, I'm sorry, I didn't get your name."

"Lance Kapowski," I extended my hand, "but you can call me Matt."

"I shall, Matt. Why don't you have a seat over there and I'll see who's available."

I started to turn.

"Ah, coffee?" she asked.

"Love some," I raised a finger, "*but* only if you have the time. Otherwise, I'm good."

"My, but you're a keeper," she mused. "Pity you're so young."

"We all bear our crosses, Elizabeth. Black, *if* you get the chance."

I sat sipping my wretched instant coffee for a few minutes, then Elizabeth came around the counter. "Mr. Blevins can see you now, Matt."

"Perfecto," I responded. "Lead the way, if you please." I held out an arm.

"Follow me," she said with a giggle. As we walked, she turned her head. "Now I'm not calling you Matt in front of Mr. Blevins. This early in the day, it'll just confuse him."

"I trust your judgment, Elizabeth."

"First time I've heard those five words inside these four walls," she mumbled as we progressed.

When we arrived at Blevins' compact work station, I knew I was getting a work-in-progress, a superstar-in-training. My guess was Blevins was pushing fifty, so right off the bat, I was not impressed with what he might have to offer. Then again, I had detailed stock market data in my corner, so if he was just agreeable, I'd be content.

"Mr. Blevins," Elizabeth introduced, "this is Mr. Lance Kapowski."

He reached almost halfway to me and waited for me to hook up with his hand.

"Pleasure to meet you, Master Kapowski," he stated condescendingly. Ah, well, agreeable would have been nice. "Are your parents due here soon?" He feebly scanned over my shoulder.

"I doubt it. They live in New Zealand." Popped into my head. No, I don't know. It just sounded good.

"Then who will be cosigning your application. Miss Clark *said* you were intent on opening a brokerage account today." He had that confused stupid look we'd all rather not witness. "How can we do that without a parent or guardian?"

"Well, I am *eighteen*. That might grease the mighty machine."

"You were never eighteen," he declared nasally. "You don't look a day over twelve, and I'm an *expert* judge on such matters." He crossed his arms and nodded with self-satisfaction.

"Mr. Blevins," I began pedantically, "if I say I'm eighteen, and you, as an *expert* in this situation, find that challenging to believe, the proper business approach to clearing the matter up is to ask for me to present you valid identification. Squealing like a pig and insulting me are not typically considered optimal customer focus."

"Are you lecturing me, young man?"

"No, I am saying good *day* to you, Blevins. If you are the only broker currently available to take new clients, I shall take my business to the Fidelity shop down the street." With that, I headed back to Elizabeth's station.

"Back so soon?" she asked with mock surprise.

"I got Blevined."

She giggled through her nose. It was endearing. "You are not the first to detect a hint of lunacy." She reached for her phone. "Mr. Blanc? Hi, yes, it's me. I have a new client up here who would like to speak with a broker other than you-know-who. Yes, sir, I'll let him know."

I set my index finger and thumb to my forehead and closed my eyes. "Let me guess. Blevins is his ... brother-in-law."

She clapped very quietly. "Impressive. Yes, his wife's favorite brother, in fact. Used to let her ride his back and whip him with a fly swatter."

"Well, if that doesn't earn him misplaced nepotism, I don't know what would," I affirmed.

"Mr. Blanc will be right out to rescue you," she assured me.

Soon I was in Blanc's office. It was a real office too. Four walls, a door, all the trappings of a business success. Importantly, he turned out to be alright. He apologized profusely, offered me more instant coffee, and only then asked for my ID so he could get Betsy to make *Xeroxes* for their records. Smooth and polished.

"So, Lance," he got down to business, "I may call you Lance?"

"Absolutely."

"And please call me Henri."

"Thank you, Henri."

"Are you certain about that coffee?"

"More than you can possibly imagine."

We shared a chuckle. Like I said, he was alright.

"So, what type of account are you thinking about?"

"Oh, pretty standard stuff. I want to park some capital in a few high-yielding assets."

"Are you fairly market savvy, or will you require some pointers?"

"I think I'm pretty comfortable with my asset management."

"And how much are you thinking to start with in terms of a funding base?"

"Oh, something like twenty thousand."

He snapped upright. "Dollars?" he wheezed.

"No, chickens. You do accept them, don't you?"

He wagged a finger at me. "I can see I shall need to be on my A-game to stay ahead of you, Lance. Good one."

I pulled out my checkbook. "In fact, let's make this official." I started scribbling. "Make it out to Merrill Lynch?" I asked without looking up.

"Yes, that will be fine."

I slid him the counter check. I automatically was issued checks with my name on them, but since they went to Brad's house and I did not, these would have to do.

Henri inspected the check. "I assume you're new in town," he said, flipping the part where my personal information would normally appear.

"Yes, brand new. And, before you are forced to tell me, I am quite happy to wait for the check to clear before making any trades."

"Thank you, Lance. That can stick in some clients' craws."

"I have a very pliable craw, as I'm sure you'll come to see."

"Fine, fine. Well, if there's nothing else I can do for you today, may I make you an appointment to see me in ten days? That's typically how long a check takes to clear these days."

"Two weeks will be fine. May I make one request?"

Henri waved the check in the air as if drying it. "You may make twenty *thousand* requests."

"Make my appointment on a day Elizabeth is here, not Dennis."

He paled. "You've met my nephew too?"

"No. Never laid eyes on him. I just seem to have a pleasant working relationship with Elizabeth already."

"Not a problem." He pulled out his day planner. "How does Thursday the eighth sound?"

I stood and offered my hand. "Thursday the eighth it is."

On Thursday the eighth, I stepped up to the reception counter at Merrill Lynch, one hand behind my back.

"Well, good morning, Matt," Elizabeth greeted me cheerily.

"Back atcha," I responded in kind.

"And how are you today?" she asked.

"Better now that I'm with a friend."

She wagged a finger at me and smiled playfully. "I'm liking you more and more." Then she acted more businesslike. "You are here for your ten o'clock with Mr. Blanc, correct?"

I shrugged. "Yeah, that too."

She couldn't suppress a grin. "I'll let him know you're here." She reached for her phone.

"Wait," I held up my free hand. "This first." I brought out a small gift bag from behind my back. "For you."

She angled and nodded her head. "For me?" she asked, accepting the gift.

"A little something to brighten up your work area," I downplayed.

She removed the tissue and removed the small plant in a colorful pot.

"Why, Matt, it's lovely. Thank you so much."

"It's a coleus."

She pinched her brow. "Never heard of them."

"I thought that might be the case. There are growing suggestions in the bag."

Then she looked over her shoulder. "But I can't keep it here. No plants allowed. But it will look great on my kitchen table."

I took the plant and set it up on the counter. "You do whatever you want. But if you asked my opinion, I'd put it right here."

She gave me a worried look.

"And if anyone questions why it's there, tell them to take that question to Mr. Blanc."

"To Mr. Blanc. What will he say?"

"That Lance Kapowski, the man who just opened a twenty-thousand-dollar account, put it there."

Elizabeth placed her palm over her mouth and giggled. "Alright, you win. The plant stays. Let me call the boss."

"Lance," Henri welcomed me warmly as he stood and offered me his hand. "Good to see you again."

"And it's good to see you, Henri. How are things?"

He slapped his hands on his belly. "Aside from a few more pounds, couldn't be better. Thanks for asking." He hesitated a moment, then continued. "Just for the record, I did offer you some of our taste-tempting coffee."

"Duly noted," I acknowledged with a finger pointing upward. "But, you know, Henri, as a man of French descent, you really should look into one of those new coffee stations a service can bring in."

He nodded. "You know someone mentioned that very thing at the club not too long ago. Said it was all the rage."

"Plus it says to the client that they deserve the very best," I added.

"Thanks, Matt. I'll look into that today." He put on his serious consultant face. "So, needless to say, your account is fully funded. That said, what are your preliminary thoughts as to how you'd like to begin assigning your assets."

"I've taken the liberty of writing them down for you, Henri." I twirled my fingers around one temple. "Too much to try and remember."

"You display excellent judgment right out of the gate. Kudos to you." He studied the single page. It read:

Philip Morris, $3,000

Pepsi, $2,000

Exxon, $2,000

Chevron, $2,000

Clorox, $1,000

VanEck International Investors Gold A (INIVX), all remaining funds, approx $10,000

Henri studied the list. As the seconds passed, his countenance grew more concerned. He rubbed his nearly bald scalp and fidgeted with his fountain pen.

I decided to speed this up. "So, what do you think?" I prompted.

"Well, this is a very interesting and ... er, *eclectic* choice of investments." He set down his pen and knitted his fingers together. "You will excuse me for being honest, but that is what you are paying me to be. Are you certain you know what a conventional strategy for asset allocation is, my friend?"

"Why, thank you for your candor. I really appreciate it and value your commitment to my success."

"But. I hear a *but* in there."

"*But* this is about the best strategy given my goals and the market we are stuck with."

"Really?" He raised a hand. "Hang on a second." He picked up his phone and tapped a key. "Betsy, could you please call over to Brasserie l'Orléans and speak with Lucien directly. Tell him I'd like a pot of good coffee and a few pastries and I want them now. Then send my idiot brother-in-law to fetch the order. But remind him twice where it is. What's that? Yes, I know it's across the street, but maybe point at it directly. Fine. Thank you." He shook his head. "My wife's favorite brother is a challenge."

"I met him."

"Well, you've convinced me of the need for acceptable consumables. Lucien and I go way back. We went to the same schools in Quebec. He'll do right by us."

"I thought I recognized that accent. Toi et moi, nous sommes une sorte de frères," I declared with a bow of my head.

"You are more remarkable with each revelation. Yes, I hope we are a kind of brother." Henri smiled genuinely. "So, while we wait, tell me how you came to this unconventional asset allocation." He sat back in his leather chair.

"Henri, have you ever owned a British automobile, specifically a snazzy sports car?"

He spread his arms. "Now what kind of a man would I be if I had not? When I met my wife, I drove a 1956 Triumph TR3, British Racing Green, of course."

"A story told a thousand times," I mused. "And on a warm

summer day when you took it out on the road and opened it up, what happened?"

He furrowed his forehead. "I don't take your meaning."

"As you sped through the countryside, everything was dreamy at first. But, just when you were losing yourself, what happened?"

"The damn thing overheated," he gruffed.

"Thank you. It was zooming along for as long as it could, but then it had to overheat. And after a thing overheats, it must cool off."

"Yes, this I experienced."

"We came out of WWII like a runaway freight train of growth. Money was everywhere, consumers wanted everything, and the economy exploded. And it continues to explode now into the mid-sixties."

"But you see a slowdown ahead?"

"I do indeed. Inflation is inevitable, so growth will slow. Manufacturing will look to cut costs, and that will result in unemployment. Consumer funds will dry up almost overnight. Then, Henri, it will be time to hold *real* assets. And I want you to think about it. There are cars everywhere, but oil is dirt cheap. How long can that situation last?"

"I see your argument, but inflation and recession do not go together. I feel that even if there's some slowing ahead, one must continue to hold all five traditional asset classes: tangible, intangible, fixed, financial, and current. They are the framework of our economy."

"Over a long horizon, sure. But my money goals are in the ten-year range."

"But you are so young," he protested.

"Henri," I leaned toward him, "what's wrong with making as much money as one can over varying economic cycles?"

He looked very serious ... for about ten seconds. Then he burst out laughing. "There is nothing wrong with that vision whatsoever." He cast his arms about. "That's why we are here, right?"

"We are indeed."

He studied the paper again. "And you feel these companies will outperform over the next decade?"

"I guarantee it," I replied with a wink. "When the shit hits the fan, there will be constants. People will smoke, cars need ever more expensive gasoline, and everyday folk will turn to comforting foods."

"And Clorox?" he asked, pointing at the sheet.

"They're a smart, well-run company that I'm betting will benefit from an aggressive expansion and diversification program."

"You are convincing me, Lance. This sounds quite reasonable. Well—"

"Except for INIVX, right?"

"Your largest position is in a fund I have honestly never heard of."

"VanEck International is basically a bet on gold."

He made a sour face. "Gold? Gold is for dreamers and gamblers. Its value rarely beats inflation."

"Henri, please remember that I told you this today. On New Year's Eve 1979, I want you to think back on this meeting. When you do, you will say to yourself, *My, God, the man was right. The answer was gold.*"

"You must be a prophet or a conman, Lance. I am coming to believe you."

Elizabeth arrived with our snack. It smelled *magnifique.*

One Year Later ...

I stepped into the Merrill Lynch office and shook the rain off. I looked back out the windows at the storm. "Who invited you?" I growled.

"As I live and breathe," Elizabeth exclaimed joyously, "it is the mysterious man of mystery, Matt!"

"You said mysterious twice there, Elizabeth," I pointed out.

"Yes. That's how *mysterious* you are." She rested her chin on her joined hands. "Shows up with a bag of money and defies all odds with his investment strategies. You're the talk of the town around here."

I waved her remarks off. "Enough," I protested. "Tell me of yourself. How has the year been for my gorgeous young friend?"

She shook her head with more than a little disgust. "Same old same old, I'm afraid."

"But you're well? Your family's well?"

"Oh, yes. But I'm still sitting here greeting old men who are the only ones who ever hit on me."

It was my turn to express disgust. "I'm truly sorry to hear that, Elizabeth. A fine woman like yourself should be properly wined and dined on a regular basis. What's wrong with the men of our times?"

"I have no idea. Then again, as you point out, I do have my health."

"Yes, you do."

"I'll let Mr. Blanc know you're here," she said, reaching for the phone.

"Not so fast. He can wait. All he wants is more of my money. I want to hear more about you. Are you taking classes at the local junior college?"

"Why, Matt, a man's never asked me *that* question." She puffed the back of her hair and winked at me. "They have asked me quite a few others, however."

"I'm serious. There's no substitute for success better than a solid education."

She pinched up her nose. "I know. By the way, you asked about my parents. You now officially sound just like them." She stuck out her tongue at me.

"Then I like your parents already."

"The problem is, I don't know what I want to be, what I'd study for."

I rested my elbows on her counter. "Elizabeth Clark. You might not know what degree you want or what subject to major in, but any of those paths begin with you taking an English class at the local JC." I reached over and tapped the tip of her nose.

"Hey," she protested, "you dripped on me."

"Not my fault." I signaled over my shoulder. "Blame the unseasonal deluge."

She pointed at me with a mischievous smile. "I'm going to *take* that English class if only to find out what a *deluge* is. You're not better than me, Matthew Kapowski."

"That's the spirit, prove your superiority."

Henri stomped up to the counter. "I thought your eleven o'clock was with me, Lance?"

I batted away at his remark. "Nonsense. I'm only here to chat with my friend. Yes, I need to drop off another ridiculously large check to you, but that can wait."

"Matt, you'll get me in trouble," she protested quietly.

"Very well," I surrendered. "Henri, what do you know of the silver market?"

"I know a bit," he said unconvincingly.

We headed back to his office.

Two Years Later ...

Well, the weather was considerably nicer than the deluge—I remember the word fondly—the last time I came to the brokerage to top-off and reset my accounts. Sunny days without a chilling breeze were rare around here. I walked through the door. Ah, the march of time. Gone was the half-partition reception blockade counter. The entire office had been upgraded to, horror of horrors, cubicles! The future was now and it was ugly.

As I took in the changes, a voice called to me from the side. "Matt, you came." It was a very different-looking Elizabeth. Her hair was down, straight, and long. She wore a white button-down shirt under a denim overall skirt, a cotton blazer, and knee-length gray suede boots. She looked fantastic, and she did not look like a committee of old men had dressed her.

"Where else would I go?" I asked playfully.

"Well, you didn't come last year. I was beginning to think you got a job or something."

I made a sour face. "Perish the thought."

We shared a laugh. "So you've been well?"

"Couldn't be better. And you?"

"My life has gone from frustrated isolation to unbridled chaos. And it's *all* your *fault*."

"Me? But I'm such a nice guy," I protested.

"*Take an English class*, he says. Now I'm carrying twenty-two units, working here part time, *and* trying to keep my fiancé from forgetting my name."

"Well, congratulations on your chaos. You are welcome."

She proffered a fist in my direction, but she was grinning too much to sell the threat.

"And this fiancé, would I approve of him?"

"Most likely. He's a recent graduate from Harvard with a PhD in EECS."

"Electrical engineering and computer sciences? How very forward-looking."

She shook her head. "That's what he's always saying too."

"And he's good to you?" I asked seriously.

"No. Better than good. He's my prince."

"Well, those don't come along every day."

"No, they do not. And if I hadn't taken that damn English class that I got a 'C' in, I'd have never taken an elective in electrical engineering, and I'd never have met Bert."

"Bert," I echoed. "I like it, a strong *masculine* name."

"I'll be certain to pass that along," she teased.

"So, what does the future hold, young lady?"

"More chaos. I'm graduating with my A.A. degree in two months. And Bert has my future all lined up. Every relative of his with two 'X' chromosomes has gone to Vassar. So, of course, I am going to Vassar in the fall." She wagged her head back and forth. *"Can't have a van Houten woman not graduate from Vassar now, can we?* That's Bert talking." She rolled her eyes.

"I assumed so. Well, I doubly approve of him now. In fact, I'd offer to send you off with a useful and expensive college starter gift, but I imagine the van Houten family hasn't left me any open opportunities."

"Hardly. Seriously, I don't know how Bert came out of all those snobby, trust-fund hyper-inflated egos so wonderful."

"I think it skips a generation every now and then."

I saw Henri walking up to us. At least he wasn't upset at my delay like last time. We shook.

"So, I assume you heard of our impending loss?" He gestured to Elizabeth. "We all blame you, Lance. Watch your back around here." He turned and retreated to his office.

"He was joking, right?" I asked her.

She took a second to focus. "Mayhap?" Then she smiled enormously. "Now *you* have to sign up for the English class."

I raised my arms in surrender. And I didn't need to worry about my friend any longer. I remembered that in 1988 Bertram and Elizabeth van Houten founded the largest, and by far the most successful, online brokerage company in history. She did good.

Step Five—Setting The Table

How does one capture a small rat? With a small but meticulously constructed trap, of course. My 1967 investments had swelled. Big surprise, right? I had more than enough money to pull off the most complex and elaborate schemes I could imagine, and I could imagine a whole lot of sneakiness. I knew a few points along the timeline where Biblico and Otto would be. I never knew precisely where they were aside from the times I witnessed them or confronted them. So my plans had to be at least semi-movable. And I had a 1975 Matt body—in fact, I was inhabiting it right now in 1975 —which I could deploy wherever I wanted to.

But I knew Biblico wasn't such a successful bad guy because he was lax and inattentive to each and every evil detail. I had to worry that he could sense my time dives into or around his position in time. Maurice hadn't mentioned that to be an issue, but I had to, as my father always stressed, hope for the best but plan for the worst. At the very least, I needed to keep the dives to a minimum. And I was pretty much on my own. Maybe I could get Rolando to help me a little. But I could really only tap him if it was after my attack on Biblico, because he only knew me well enough to trust me after that fiasco. And my first impressions were to attack Biblico before we ever met.

Don't you just love time talk?

I had two broad options. One was to keep it simple. I could just blow his Mercedes to kingdom come. But there were problems with that. First, as with any large explosion, I risked damage to innocent bystanders. I remember hearing about the rental truck used in the Oklahoma City bombings. A couple was nearly killed blocks away by some heavy part of the truck. Plus, I wasn't eager to join the murder-one-club. A double homicide would be a firm step into the Dark Side for sure. Finally, what the hell did I know about blowing up a Mercedes 600 on a public street? What, did I crawl up and affix a bomb, then run away? How much of what explosive did I need? Yeah, I was knowledge challenged.

Plus, if my plan included safely capturing Biblico, there was a chance I could pump him for some useful information. Otto, probably not so much. But if I put a fright into the boss' heart, he might sing like the proverbial canary.

So I came up with a three-part plan. I was fairly certain it would work, mostly because it was simple. No *Mission Impossible* complexity for me, thank you very much. And as I got into the execution phase, I was sure glad I had a fortune in my bank account.

I spent a day driving around Reseda. I wanted to know the lay of the land very well, but I also needed to find a good secure location to use as a base. I finally found a fairly isolated, one-story industrial park that looked only lightly rented. I called the agent and arranged a viewing later that same day.

I hung out by the locked entrance. A Mercedes—grr—pulled up right on time. A serious-appearing woman of advancing years stepped out and walked directly to me.

"Mr. Kapowski?" she asked dryly.

"Yes." We shook.

"I'm Dorothy Lamonica, not related in any way to the famous football player," she said, sounding all the world like a tape-recording of an Italian grandmother. "Let me unlock the door," she said as she reached for the realtor's lock box. She was a right-down-to-business kind of gal. "We can access the shop via the main office."

Oh, I thought there was a wall of live piranha separating them, I thought idly.

She shook the stuck door and it jerked open. "A lot of these industrial properties are well used," she remarked, as if that justified the poor repair.

We walked in. It was basic. A fifteen by fifteen space with a restroom, a sink, and a door leading to the shop area.

"This is a triple net rental, so you know that up front. The owner's asking twelve thousand a month, first and last months' rent up front and a six-month lease. I'm sure if—"

"I'll take it," I interrupted her preprogrammed rant. "How soon may I take possession?"

"But we haven't even seen the shop yet."

"I know. Isn't it amazing?"

"Isn't what amazing?" she asked with no hint of humor or warmth.

"Everything. Now, about taking possession?"

She was flabbergasted. "I ... well, I'll need to get a FICO score on you, and there're papers to sign. Maybe a couple months?" she asked someone.

"How about tomorrow? A FICO update will take too long. Tell the owner I'll pay for all six months upfront, so they don't need a FICO. If they want to get one to extend the lease, there'll be plenty of time."

"But, Mr. Kapowski, if we don't know you have a good credit history, how will we know if you'll pay your rent on time?"

I took out my checkbook. "Because I'll pay for it right now."

She frowned. "That's not how things are done. What if you have a history of using rental property for nefarious reasons?"

"My dear, a credit score wouldn't reveal that information. Now am I going to be able to rent this space or not?"

"There are the forms."

"Do you have them in your briefcase?"

"Yes."

"Then pull them out and let's make this happen."

"I cannot guarantee the owners will be willing to rent without due notification."

"I'm sorry, what is that?"

"You know, warning."

"Of what? That the property they wish to rent has rented?"

"Possibly," she replied uncertainly.

"Well, who is the owner? Perhaps you could go next door and borrow their phone and call them?"

"I'm the owner. My late husband and I built the entire complex."

Why were we dickering like this? "If you are the owner, why do you keep saying the owner this and that?"

"You're scaring me. This building's mostly empty. No one's ever rented this space. I'm trying to figure out what I'm missing here."

Business sense, I thought to myself. "Mrs. Lamonica, you're missing renters. Bring me the paperwork, take my check, and give me the keys."

"I suppose so. But I want to go on record that this is not the way we usually do business."

No wonder most of the spaces here were unrented. The owner

was an idiot. In any case, by week's end, I had all the furniture and equipment I needed moved in and operational. Best of all, I found the building really to be very quiet. Fewer witnesses was a good thing.

As I drove down the streets of Tijuana, Mexico, I remembered why I rarely came here. The city was grim. Dirt poor. Dirt everywhere. Hustlers, pimps, and pickpockets everywhere. Unless you were young, drunk, and stupid this was not a nice place to be. But I was not on vacation, so I focused on why I was here. And as I thought that, the bright green sign with a cross in the center came into view. I parked out front and went into the pharmacy.

"Good morning," the pharmacist greeted from the back of his small shop. He'd surmised immediately I was American and didn't bother trying Spanish first. "What might I help you with today?"

"Hello. I'm putting together a home medical kit and wanted to obtain some basic medications and supplies."

"Are you a doctor?"

"No. Is that a problem?"

He gave me a toothy smile. "Of course not, señor. I am just making pleasant conversation."

"Here's a list of what I'd like to buy."

He ran a finger down the short list. "Should not be a problem. But, I'm not sure this is what one keeps in a family first aid kit."

I smiled. "You haven't met my family."

I strolled around the yard of Ace and Sons Towing in Burbank, California. I was in what Johnny Carson referred to for years as *beautiful downtown Burbank.* In case you didn't get it, he was kidding. Nothing beautiful within miles and miles of downtown

Burbank. I was impressed with the fact that Ace, whom I'd spoken to over the phone, had designed his business. It was very much in keeping with the style of design Johnny joked about. It focused on decaying sprawl and deferral of routine maintenance, not to mention never decluttering or cleaning, and heaven forbid a new coat of paint anywhere.

"You da guy what called earlier?" barked a Marine sergeant voice from behind. I nearly saluted.

I turned to see a parity of a man. It was as if a casting agent at the nearby Burbank Studios had instructed Ace how to appear like a gruff, filthy, likely vulgar owner of a tow truck company. He was art-in-motion. Not good art, but art nonetheless.

I looked sternly at him. "No, I'm a process server."

In spite of the layers of dirt, grime, and sun-scalded skin, Ace blanched. It was wonderful.

I threw up my arms. "Just kidding. Yes, I'm the interested party."

He pulled the cigar stub from his mouth and pointed to me with his thumb. "And the price a whatever just fuckin' went up."

It was worth it, that look on his face. Plus, hell, I was rich with other people's money.

"Can you show me the rigs?"

He stared at me, deciding if screwing me over in a sale was worth it, pissed as he was. Such a shallow businessman. He relented. "Over here, Don Rickles." He turned and lumbered away.

He stopped and waved a hand. "I got two. Dis 1963 Ford two-fity an dat 56 International S1700 Wrecker Tow ova der."

They were both correctly located in a tow/wrecking yard. Both vehicles were piles of junk.

"Do they run?" I hazarded a question.

"Depends on ya definition. To me, day do. To a sissy, maybe not as reliably."

"How much are they?"

"Twel hundred for da Ford and twenty-seven fity for da Wrecker."

"Wow, you're a very optimistic man."

He scrunched his face into a fist. "Keep it up, buddy, an' dale never find da body."

Now, you don't live all the lives I have, as passionately as I often have, without learning a thing or a thousand about personal defense and the anger management of others. Faster than a cobra, I threw my arm around Ace's shoulder and neck—yuck—and pulled him in close.

"Funny story here, Ace. I have *literally* killed men for lesser affronts." I turned my head and was so close, I knew he thought I was going to kiss him. "*Affronts*, those are big threats by men with tiny dicks in their crotches, Ace." I shook him and pulled him in very tightly. "You're not a man with a tiny dick, are you, Ace?"

Yeah, big bad Ace, who was blowing a very high blood alcohol by the way, was all bluster and no go. He started trembling like a teenager in a horror movie.

"Hey, pal, I was just kiddin' 'round. No hard feelings." He added a three-toothed grin.

I shook him once more and released his unwashed body. "So, on the Wrecker, do you think you could do thirteen five?"

"As God is my witness, Dutch from Simi Valley Towing offered me twenty-one three for it not a week ago. An dat's da honest trute. An *dat* man knows his trucks."

"Well, if Dutch said it, who am I to doubt it. Twenty-one three it is. Shall we shake on it?"

He got a weak grin. "My hand, not my neck, right?"

That Ace, you just have to not love.

The next morning, I was sitting in the bare-bones office of my rental, waiting for yet another delivery. The iron workers I'd hired were slamming hammers and making an awful racket. I hoped the last of my orders would be on time so I could escape the noise. Partly they were erecting structures, but partly they were trying to reattach the tow bar to the truck's frame Ace sold me.

I was in luck. The San Gabriel Welders Supply truck pulled up early. Hallelujah. I went out to meet the driver.

"You're early. Thanks," I said as he got down.

"No prob. You're the first call of the day. I figured why not start off the day nice and easy."

"Glad to oblige."

"So where you want the cylinders?"

"Right in there." I pointed to the open shop door. "Ah, sorry about the work. It's pretty noisy in there."

"Not a prob," he repeated. He went to the rear of his truck and shouldered two tanks. As we walked, he remarked, "We don't get too many calls for these ten pounders."

"I'm not planning on using too much. Any heavier and the tanks become impractical."

"Impractical? What, you going scuba diving with this stuff?"

"It's to be a memorable dive."

"Memorable up until you *drown*." He chuckled darkly. "Once I set these down, I'll bring in the valves and tubes. You know how to use them?"

"Yes, shouldn't be a problem."

This was coming together. Now it just needed to work.

Hey, I thought, no prob.

Step Six—Trapping The Rodent

I bought the most boring, anonymous car I conceive of, a used 1973 white Ford Pinto. It was impossible for that car to stand out in any way, in anyone's mind, or in automotive history. I knew I could tailgate Otto and he wouldn't realize I was back there because of the car's superpower. Dullness defined. If the Romulan fleet had designed their ship to look like 1973 Pintos, they wouldn't have needed those fancy cloaking devices. A penny—or whatever—saved is a penny—or whatever—earned.

I was not so certain at first, but I finally began to determine where and when Biblico's car would turn up to torment poor Rolando. As far back as March 1975, that black Mercedes 600 began to turn up in front of locations Rolando would frequent. They started observing him at church, and expanded their patrol area to his work places. They finally settled in on longer stops, presumably for Biblico to mess with Rolando's mind, at three locations. The church, that second job, and in front of his house when he left for his full time job. That was the briefest interaction they had with him, but it could be as often as five days a week. Toward the end there in late May, it was daily. I guess Biblico was whipping him up into a frenzy.

I followed the car up onto the freeways almost every time I tailed them, but, guess what? A really expensive German driving machine outperforms a used 1973 Pinto ten times out of ten. I was lucky to have them in sight one freeway exit later. Rich bastards. So I never did find out which wet rock Biblico lived under. That would have been nice to know.

And you know what's like the second most intense experience after tequila shots with Farrah Fawcett when you're both naked? Watching yourself follow Rolando. Yeah, I obviously knew where and when I'd observe him, and when I made the move to befriend him. So now I was ready when the 1975 Matt, possessed by the 1987 Matt, would bumble about. What a rookie! He would not have been more conspicuous if he wore a Folies Bergère dress and lit his hair on fire ... excuse me. I was thinking about Farrah again. Sorry.

After a few weeks, I determined that the longest the Mercedes remained in one spot was at the second job site on Saturdays. I presumed Biblico wanted to take a shot at Rolando both before and after work, really screw with him. That would be where I took him down. Maybe. Well, you know when they say or die trying? Yeah, it was kind of like that.

The neighborhood around the office building Rolando cleaned on Saturday afternoons was mostly forties and fifties bungalows, with shade-tree lined streets. It was a nice enough area, and it was definitely quiet. There was not a lot of car or foot traffic, which suited my purposes. I didn't need a misdirected good Samaritan rallying to Biblico's aid.

I had no idea what Biblico did while he waited for Rolando to be visible. The brief glances I'd gotten of him told me he was just sitting there waiting. There weren't cell phones and wi-fi back then and I don't recall seeing any books or magazines. Otto, on the other hand, was presumably on the lookout for trouble. So I had to get close enough to spring my trap without being seen. Just because they didn't know me yet didn't mean they would ignore me, especially when I got up-close-and-personal with their ride.

I wore unremarkable clothes. Jeans and a dark blue tee shirt, along with a backpack that was too large to not go unnoticed if given more than a perfunctory glance. I approached the Mercedes from the rear, using the mature tree trunks as cover. Even if Otto was concentrating on his mirrors, he'd only get quick snippets of my progress, which I made sure was slow and relaxed.

The real operation began when I had to duck down and then begin crawling. I needed to get under the car unnoticed. I stopped at the tree closest to the car that blocked any visibility. I dropped to one knee, peered around the trunk to make sure the car doors didn't fly open, and eased to lie prone on the grass. I removed my backpack and slid it ahead of me and inched toward the back of the vehicle. So far, so good. Just as I arrived at the rear bumper, I rolled onto my back and slid under.

I'd be working on the passenger side toward the back, so I curled up to tuck my legs in from being seen by a passerby. Once in position, I listened to see if the occupants were talking. It was very quiet, which I assumed was normal. I doubted Biblico was the chatty type, especially with the hired help. To make certain, I got out the stethoscope I'd brought along and applied it to various hard surfaces.

Nope, all was quiet north of me. Wouldn't it be great if they were napping?

My first target was the undercarriage drain plug. You may have wondered how you can get water out of your car if it's flooded. Well, I'll tell you. There are drain plugs scattered about your car. There are usually ones at the bottom of your doors and one or more under the cabin. To get unwanted water out of a vehicle, all the mechanic needs to do it remove the plugs with a screw driver and, whoosh, the water pours out. I needed a cabin drain opened for somewhat different purposes. Cue the muahahahahas.

I checked ahead of time, so I knew right where the plug was in a 1965 Mercedes 600. Since the car was new, hopefully, the plugs would pop off easily. This was the most likely step to get me caught, or run over where I lay. I squirmed over to where the plug was. Damn, the undersurface of this car was clean. If gravity didn't say no, I felt like I could've eaten off it. Question. Who keeps the *bottom* of their car spotlessly clean? Answer, apparently, Biblico Hoxha does.

Unzipping my pack, I retrieved the flathead screwdriver. It hit me then, I was absolutely the only good guy to attack Biblico with a screwdriver *twice*. I have no idea why that's important or even worth mentioning, but, oh well, there it is. Very, very, very carefully, I inserted the tip under the edge of the plug. I waited a few seconds, and then, as gently as a lover's caress, twisted the handle.

POP!

OMG, the damn plug snapped off like one of those lame poppers your parents tied to pass off to you as a firework. Craaaap.

I heard a muffled voice. "What was that?" It was from the back, so it had to be Biblico.

"What was what?" came the confused answer from the front ... no wait. That was the back seat also. But it was definitely lower and Otto's.

"That sound from beneath the car, you idiot."

"I didn't hear a thing."

There was a distinct slap. "I was distracted. You were supposed to be paying attention."

"It's ... it was probably a squirrel, sir."

"You think it was. You'll know as soon as you get out and check." There was that distinct slap again. I'd have been intrigued if I weren't in such deep shit.

Since Otto was apparently in the back, I had to wait to see which door he'd exit. My only chance was if he came out the driver's side and into the street. Thank the Maker, the rear driver's side door clicked open and two heavy black shoes slammed down on the pavement. I was just about to dive out from the sidewalk side, when a detail froze me solid. Otto's trousers were down around his ankles. Ah, somebody help me because I was zero-to-sixty grossed out to the max. I was smitten by TMI. A pair of hands came down, the pants went up, and I flew belly down up onto the sidewalk.

I knew Otto's first move would be to kneel down and look under the car. From where his head would stop, he could maybe see all the way to the curb, but unless he actually lay down in the street, he couldn't achieve the angle to see me. I was able to peek under the chassis and watch him. If he did actually place his fool head on the pavement, that little of a cheat wouldn't have mattered.

I was in luck. Otto was a lazy bastard. I barely saw his chin bob down quickly before he set a hand on the concrete and rose.

"Nothing, sir," he said. The car door was still open. He then stepped toward the rear of the car to check the perimeter. This was going to be dicey. I shot to my knees and crawled toward the front of the car. I had to keep the vehicle between me and the driver. That open door was going to bring a crisis if something didn't give.

I guesstimated his speed and stayed eclipsed by the car as I rounded the bumper to the driver's side. Yup, that door was still open. I shot a glance across the street. Too far and likely in Biblico's line-of-sight. I peered under the frame. Otto's clompy shoes were about to step to the front of the car. I shot to the ground. You know those nature documentaries where two bull sea elephants fight to win the rights to a harem of females? How they slam their heads, teeth, and torsos together? Yeah, that was me and the pavement. Nonetheless, though slightly bloodied, I was able to slither under the car quickly.

Otto's feet were right next to the open door when I was able to glance under the car and check.

"Nothing, sir. Like I said, probably a—"

"Yes," Biblico dismissed. "I heard your *zoological* opinion the first time. Get in the car."

"Er, the front or—"

"Up front, you perfect moron. It's almost time for that black bastard to finish up."

"Yes, sir. Right away, sir."

Wow, Otto was an infinite reservoir for insults and abuse. Maybe the job had too good a retirement plan to walk away from?

He closed the boss's door and got into the front. Once his door was closed, I slipped under the car and shimmied over to the plug ... Oh, my, the plug. It was just lying there for all the chauffeur drivers of the world to see if only they were not lazy bastards. Next time, Matt, pocket the evidence. In fact, I did just that.

Now for the trickiest part. I removed a set of heavy needle-nose pliers and the knife. I'd chosen what's called a Number 11 size scalpel. Those have an elongated triangular blade sharpened along the hypotenuse edge with a strong pointed tip. They were designed to make stab incisions like the ones needed when lancing an abscess. I reached up with the needle nose and took a firm bite of the underside of the cabin carpet. I then said a half dozen Hail Marys and shoved the blade through.

Don't hit Biblico's foot ... Don't hit Biblico's foot ... I repeated as I stabbed through the tough fabric. The cut was surprisingly easy. Thank you, surgeons of the world, for insisting on superb craftsmanship. Holding the carpet down with the pliers, I made another cut at ninety degrees. Then I split each piece of the attached carpet pile one more time, so that the opening was a loose tattering of woolen fabric. I returned the tools to my backpack and retrieved the next items I needed.

Careful not to let it scrape or hit anything, I removed a ten-pound canister of gas and a short length of one-inch PVC tubing. I attached one end of the tube to the valve and started to slide the other up to the hole I cut in the carpet. That was when my eye strayed to the label on the tank. NITRIC OXIDE it read in bold lettering. Oh shit. I needed nitr*ous* oxide gas, you know, laughing gas. Please note, at that late stage, I was not laughing. Those two chemical terms are very similar, but the molecules are not similar in action.

Nitric oxide is used in industrial production, causes lung irritation and nausea, not the almost instant sedation I desired. I ... was ... such ... an ... idiot! I know I'd ordered nitrous oxide from the gas company. Apparently, instead, I received an easy-enough-error-to-imagine. I repeat, shit.

I detached the PVC tube and slid the tank back into the pack. I pulled out the one backup tank I'd brought because even though nothing could go wrong, what the hell, they were only ten pounds each. I closed my eyes, then squinted one eye open a tiny crack. NITROUS OXIDE. Oh thank you, backup plans. I will never undervalue you in the future. I promise I'll find out who is the patron saint of backup plans and erect a huge shrine to him or her. Massive, with lots of gilding.

Again I attached the PVC pipe to the valve. I then inched the business end of the tube up into the hole I'd crafted. I rested the tube so that it just parted the leaves of carpet. Then I tore the pre-cut lengths of duct tape off the plastic board they were attached to. I gingerly affixed them to the pipe and the metal rim. When I was convinced the connection was secure, because I was attentive enough to detail this time, I applied putty to the entire tape-tubing complex. I did not want to knock *myself* out while gassing my quarry. No, that would have been counterproductive.

With the setup in place, I slowly opened the valve. Nitrous

oxide is an interesting compound. It's odorless and colorless, so if introduced quietly enough, the recipients don't know they are being exposed. It's called laughing gas, and, yes, it can have that effect on individuals at modest doses. But at a higher dose, it quickly—as in less than a minute quickly—renders the person unconscious. The beauty of it is that its effect reverses itself very quickly and there is very little risk of toxicity, like, say, the victim stopping breathing and dying.

With the valve open wide, I checked my watch. With any luck, the pair'd be out soon enough. The flow rate I aimed for would make it reasonably certain that they passed out at the same time. Plus, now that Otto was back in the front seat, where I assumed he'd be the entire time, his back was to Biblico, who was closer to ground zero. Seriously, though, I crossed my fingers.

I knew ahead of time that I'd have to risk going up top sooner or later to verify my targets were neutralized. Obviously, if I poked my head up too soon, I'd blow the element of surprise and Biblico would have a chance to fly the coop. I was just trying to work up the nerve to look when ...

The car horn blared loudly. I'd never been under a car when the horn went off. My, but it was loud down here.

Otto had slumped forward onto the steering wheel and was pressing the horn. Someone was going to notice and they were going to notice soon. I shot out and stood up. I unzipped my black one-piece jumpsuit and clumsily kicked it under the car. Now I was Composite Towing & Storage Company man! I had the uniform tailored, then I spent two days trashing it to make me look like a prototypical tow truck driver. Why Composite? Ah, you got me. It was the only name I could come up with. I didn't want the police, when they eventually tried to figure out what the hell had happened in Reseda, to go after a legitimate towing company. So I had to pick a name no one anywhere would have. Anyway, I thought it sounded scientific and dutiful to any prospective customers, even though they couldn't call since the phone number on the truck was made up too.

I scrambled to the driver's door and opened it. I wrestled Otto off the wheel and the alert blessedly ceased. But a couple of pedestrians were already heading toward me.

"No, problem," I said very loudly and clearly to the unconscious Otto. "I can get you guys to the shop in a jiffy." As I spoke, I had to be careful not to let any nitrous waft up into my face. The inflow of gas was off, but I didn't know how quickly it would vent to safe levels. Actually, I was banking on it *not* dissipating too quickly or my sleeping beauties might rise from their slumber.

"You a ... everything okay?" a mailman asked as he cautiously approached from the other side of the car.

"Okay? Oh, that, the racket. Yeah, these German cars are trying out some newfangled car alarm systems." I wiggled my open hand in the air. "Got a long way to go 'til they're any good, if you ask me."

He nodded. "I thought those alarms made the horn go off in little fits."

"Thank you! That's just what I was saying. Long way to go to good."

"Sure thing," he responded as he turned to leave.

I trotted over to my tow truck, which, wouldn't you know it, just happened to be parked across the street. I did a U-turn and backed up to the front of the Mercedes. I then began lowering the tow bar and untangling the chains. When everyone who'd taken notice was moving along again, I whipped the face mask and tiny air canister from my chest pocket and dashed back to the Mercedes. I slipped my protection on and thumbed the valve open. Again, I didn't want to accidentally pass out.

Biblico and Otto were still out. They weren't stirring, which made me proud I'd thought to include the fresh air for myself. From another pocket, I took out a small metal box. Inside were two large syringes. One, the more full one, was labeled "OTTO." The smaller one had Biblico's name on it. Right through their clothes, I injected each with his dose and tossed the empties onto the car floor.

I was almost done. I closed the door and checked that the

windows were both closed. I returned to the front of the vehicle and attached the chains. While on my side down there, I opened the nitrous valve again, flooding the cabin one more time. Then I jerked the PVC out and stuffed it in a pocket. I jogged to the tow-control panel and hoisted the front end of the car. Then I double-checked the attachments to make sure they were secure.

Hot damn, I was in business. I climbed up into my truck, signaled that I was pulling out, and the three of us were off to our next adventure.

PS: I figured *I'd* be enjoying the next part of that adventure one hell of a lot more than my two guests.

Re-cue the muahahahahas.

To Be Continued in Book 3, *Heaven Says Wait*.

EPILOGUE

Before I left 1967, at least for the time being, I had one more thing to do. I needed to make a wrong I'd done partially right. I've had to act out of expedience quite a lot. But that didn't remove from me a moral obligation I couldn't ignore.

On a stormy day, I lowered my umbrella and stomped my feet on the worn out mat outside of the Whistle Stop Club. It was not Sunday, so I knew Fast Eddie would be in his office. I checked my watch. 10:01. The establishment was open for business. I stepped across the threshold for what I hope to high heaven would be the last time ever.

Even before I closed the door behind me, what little noise there was in the bar fell away. It was like a western and I was there to call out the guy with the black hat. My eyes landed on the barkeep. Yup, it was Alphonso. I had the impression that he never liked me. Then again, I had the impression he didn't like anyone, so I tried not to dwell. Without missing a beat in his wiping of the counter, he nodded silently to where I knew Eddie sat. I turned and headed over.

"Well, if it isn't the luckiest kid in the whole wide world," Eddie basically shouted in my direction.

I continued to approach him. Sure, I'd won a big bet, but I didn't figure Eddie to be a dangerous man. If he needed someone hurt, I had a feeling he outsourced that type of work.

"Hey, Eddie," I asked, "how's it going?"

"I can't complain."

"Happy New Year," I wished him.

"Happy New Year to you too, kid," he returned warmly.

His ever-present mousy companion, Miles, no last name, flashed me a toothless grin. "Happy New Year, he says." Then he laughed like the idiot he surely was. It was a bit hard to know what Miles was trying to communicate.

"May I?" I asked, pointing to the seat across from him.

"Take a load off," Eddie invited expansively. "Let me see if I got a nickel here left in my pocket for you to relieve me of." He then laughed just a little bit less idiotically than Miles.

"So, Eddie, how's the family?" I asked. Over the short time I'd known him, we'd chatted about his wife and kids.

"They're fine, thanks for asking. And you?"

"I'm good, thanks."

That was it for jibber jabber between us.

"So you here to place a wager?" he asked very seriously.

"Nah, my gambling phase is kind of over."

"One bet too late for me." He chuckled humorlessly. "You know that bet you made on Ali? It was big enough I had to share some risk, pass it up the food chain, if you will. That guy keeps asking why I took a bet from a asshole who had a tip. Can you imagine that? He thinks a thirteen-year-old kid has a contact close enough to the champ to get a tip like that." Eddie wasn't laughing.

"That's kind of why I'm here," I stated flatly.

"I'm listening."

"I was very lucky winning that bet. I had a strong feeling. That was it. But I know how easy it'd be to let your imagination run wild. So I came to tell you about another strong feeling I have."

"What, so I can make a bet with myself?"

I grinned. "If you really wanted to, sure. But seriously, I want to make it good between us."

"As in *no hard feelings?*" he asked dubiously.

"Exactly. Like that."

"This ain't never come up before, but I must admit I am intrigued. Go on."

"I got this feeling about the NCAA finals this year."

"Don't we all." He laughed nervously.

"But this feeling I got, it's as strong as the Ali one I had."

"But you're not trying to put some money on the hunch?"

I shook my head. "Nope. I'm just going to pass my hunch along to you. I figure a man in your profession could make a little extra coin knowing a thing or two."

"Knowing, sure. But the tournament's over two months away. We don't even know who's in it yet. There's no knowing where nothing is known."

I smiled. "Mind if I quote you on that? You sound like Yogi Berra."

"Be my guest," he invited with open arms. Then more seriously, he asked, "So what's your prediction, the one you want to share with your bookie?"

"In the finals on March 25, UCLA wins over Dayton."

He stared at me for thirty seconds. "That's it. UCLA, with Lew Alcindor, the prohibitive favorites, win the finals? That's not much of a gypsy fortune, my young friend."

"It is what it is," I replied, shrugging.

"Who's each team beat, and what will the score be? Now *that'd* be worth knowing."

"Where I come from, we have a term. It's a thing with us. *Spoiler alert.*"

He pooched out his lower lip. "Never heard that one. What's it mean?"

"It means if I tell ya, you'd hate me for spoiling the thrill of watching the game. So I won't." I grinned impishly.

"Hey, kid, I'm a bookie, not a fan. *Tell* me already."

I shrugged. "Nothing to tell. My premonition doesn't go into detail. But I figure knowing that much for a clever businessman like you, well, that's powerful information."

He nodded slowly, thoughtfully. "You know you're probably right about that." He reflected some more. "I bet I can finagle that piece of information to my advantage."

"Maybe pass it up the food chain, get whoever off your back," I added.

Eddie slapped at the words as if they were still in the air. "That son of a bitch? Forget about him. He complains more than my mother-in-law, and she complains too damn much."

Miles and Eddie shared a knowing, if inebriated, laugh.

"So, Eddie, I need to hit the road. But, we good?" I asked.

He reached his hand across. "We always been good, kid of mystery."

We shook and I left. I did feel better. I'd basically stolen Eddie's money. Sure, I'd only spread the pain out thinner now, but without Eddie's cash, my plans to take out Biblico would've never gotten off the ground.

Kid of mystery. Hmm. I wondered. Would that make a good comic book hero? Eh. Probably not. But it *was* my first true moniker. I liked it.

AND NOW A WORD
FROM YOUR AUTHOR

Thank you so much for joining me, Matt, and the whole gang on this ongoing journey! *Time Diving* is a blast, and it's even better with *you* along!

The outstanding people at Podium Audio will produce all the books of *Time Diving* into audiobooks. If you're having any trouble locating a book, check out their website.

I have written three books in the Time Diving universe. *Letters From Hell*, Book 1, this one, and *Heaven Says Wait*, Book 3. If this initial trilogy is well received, I will write more books in the series. So if you're a fan, spread the word!

Three favors. One, let me know your impressions, thoughts, or suggestions. You can do that by contacting me by email (contact@ craigarobertson.com) or on my Facebook Author's Page. Second, please post a review on Amazon/Audible. Those are more precious than gold to us authors. Third, email me to be placed on my mailing list. I promise to only send useful information. No cheerleading-please-don't-forget-about-me material. I am not that needy.

Finally, if you like *Time Diving*, check out my fantastic books in the Ryanverse. Beginning with *The Forever Life*, follow Jon Ryan after he has his consciousness transferred into an android. Then he begins his truly epic journey to save humankind time and again. The adventures are just the best. The books, twenty-eight of them so far, are available on Amazon. The audiobook, narrated by the brilliant Scott Aiello, are all on Audible.

Craig ....

www.ingramcontent.com/pod-product-compliance
Lightning Source LLC
Chambersburg PA
CBHW071803020726
47502CB00004B/987